Empire of Sin

By R.C.J. Dwane

Published by Crumpled Papers
https://rorydwaneart.wordpress.com/

Part 1

"To us—richer and cleverer than everyone else!" – Scott Lynch, 'The

Lies of Locke Lamora'

Introduction

The old verbiage goes that if it seems too good to be true, then it probably is. So, it's my job to *make* you believe.

I'm sitting at the bar in a tavern, not my local, as I'm from the Bronx, and I'm stood beside a beautiful woman who is pretending to be my wife. Why, might you ask? Well, that's a story for another time. Right now, you need to focus on the man to my left. He is a wealthy merchant from Queens, and when I get up to use the men's room, he will try to coax my wife, who isn't my wife, nor originally a woman, I might add, into bed.

She's been flirting with him on and off when I've been going toilet throughout the day, and her batting eyes are giving him the *come-hither* vibe.

Let's watch and see what happens, shall we?

"Where are you going, honey?" asks Belladonna.

"Gottatake a leek, babe." I kiss her cheek and stumble off to the toilet once again, and glancing back, I see the merchant shuffle over and take my seat.

We already organized the final conversation. The nail in the coffin. Right now, Bel' is saying how mighty fine the man's suit is, and how much a fine suit like that might cost? And what a gal must do to

see a man out of a suit like that. And the man, let's call him Mark, since

he *is* the mark, after all, is giving Bel' the eye, gliding his hand down

the back of her dress, along the outside of her thigh.

The ring, look at the ring, as she places it so ever blatantly on the

bar, and she flashes her shiny smile also.

The man leans in, whispers in her ear, telling her sweet nothings,

of how he'd love to see her out of the silk dress, because it is silk, we

don't skimp on the outfits. She blushes, and slaps his chest playfully,

telling Mark that she's a newly married woman.

And that only serves to make him hungrier, because a man only

wants what he can't have.

He slips her his room number and tells her to get rid of the ball

and chain. Then he takes his drink and wobbles up the stairs, for we've

plied him with drink. Our drinks are watered down, as I slipped the

barman a hundred earlier to do so. I'll tell the truth, I don't normally

drink, but the con demanded it of me. I can't deny that I miss it though.

I meet Bel' by the stairs and swap the ring on her finger for a

cheap imitation, then kiss her on the cheek and slip out the back.

I wait in the back alley for ten minutes.

The skyline from Brooklyn is a thing of wonder. The old

Brooklyn Bridge still stands majestically over the waterway, which if polluted before, is sure to be today. What it must have looked like a thousand years ago? When the streets were filled with business, with life, and not the wasteland it is today, a shell of a ghost, ripped apart by nuclear war and a thousand years of crime afterward.

Anyway. I need to keep my mind on the con, so I climb up the fire-escape and I can peek in through the window. I see them on the bed, ca-noodling, as Bel' calls it. She's left the window open, and I silently open it, go to the man's discarded coat, find his set of keys, copy each one by pressing them into wax tablets I have readied, and then I go to the window and clear my throat.

Bel's a Grade A actor. What we in the business call a Beguiler. She jumps up from the bed and begins pleading with me, telling me it was just the drink, that it didn't mean anything, and I fake a tear. Mark stands by the bed, judging on what to do, whether to flee or not, but I rip the ring from Bel's finger and tell her to get stuffed, that I want nothing to do with her.

After all, marriages haven't been a thing for a thousand years, as there is no religion anymore, so if we say it's a dead thing, then it surely stinks of carrion.

Bel grabs her things and runs from the room. I turn around and face the window.

"And this piece of crap can go too!" I shout, ready to fling the jewellery out into the street. Mark shouts for me to stop.

He is a merchant after all, prone to greediness. He's had a good look at it the entire night, and to think of wasting money...

"What?"

"For Christ sakes man, don't be daft!"

I hold the ring out, looking down at it with tears in my eyes.

I've rehearsed this moment at least a dozen times in my mirror.

"I can't keep it. It reminds me of her."

"Then... Then sell it. I'll give you a fair price. How about a hundred?"

I clench my fist around the ring. "A fair price? You know I paid three for it, my wife let every fool in Brooklyn know how much I parted with." I take a step towards him, anger flashing across my face.

I'm a big guy, after all.

"I'll pay more than what you paid," Mark says quickly, "two hundred, the extra for causing you any trouble."

"Three is better."

I watch as Mark goes to his discarded clothes and takes out his wallet. Note how I didn't just take his money and exit the room. There's a reason for that.

He counts out three hundred bucks and offers it to me. There's at least another five in his pocket. I did check, after all, I'm still a thief at heart.

I go and take the three, then open his pocket and count out another three. I'm not greedy. "For being a cheating, pompous asshole."

Mark nods his head. "C-Can I have the papers?"

"The papers?"

"Of... authenticity?"

"Right." I take the papers, forged of course, and place them on the bed beside the ring. I open the door and look back.

"I hope it brings you better luck than it has me." I gently shut the door closed behind me, leaving the sweating mark alone in the room.

He thinks he's gotten himself a deal, as the ring in my pocket is worth at least a thousand in materials alone.

I swiftly flee the bar, slipping the bar man another hundred as arranged earlier, and meet Bel' outside. We take a carriage back into the Bronx. The bridge creaks and moans as we pass over, the water gurgles by beneath, and the empty streets so late at night seem filled with a presence, as if the ghosts of the city still inhabit this dwelling, one thousand years on.

Some said it had been a total global disaster, but then how had we survived? The remnants of society clung to the cities now, walled and

9

warding off all mutants who riddled the plains between the places of humanity.

My home wasn't perfect. But at least it was safe. From mutants. Otherwise, it was a crime infested den.

But it was home.

*

People always ask me why I do it? Stealing, conning, etc. And in a way I want to say it's for my little girl. You see, the water is radiated, as is the foraging where we can find it, and most of the animals outside of the city are mutated, as are those unfortunate enough to live there. We grow crops on farms places throughout the city, as is livestock raised. So, I steal in a way for her, to feed her, give her the medicine she needs, buy the rations and clean water.

But at the end of the day, I just like to steal.

There are a few other cities which we could live in, of course, Boston, Detroit, but those are run by other organizations. Say what you will about criminals, but at least they look you in the eye when they take what's yours. Politicians on the other hand tax you and expect you to kiss their ass for it. No, I'll lay my hat with the criminal every time.

The New York that I know and love is run by five crime lords, each one rules it's borough like clockwork—if that clock was prone to snatching tax jumpers from the dead of the night and leaving their bloated corpses to fester in the Hudson River, I mean.

The crime lords guard their identities, and you could only guess who ruled the boroughs, silently, of course, for it wouldn't do to be caught in a tavern naming off the most notorious men and women in the city, now, would it?

Me, I'm small time. But I choose to keep it that way. I pay my taxes, stay under the radar. Yeah, I put some away for a rainy day, but who doesn't? Just in case me and my daughter have to skip town suddenly, but the thought of the two of us trekking across that mutant ridden land keeps me up at night.

The five boroughs are each surrounded by a wall, and the five crime lords' man each wall, respectively, guarded by men armed with flintlock rifles. The crime lords might disagree about a lot of things, violently, but it warms my heart to know the most vicious men and women in the immediate vicinity care about the city's inhabitants.

Anyway, I'm getting off topic. Where were we? Oh yeah, the con…

*

I guess this is where I should introduce you to the gang, right? After all, it wouldn't do for one of them to mistake you for a mark and try slipping their hand into your pocket.

11

You've met Belladonna, as dangerous and beautiful as the plant she's named after. I know Bel' since before she called herself Bel' and went by the name of Benjamin. She's still one of the most beautiful women I've ever met and can stun most men in the city with one glance. Bel' used to be an actor on Broadway. Yes, it's still in existence, a simple nuclear war won't stop the theatre, as Bella jokes.

Then there's No-Name, who won't tell anyone his real name, even me, the cheeky git, but since he is one of the best Disguiser's I've ever met, I let that slide. You'll meet No-Name soon enough, but you won't know it.

Thirdly there's Gamma, she's the brains, or so she likes to think. Anything that happens, Gamma knows about the day *before* it happens, and she knows everyone in the city. I mean everyone. She sorts out the keys, susses out the maps, works out the kinks, and all that boring stuff that a con man like me doesn't have to, because we have people like Gamma to do it for us.

The last person, I can't introduce you to yet, as I'm still getting to know you, and can't trust you. But that might just change after the job.

Let's get going, shall we?

Chapter 1: Queens, Month of the Warden,

3023

The Bronx, Month of the Warden, Beneficiary to those who hold the keys.

And for us that was Gamma. Gamma is small of stature, but don't tell her that, as she has the worst temper I've ever seen.

"Hey." Gamma lets us into the safehouse, as we've the front door barred. No-Name is already out, scouting down the disguise needed for the con. Bel' and I step through into the courtyard and then into the safehouse. I find Rayah feeding the raven. Damn thing cost me an arm and a leg. I called it Edgar Poe, after the poet.

"Hey honey," smiles Bel' to Rayah. She goes to clean up and get changed for part two of the con. I hug Rayah, slip her a chocolate bar I'd picked up the day before for her.

"Thanks, Dad."

"Happy birthday, chicken."

"I thought you'd forgotten."

I lift her chin and smile down at her. "Never."

"Is the job finished?" She looks away, not liking the fact of who I am, just like her mother used to. Before…

I push it down. It's her birthday, and tonight I have something special planned for her. So, I nod. "Almost, chicken, almost. Daddy's playing it small, don't worry."

"OK, Dad." She goes back to playing with Edgar. She loves reciting poetry to it, and those cost me a pretty penny also.

I suppose you're wondering what happened to her mother. Well, that's none of your damn business.

*

Queens, later that day. Bella has changed into a foot servant's uniform, and she's driving the carriage. No-Name is inside of the carriage, dressed in a warden's uniform, along with a fake beard. There's also myself and the fourth member of the group. You might recognize him, if you do, stay silent.

We pull up outside of the merchant's place of business, and No-Name checks to make sure he's still out. He is.

Wardens are something akin to what you called policemen. Only they are infinitely more brutal with the wooden baton they carry and answered only to the crime lord of their borough.

Today is Sunday, and that means all places of business are closed. But Gamma has intel that there's a special delivery coming in. Hence the need to copy the keys, which Gamma has also done. In case you haven't realized it yet, Gamma is fucking awesome.

I let myself in through the back, slipping on the sign that the door is busted. Bella parks the carriage and awaits the delivery. The mystery member of the group takes the small chest he's carrying and places it onto the store's desk. No-Name goes outside and patrols the street. It's only a matter of time until the mark arrives, and the second act of the con can begin.

I suppose while we're waiting, I can fill you in about who I am? As I'm sure you're still guessing. Fine, I'll tell you something, but quickly...

*

What's my name? I'll never tell you. But I can tell you about someone else. Someone else's story, which is so like mine that we are one and the same. His name was Guy, let's call him that.

Guy was one twin, a pair of brothers, left on a doorstep one night during the Year of the Crook, and that's an omen if I've ever seen it, because a bigger pair of crooks the Bronx has never seen.

We stole small at first, living in an abandoned warehouse. We grew up living off the streets, stealing bread, rations of dried meats, all that sort of thing, which developed into stealing wallets from the citizenry, which then developed into robbing jewellery from the more well-off members of the community, who mostly reside in Manhattan. This is where our story takes place...

15

Manhattan, Year of the Pickpocket, 3003.

Two brothers walk along the riverside, following a drunk jeweller. One is much like the other, dark of hair, tall and broad-shouldered for their age. They follow him into an alleyway and rush him, bludgeoning him with the batons they carry.

On the unconscious man they find a roll of diamonds.

"What do we do?" asks the first twin.

"What do you mean? We take it, of course."

"I don't know, this will be missed."

"Long after we're gone, yeah. C'mon, let's get back to the Bronx before anyone—"

"Hey, you!"

They turn to see a duo of Wardens striding up the alleyway. They turn and flee.

The alleyway rushes past, bystanders take note of the panicked eyes above the cloths masking their faces. But nothing stands in their way as they are chased out onto the boulevard, down along the main thoroughfare, and back into the network of alleyways. The Wardens are closing in, their batons promising pain with every step they gain, until the twins rush out onto the far side of the island. There's a boat pushing off nearby, heading upriver, and they jump the gap, brandishing their weapons to the boatman.

"Take us to the Bronx!"

"Get the fuck off my boat!" shouts one of the boatmen, going to grab a wooden club nearby. One of the brother's beats him over the head, knocking him unconscious. The Wardens jump into the river, kicking their way closer.

"Get us moving!" the other brother shouts at the remaining boatman.

"How can I?"

"What?"

"You've knocked out the driver!"

The Wardens are reaching the boat, when the boy named Guy grabs his brother and together, they jump into the river, letting the current wash them away from a savage beating.

But the current is stronger than expected, the river swelled from the rains from the north, and they are separated.

The last thing the brother sees is Guy going below the waves, sinking with the precious stones...

*

There's movement at the front of the shop now, so I'd better stop there. But you get the drift. My life has been like pretty much everyone

17

else's who call this miserable city home. I lost a brother, but also a sense of self that day.

Poor me, right?

Let's get back to the con. The mark's here.

*

No-Name precedes the mark, the man from last night whose real name is not Mark, but let's call him thus.

Mark enters, chatting about the weather, offering the policeman who is not a policeman a drink.

The Mark steps behind his till and notices something isn't right. The sight of a flintlock pistol and masked men isn't a normal sight, I guess.

"I'd appreciate if you opened the safe," I say, calmly.

"Warden!" shouts the Mark. No-Name steps in and whips the Mark across the face with the palm of his hand.

"Shut the fuck up and open the safe." No-Name has a way with the marks.

The mark opens the safe.

But it's not what's in the safe that we want. You see the first rule of a con is distraction.

We take the measly stock of coin, a few bonds.

"You came at the wrong time," Mark smiles, and in the face of a loaded flintlock pistol, I have to give him credit for it.

I smack him across the face with the butt of the pistol. "Where's the rest of it?" I have a way with them sometimes myself.

But I already know it's all there is. I hand Mark a letter of authenticity. "Sign it."

"You'll never get away with this."

"That's yet to be seen."

He signs, and we tie him up and gag him, locking him away in a backroom. Step One, complete.

Soon the delivery arrives, and I hide behind the counter. I hear as the delivery man is pulling up in his carriage. Three of four men enter, guessing by the sound of their footsteps, and I know each one will be armed and dangerous. One of them greets the mystery man of our group, they chat, and then they take the payment of fake notes, the top quarter are real, mind you, and they leave, content in the transaction. It will be some time before they find the fakes below the real notes, hopefully long enough for us to make a run for it.

Step Two is complete.

We swap out the bogus bullion of silver that we brought with us and swap them for the real thing, then place the letter of authenticity on top of them and I go to retrieve the Mark, who by now has gotten his gag halfway down his chin and is shouting for help.

I point the pistol at him. "We're not finished with you, sir. I'd appreciate your John Hancock."

The Mark looks at me, confused. We enter the front of the shop just as the next part of the con comes rolling up. We hide in the back as the men enter the shop, and my pistol never leaves sight of the Mark's back. He doesn't know we've swapped the silver for fake bullion, and the people purchasing it won't know as the lead has been dipped and plated in silver, so we'll be long gone before they become any the wiser. The Mark is tense, and I think he'll give us away, but he comes through, signs the documents and smiles as the men carry away their bullion of fool's silver.

I nod my thanks, before knocking out the Mark with the butt of my pistol and tie him up once more in the backroom.

We leave. The fourth member of our group departs with his share of the bullion once we re-enter the Bronx. He won't be seen again for a while, so don't worry about him. Yeah, he'll keep his head down, he's no fool.

*

Right now, you're probably wondering why I've carried out such a con if I'm small time?

The answer is one word: Opportunity.

The man selling the bullion got conned, but so what? He was a jeweller from a different city. Serves him right to try to make a deal in New York without one of the crime lords' say so. So, we have nothing to fear there. And the other half, the buyers, were a medium-sized group of jewellers from Queens. They would have melted down the bullion, cut down its quality and re-sold it for an extortionate profit. Where's the harm?

I might be pissing off one of the crime lords, I hear you say. Well, that would be true enough if I had to worry about more than one, and that's the crime lord of the Bronx, as it's where we hang our hats.

Gamma takes the bullion and gives a piece of it to a guy, who gives it to a guy, who gives it to the crime lord, and we are home-free, as they used to say when a thing such as baseball existed.

And who says crime doesn't pay?

*

Tonight is Rayah's birthday party.

After I give her medicine, we take a boat out on the river. She loves the architecture of the old world, the skyscrapers which are crumbling in Manhattan, and the old Brooklyn Bridge. We anchor the boat between Manhattan and the bridge and take in the view. She knows I hate the water, so the act of taking a boat means the world to her.

As I've told you already, I have a good reason for hating this river, as it took two precious things from me.

What's the second? That's a story for another time. Right now, it's time to focus on Rayah, as we don't get to spend enough time together.

I take out the two bundles I've brought out with us. One is a picture book, of places from around the world, places she would never have seen if not for the existence of books. She smiles as she flips through it, to pictures of pyramids on sand dunes, of ice glaciers, and scenes filled with animals that no longer exist.

"Thanks, Dad."

"No problem, chicken."

I take out the second item. It took me weeks to get the rations of flour and milk. I hand her the chocolate cake. It isn't big, but she is grateful, nonetheless.

"Dad?"

"Yes?"

"Why don't we ever talk about Mom anymore?"

That catches me off guard, and I feel guilty, because I know it's the truth. I've been neglecting her memory, from pain or cowardliness, I'm not sure.

"You wanna talk about her now?"

Rayah nods.

"Ask away and I'll tell you."

"What was she like?"

Rayah's mother died early. When she was three. You see, I can't even say her name. How much of a coward does it take to not even be able to speak about the mother of your child?

I shake my head.

"She was beautiful. Just like you, chicken."

"And she liked architecture, right?"

"Yes she did. She told me she wanted to go explore the world one day, find one of those old airplanes we used to read about in the storybooks."

"I wish I had a picture of her."

"Me too."

"Dad?"

"Yeah, chicken?"

"Did she die because of me?"

I sit up and face her, not hiding the tears in my eyes.

"No. She was sick. It had nothing to do with you."

"OK, Dad."

She shares her small chocolate cake with me because her heart is bigger than mine. I still don't know what I done to deserve someone so caring as her.

"Dad?"

"Mm-hmm?"

"Tell me how she died?"

I nod. "OK, chicken."

*

It was three years after you were born. She had never been the same after it. Some said it was the Sickness. I got her the medication, but it did little to help. Yes, the medication is working for you, chicken, and don't you think differently.

Anyway…

She grew sicker and sicker, ate less and less, until one day she vanished. Some said they'd seen a woman fitting her description jump off the pier and into the river, others said they saw a woman like her cross through the Gate of No Return. Whichever it was, she was gone. There's no easy way to say it.

Don't cry, chicken. It's OK.

Let's talk about who she was before she got sick, huh?

24

Your mother was smart. So smart. She was the only one I ever told I had a brother. She helped me heal from the time in my life, and in a world like ours, that is something special. She loved art, and music, and I spent a lot of money getting her those records she loved, of Beethoven and Chopin, she loved all the classics, just like you. Yeah, you both are so alike that it hurts me sometimes, chicken.

She loved chocolate too, and writing, she used to write these short stories, inspired from the books she would read, and would read them to you when she was pregnant. You would move around to the sound of her voice and kick your feet when the exciting scenes happened, it was like you understood what she was saying, even from inside.

And in those first few months you were born, she was the best mother anyone could possibly hope for. We painted your room, and she cooed over your crib, spoiling you in every way imaginable. And look at me, chicken. I know if she was here today, she would be proud of the little woman you're becoming.

OK?

That's it. Let me see that smile.

I love you too, chicken.

Chapter 2: Bronx, Month of the Owl, 3023

Those weeks following the con were some of the best of my life. It was filled with happy memories. Between myself and the gang we laid low, waiting for Gamma to unload the bullion of silver.

We had a picnic on the Brooklyn Bridge, the whole gang, even Gamma was there, and No-Name even splurged and bought us some champagne. Or perhaps not bought, knowing him. But I don't drink. Not since Rayah's mother.

Funny, isn't it? A thief with scruples. But there you go.

That evening the sun crested the horizon, spilling blood across the landscape and little did I know that it would be an omen for the weeks ahead, filled with moments of bloodshed and violence…

*

But that's not yet. There's one more con before we come to the now of our story.

How does a con get set up? I hear you say. Let's take a look and see.

First off comes the intel to our so-called brains of the operation, Gamma. She keeps her ear to the street and listens, and when something comes knocking on our door, we don't turn down the offered chance of making a living.

So, when a guy who knew a guy came a-knocking, it was with an eager ear that I listened.

"The boss wants your gang to take on a mark." The man had silver teeth, an omen I took to mean forthcoming wealth, and not the cold snapping door of metal bars, which would surely happen if we failed in a con for the crime lord, or worse, got caught.

"Who's the mark?" I ask.

"There's a new boss in Manhattan. The Duke wants you to take him for all he's worth."

Oh yeah, haven't I told you about the Duke? Foolish me.

If you haven't heard of him before or have been living under a rock the past thirty years, then OK, but everyone should know the Duke. Word was that the Duke ruled the Bronx.

What about the bosses of the other boroughs, you ask? Never mind them. Your problem is the Duke, plain and simple. We turn him down and we're finished.

"Manhattan," I say, trying to keep the shakiness out of my voice. It's been years since I was there. I've avoided it ever since Guy took a dive into the river with a pocketful of diamonds.

Did I have the nerve to rob the most powerful man, or woman, who lived there? Wouldn't it be a nice 'Fuck you' to everyone who called it home, in revenge for my brother?

Perhaps. But that's not the only reason I said yes.

As I said already, I simply like to steal.

"Of course, yes. It wasn't a question. The Duke wants you to go to the House of Power tomorrow. Just you."

Gamma sat up. No one ever over spoke when she was around, I'll give her that.

"Fuck he is. We go together or not at all. Maybe your Duke can come down here and tell us himself?"

"Easy," I say, trying to stop her from earning herself a beating. The man smiles though, and something about those silver teeth seems unsettling to me, and just can't understand what.

"You can tag along too. Just the two of you, tomorrow at sundown."

"You sure not High-Noon?" says No-Name. He has a penchant for Westerns.

The man ignores him and puts back on his cloak, then leaves. Gamma can only stare at me. Everyone knew nobody ever got to see the Duke. Nobody ever got to see any of the crime lords. So why now?

*

I allay my fears that night by of course spending time with my Rayah. Bella listens in as I read to her from Herman Melville's '80 Days Around the World', one of her favourites.

"I wish we could get a balloon and go traveling," she says.

"Better not," says Bella, who's been quiet so far. "Or else the mutants will eat your face!"

"Bella!" I scold her.

"What, I'm only joking."

Rayah giggles. She loves a bit of mischief. I guess there's more than a bit of me in there.

"I would like that too," I tell her. "Perhaps one day."

I know this is a lie. The only people that travelled the land were heavily armed caravans, and most of the time they didn't make it back. It was a far distance from here to the nearest city, which was Detroit. And if you think the stories about the mutants are bad, you should hear about that city's inhabitants, as rumour has it that many have turned to cannibalism.

I shudder and continue with the story.

Rayah falls to sleep on my lap, and I carry her into bed and tuck her in. She mumbles in her sleep, and I just make out the words, Alyssa.

My voice catches in my throat as I kiss her forehead and whisper to her goodnight.

Think beautiful thoughts of far-off places, my sweet angel, and not of those ghosts that roam these planes of existence.

I sit down beside Bella outside.

"How is she?" Bella asks me.

I shake my head. "She asked about her mother on her birthday."

"And what did you say?"

"What could I say? The truth."

Bella nods. "That's for the best. She's a smart girl and deserves to know the truth."

"How can I protect her, Bel'?"

"What'cha mean?"

"I mean look at us. We're thieves. How can I raise a child in a place like this?"

Bella puts her hand on mine and squeezes it. "But you are, OK? You already are. That's a fine little woman you've got there, so don't you think for one moment of speaking like that. You're one of the best men I've ever met."

"Like that's something to be proud of in this cesspit."

"But it is… it is."

"Thanks Bel'."

She puts her head on my shoulder and we watch outside of the double windows at the rising moon. "Anytime."

*

The following day we head for the House of Power, stronghold of the Duke, situated somewhere in the Bronx. I say somewhere, because we get there by entering a carriage outside our safe-house and be blindfolded, much to Gamma's disapproval.

Each borough has its strongholds, with their locations just as discreet as the crime lords who inhabit them. I count the minutes as they tick by, and soon we stop and are pulled out into a narrow courtyard. Men watch from the roofs, armed with flintlock rifles. I count five stories, with bars on the windows. It's a fortress, simply said.

We're searched before being shown inside into a waiting room. We're searched, again, this time in separate rooms and I have to disrobe. I don't mind, I've nothing to hide.

Once they're happy we're not holding any hidden weapons we're shown to an elevator. I've heard about these things but never seen one. I know it's powered by men below pulling a wheel which raises the box and those inside of it. Back in the day it had been powered by electricity. But since all the power stations had been wiped out there was no such thing.

Too bad, as Rayah would have loved to have seen it.

I give Gamma a nod as we're lifted to the second floor.

"You OK?" I ask her. She's not used to leaving the safehouse. Not on business, at least.

"Yeah." Her face is a picture of panic, but she slips on a mask of calmness as the ground rolls past and we come to a doorway. Two large men pull it open, on their belts are two pistols. I try not to stare at them.

A flintlock pistol is worth more than a horse these days. And they alone cost the same as a year's tax. What happened to the flintlock pistol I had during the con? It wasn't mine. I wish it was. Perhaps one day.

I reprimand myself. Pistols bring danger. That pistol hadn't been loaded. It had just been for show.

We're shown to a stairwell and told to wait. One of the men climbs the stairwell. The other stands and watches us, his hands resting on his belt, just in case we needed reminding.

We didn't.

A sheen of sweat covered my forehead as the second man reappeared and waved us up. We're on the third floor now, and my heart is beating in my chest.

What if I make a fool of myself somehow? Or say the wrong thing. I could just picture Gamma returning to Rayah with a long face.

I'm sorry, but your dad is sleeping below the Hudson.

Great. Leave it to me to think up this shit right now. I really hated my mind. It betrayed me at the worst of moments.

"You OK?" Gamma asks me. I nod and try to give a reassuring smile. I know it doesn't look right.

"We'll be fine." She pats me on the shoulder. Since when was she the reassuring kind?

We pass through a corridor, through a heavy double door, and into a library. My jaw drops at the number of books. I've never seen more than the few I bought for Alyssa and Rayah. What was that, five, six? There were hundreds here. Rayah would have a blast...

I shake my head and tell myself to focus on the task at hand. A man sits at the table, holding a book, and he is the image of the Duke I had pictured. His moustache is waxed, sitting in a heavy wooden armchair, dressed in a pinstripe suit, with a cigar smoking in an ashtray on the table. He's holding a book, and I can't see the title.

I stop and bow briefly. "We're honoured to meet you, Duke."

The man smirks. Shuts the book, and I see it's titled *Art of War*, and he picks up his cigar, taking a long drag and blowing the smoke towards me. I wait, silently.

"He is not the Duke." I turn to see a woman standing on the far side of the room, flanked by two tall, slender men dressed in overcoats which bulged at the waist. Weapons, no doubt.

33

"I am."

"But… But you're a…"

"A woman, yes. How observant of you."

"Forgive me, but the Duke entails the title of a man."

The woman smiles. "A useful ploy to confuse my enemies."

"Clever."

"I know. I suppose you're wondering why I called you here?"

"The thought crossed my mind."

"As my man told you, I need a favour. I've been following your group's con's these past years and find them… interesting. They stand apart from the rest of the rabble."

Gamma took a step toward the woman. "We're not the best you could hire, if you forgive me saying so. So why us?"

"You owe me." The woman slipped out a packet of cigarettes and lit one up with a golden gas lighter. Everything about her dripped of money. I could only wonder what privileges getting onto her good side might provide, and Gamma's tone of voice snapped me right out of my daydream of living in luxury.

"What my friend here means to say is one so exalted as yourself deserves the best in the business." I look at Gamma, silencing her. Now isn't a time to prick fingers.

"As I said, you owe me. And if I tell you that you need to do this for me…" she let it hang in the air.

Then you bloody fucking do it.

I nod. "Of course. We'd be happy to. Might I ask who the new boss of Manhattan is?"

The woman holds out her cigarette and the man to her left holds out his hand, letting her tip ash onto it.

"You might."

"Your man said there was a new boss."

"I'm not sure of his name, but he goes by the alias Crystallini. That's all I know so far. I need your gang to infiltrate his organization, gather intelligence, and come back to me when you know more. I need to know precisely how many men he has guarding him."

Gamma looked at me, the question obvious in her eyes.

What's in it for us?

"And what type of payment might we be expecting?"

"Oh, you'll have something which you'd die for, chicken."

My heart skipped a beat.

"Ex-Excuse me?" My mouth was suddenly dry. My legs feeling like they were slowly giving way, and the room spun in dizzying circles.

"My man has taken your daughter into his possession. I will oversee her medical treatments, so far as you and your gang follow through with my requests." The woman tapped her cigarette out onto the man's hand. "Understand?"

"I... Yes."

A battle raged within me. On one hand I wanted to run at her and begin choking the life from her. But I knew I would only make it two steps before being shot down. And then where would Rayah be?

Gamma had her fists balled. I shake my head, telling her not to think about it.

"Good. My man will be in contact with you soon. I advise you get working on your first plan of action by tomorrow. I'm sure your daughter would agree."

I nod, fists clenched. We're shown out of the building and re-enter the carriage. I want to throw up. Gamma looks like she wants to cry as they slip the bag over head. My only thoughts as they slip the bag over my head is of Rayah.

I do something I haven't done since I was a child.

I pray.

*

Gamma helps me inside of the safehouse. I stumble into Rayah's room. It's empty.

Of course, it is.

Then it begins to sink in. Really sink in.

She's gone. My baby girl, taken.

My fists begin to shake, and shock turns into anger.

How fucking dare she! Who the fuck did she think she was?
Duchess or no Duchess, no one, and I mean *no one* fucks with my little
chicken.

"You OK?" Gamma asks me from the doorway.

"No." I shake my head. "They took her."

"You know what we do then?"

"We make her pay."

Gamma approaches me and puts her hand on my shoulder. "We
do what she asks. I'm normally the one getting us into trouble, but
listen to me when I say, the best thing you can do is do what she asks."

"Hmmph."

Bella comes in then, and there's tears in her eyes. "I just heard."

"Heard?" I realize it before she even says it.

"It's all over the borough, honey. The Duke has made an example
of you for stealing the silver."

"I need a drink." I go out to the living room and open the cabinet.
It's been years since I've drank, but if I don't kill the panic building in

my chest, I think I'm going to have a heart attack. I pour myself a glass of whiskey and my hand shakes as I lift it.

"You're sure you want to do that?" asks Bella, rubbing her hand against my back. I nod.

"Anything to kill the pain." I toss it back and pour another. The liquid burns going down, and it feels so good. As does the next one.

"Take it easy, cowboy," says No-Name, entering the room.

"Fuck yourself," I cough past the burn. I go to pour another, and Gamma stops me.

"That's enough, for now. Let's get a plan going before you drink yourself stupid. I don't want the old you right now, I need the man who can con like the best of them. OK?"

I nod. "OK."

We enter the courtyard and sit at the table. I look at the wall, where chalk lines mark Rayah's growth spurts over the past seven years. I can't believe she might never...

No. I can't think like that. I'm going to get her back.

"So, what's the plan?" asks No-Name.

"We do as the Duke asks," says Gamma. "We get in close with this Crystallini, prove ourselves, and then check back in with the Duke."

"Easier said than done," says Bella.

38

"What you mean?" I ask.

"Haven't you heard?" Gamma asks me.

"No. Heard what?"

"Sit down."

I sit.

"This Crystal, he's no push over. He took over Manhattan by force, made an example of the last boss by sending one limb to each of the other four boroughs. Now he has the rest of the old boss hanging on the top of the skyscraper he calls his base of operations."

I shrug. "It's nothing out of the ordinary, is it? The crime lords have always been prone to violence."

"But this guy has them all riled up. He hit each of them all at once, stealing money, jewels, bonds, you name it. In the space of a week, he went from a ghost to the most notorious man in New York."

"Then we find out more about him. We find out who he is, what he wants, what his fears are. We wait, and we watch, and we find an opening. Same as always."

Gamma nods. "OK, we can do that. But we need to be careful."

I ball my fist on the table. "We do as the Duke asks and get Rayah back, and may the devil help anyone who touches a hair on her head."

Bella reaches across and places her hand on mine. "We'll get her back, she'll be OK."

So, there I was, backed into a corner. I just had to steal my way

out of it, and anyone who stood in my way didn't stand a chance.

Or so I thought.

Chapter 3: Double Take

The Manhattan skyline dominated the city, like shards of broken teeth, shattered columns, they clawed their way up into the sky, speaking tomes of a greater time. Staring at the broken architecture, those relics of the past, I couldn't help but think of Rayah, of all the times she's cooed over the old world's creations.

"Gamma set up a meet with a member of Crystal's organization," I say to the group, looking away from the skyline. We're all there in the carriage, Belladonna, No-Name, Mystery Man, who I'll fill you in soon about, and myself.

"We going to work for this Crystal now? I thought we stuck to ourselves?" says No-Name.

"We're doing it for Rayah, No-Name, don't forget that."

I nod my thanks to Bella.

"We keep our heads down, work hard, collect information and report back to the Duchess. She just wants to know how many men this Crystallini has got guarding him." The group seem content with what I say.

I'd filled them all in about the Duke's real gender, seeing as we'd probably be dead within the month anyway I saw no harm in it.

The Empire State building had been an icon of its time, or so I

read in some of the books I'd collected, and it was this building that we

slowly made our way toward. It was mostly foot traffic, businessmen

and women of leisure strolling about.

"You'd think they didn't live in the middle of a wasteland," Bella

shook her head.

We pulled up outside the Empire State building, and a shudder ran

across my spine as I stared up at the towering house of gambling,

prostitution and every vice known to man.

A large sign outside proclaimed this as the House of Two Faces,

and its reputation preceded it. Out of the five boroughs there was no

better place to piss away a fortune. Or so I've heard.

OK, I might have spent many of my younger years here. But that

was before Rayah.

Two men in overcoats clutching flintlock rifles and maces on their

belts pull open the door. More guards stand around inside, and we

eventually get past them after being searched and enter the foyer. A

dual sweeping staircase leads upstairs, and we pass by revellers

enjoying a game of dice and a drink. My neck itches at the sight of the

dice.

It's been too long since I've placed a bet. Not since Rayah…

"Eyes on the job," Bella whispers in my ear as she presses close to me, she knows it's my weakness, cards and dice, and I nod and turn away from the table. We're shown to an elevator and enter, the guard inside shuts the grate and we begin ascending, the ancient metal screeching with every turn of the wheel. We eventually stop and exit, and the scene is one of luxury and debauchery, all rolled into one. Bare-chested women carry drinks trays to and from the tables, where card games are being played. One man leans onto the table and snorts something from it, much to the dealer's bemusement. There's a band playing up on the stage, with a bar bordering the far side of the room. This is where we make towards, and I lean up against the bar and take in the men sitting there.

A minute passes by before our contact spots us and makes his introduction. He's an effeminate man wearing nothing but skin-tight leggings, and he shows us past the partygoers and through a metal door at the back of the room. We pass through a series of locked doors, with guards outside each one, armed with dual pistols and cudgels.

"Wait here, if you please," the man says to us, then enters a room and shuts the door behind him. A few minutes pass by, until the door opens, and the man asks us to enter.

He shuts the door behind us, leaving us in a richly decorated room. There's a screen at the far side, and a silhouette is visible behind it.

"Please, take a seat." It's a man's voice.

I take the seat nearest to the screen, No-Name, Bella and Mystery Man sit behind me.

"So, Gamma tells me you're looking for work?"

I nod, then remember he can't see me. "Yeah. What do I call you?"

"You can call me Ghost if you like. I'm the right-hand man for Crystallini. Anything you hear through me comes straight from the top. Got it?"

"Yeah. What can we do for you?"

The man, Ghost, clicks his fingers and a secret compartment opens in the wall. A man enters the room carrying a tray. There are documents on it. He places it on the table in front of me and disappears back into the secret compartment, but I have an inkling that if I chose to attack Ghost then I'd find myself with a couple balls of lead in me before I reached the screen. I lean forward and look at the files.

It's a con, alright. Maps, timetables, the mark carriages contents.

"You want us to hit the Staten Island cartel?" I ask. No-Name looks at me incredulously, but I ignore him. He can't hold a poker face for shit, it's why he'll never reach the top.

"Can you do it?" asks Ghost.

"Perhaps. It depends on the price."

"We'll give you ten points of the total."

"Twenty."

"Fifteen."

"Done. But this is gonnapiss off a lot of people in high places. I hope you're ready for retaliation." I pick up the files and slip them under my coat.

The figure seems to smile, I can almost feel it, and it makes me think of serpents slithering at the bottom of deep, dark holes.

"I am counting on it."

*

"You're fucking kidding me, right?" says Gamma, not at all happy that I've decided to give a yes on a job without her say so. She likes to think she's the boss, but the hell she is.

"No. It was a take-it-or-leave it moment. I couldn't hesitate."

Gamma grimaces, then looks over the files once more and thaws a bit. "I suppose we could set ourselves up well if we carry it out correctly. But that means no murders, No-Name."

45

No-Name shrugs. "That was one time, and he was asking for it."

"No murders," Gamma reiterates.

"She's right," I say. "We do this calm and collected. We plan accordingly and get away clean, make a good impression, and we have our foot in the door with this Crystal."

The gang nods.

Now it was time to set up the con.

*

I guess it's time I introduced you to our mystery man.

He's what we in the business call a Chameleon. He doesn't do disguises because he doesn't have to. He just fits in. The Chameleon is crucial to this next con. But it will be his last.

*

Staten Island. Month of the Wolf, Beneficiary to those who hunt in the night.

It's been weeks since they took my Rayah, and weeks since we've started working the con, but the route has been set, the outfits donned and now the wheels of fortune have been set in motion.

I take a swig from my flask of whiskey and earn myself a frown from Bella.

We're dressed as Wardens, me, No-Name, and the Chameleon. Bella is dressed in her finest outfit, which gives just enough of her bust away to distract any unforeseen disturbances.

The destination is the bank of Staten Island. Chameleon has all the documents of the security patrol, and we stop our carriage by the bridge, park it under the eaves, and wait.

It's not five minutes before the mark comes rattling up the street, timed to perfection by Gamma's Intel, as usual. We roll our carriage out onto the street, me and No-Name hide by the wall. We watch as the loose nut rattles and falls off, and our carriage grinds to a halt, blocking the road.

"Get the hell outta the way!" The driver shouts.

"You blind?" shouts Chameleon from the driver's seat. "How my supposed to move a carriage with three wheels?"

The driver curses and hops off, the guard beside comes to help as they lift the carriage, and me and No-Name move out.

Gamma has loaned us two pistols, and these are loaded. I half-cock back mine and rest it against the back of the guard's head.

"Holy shit," he says. "You guys know whose stuff this is?"

"Yeah, ours." I butt him into the back of the head and knock him unconscious. The driver has his hands up.

"Just take it, don't shoot."

No-Name whacks him over the head with his baton and knocks him out. We drag them to the mark carriage and lean them up against it.

"We know there's only one of you in there," I say, pointing my pistol at the driver. "Open the door or your friends eat lead."

The door rattles as the guard opens it up and jumps out.

He sneers, a scar running across his face. "Never been robbed by dead men before."

"There's a first for everything," I say, as I climb in and grab the case. I check the code Gamma's given me before entering it, as the case is primed with ink and if I enter the wrong combination, it will spray the bonds inside and make them worthless, but the clerk on the other side is crooked and he's in on the con.

I open it up and check the bonds. Ten in total, each worth ten-thousand dollars. I do my business and then shut the case. We knock out the last guard and hide the three bodies trussed up behind the bridge. Bella is driving the spare carriage, and she'll meet us at the rendezvous. I sit up and drive the carriage, Chameleon is riding shotgun and No-Name in the back. We continue along the route, the exchange has us late by two minutes, but I peg the horses along the streets at a break-neck pace and by the time we reach the bank we're still on schedule.

"Identification," the guard outside the gate says. I hand him the forged documents and he passes us through.

There's a score of guards inside the gate, all armed to the teeth. We park the carriage by the platform and No-Name hands the case out through a compartment in the side of the carriage. We meet a fat gangster by the doorway, there a massive gold bands through his ears, a sign he's a made guy in the Staten Island cartel.

He relieves me and Chameleon of our pistols. We enter the building. Down a hallway, we pass three armed guards sitting at a table. Into a room with a massive chandelier hanging over a table, where two men are sat behind. I know one of them is the boss, but which I'm not sure. Neither speaks, so I place the case on the table and stand back. The fat gangster goes to the cabinet in the corner and takes out a case, places it beside mine.

"Please, open it," says one of the men sitting at the table.

I open their case and inside if a small black bag. I open it, spill out its contents.

Diamonds.

My mind flashes back to that day on the Hudson, Guy sinking beneath the waves, along with a small fortune. My hands almost shake, but I catch myself just in time and look up, giving both men a nod. I enter in my code and pop open the case and slide across the bonds. The man on the right inspects them, and my heart is beating in my chest like an alarm. I force myself not to blink, not to look at Chameleon.

But then the man nods and closes the briefcase, and I stifle a sigh of relief.

I pick up the case of diamonds and we're escorted back through the building, to the carriage. My hand is steady as I take back my pistol, and there's a smile in Chameleon's eyes as we climb back onto the carriage and make our way out of the compound.

*

We park the carriage behind an old, abandoned warehouse. Belladonna is there with the getaway carriage. We pour flammable liquids on the carriage and set it alight. Then climb into the carriage and we head back towards Queens, because the final leg of the con is happening there.

Bella has arranged to sell the diamonds with a familiar merchant, remember Mark? Yeah, well it turns out that the sleezeball has just sold a bullion of gold and he is sitting on a fat stack of cash, but the place is riddled with Wardens since we pulled the last job and you'd be better off trying to steal the holy grail than that place right now.

But we're not trying to steal it. We're going to have them hand off the cash and the diamonds to us, without any trouble.

We enter Queens and stop at the corner, and there's Wardens patrolling the street outside the Mark's shop. This is where Chameleon comes in. He's changed into the Chief Warden uniform and holds documents that places him as the head of security for Manhattan. While in a different borough, and as said earlier the Wardens only answer to the crime-lords of their territory, the Intel said that the diamonds were being shipped to Manhattan, and me and No-Name were already changed into Warden uniforms. The three of us slip out of the carriage unnoticed and into the side-street. Bella parks the carriage outside the shop and enters carrying the case. Minutes pass, and she's no doubt being shown into the backroom where the transaction will take place, along with some mandatory flirting, of course.

Bella eventually re-emerges carrying a different case, and she climbs onto the carriage and is being escorted to the bridge back to the Bronx by three Wardens.

This is show time.

Chameleon leads us along the street and the Wardens that pass us by salute him. They might not answer to him, but the Wardens are seen as a brotherhood, even though they are prone to beating each other senseless if found in another's territory. But the Chief Warden of each borough couldn't be touched.

We enter the shop and the Mark nods at us. He turns the sign on the door to *closed* and we enter the backroom. Here he takes the diamonds and places them in a new case, along with a letter of authenticity, of course, as good as that done him before. His reputation had taken a beating from the time we slipped the fool's silver to the jewellers, and we were looking to finish him off.

After all, he did try cheating with my wife.

"Do I know you?" he asks me. I've contacts in my eyes and a beard, and there's shadows under my eyes since Rayah's been taken, so he didn't place me.

"Can't say your face rings a bell," I say, smiling inside.

We are escorted by him out the back and he bids us a safe journey. A Warden escort is coming down the street, so we slip into the side-alley and head north, coming to the bridge, where Bella is waiting for us beneath. We climb in and head back towards Manhattan.

*

"Very impressive," says Ghost from behind his screen after his man placed the diamonds and cash behind the screen. He doesn't know anything about the fake bonds. We hope he doesn't as we've decided to secret them away in our safehouse for a rainy day.

We are thieves, after all. Don't trust us.

Chapter 4: Doppelganger

We're sitting in the Duchess' compound, the whole gang, and this is how my world comes crashing down around me.

So no more stories, this is how the beginning of the end happens…

*

"How many guards in the House of Two Faces?" I ask Gamma, repeating the Duchess's question to me.

Gamma thinks, she's only been there once but the woman has an eidetic memory.

"Three on the front door, six inside, two to each side of the stairs with another in the elevator. There's one hidden on the elevator roof, and two large bodyguards on the corridor outside the elevator, with six more between the locked doors. So, in total, twenty."

"I'm impressed," smiles the Duchess. She waves for a servant and he carries in a tray with drinks. We each take one.

"But that doesn't include the men hidden in the walls of the Ghost's room. And that is just to get to him. The devil knows how many men are between him and Crystal. You'd need a damn fucking army to get to him." Gamma blushes as the Duchess' eyes narrow at her.

"Thank you for telling me that. I hadn't known."

I sit forward. There's something that'd been bugging me, and now was as good time as any. "What's your deal with this Crystal? Why are you so bent on taking him for all he's got?"

The Duchess thinks for a moment, then nods. "I suppose you should know the facts." She stands up and goes to the cabinet behind her, takes a photo frame and hands it to me. In the picture is a younger version of the Duchess, holding a young boy.

"This Crystallini killed my son."

I put two and two together. "So the boss of Manhattan was your son?"

"Yes, we'd grown apart the past decade. I tried to warn him that he wasn't ready to rule, but children will be children."

"I'm sorry for your loss," I say. "I too know what it feels like to have my child taken from me." I can't help but clench my teeth. It'd been a month since she'd taken Rayah from me. She was probably somewhere, with that silver-toothed fuck, scared and crying for me.

"I'm sorry I had to take her, I really am. But it was a means to an end. Now we're nearly finished, and all you have to do is kill this Crystallini and you will have her back."

I laugh. I can't help it. "I'm no hitman. If you want someone to kill him, you may find someone else."

The Duchess clicks her fingers, and the servant hands me a photo. It's of Rayah, and she has a pistol pressed against her head. "I don't have to remind you of the stakes here, do I?"

My hand shakes as I take the photo. "I don't know how, or when, but one day I'll make you pay for this."

The Duchess laughs. "That's what I like to see, some backbone. You won't be alone in the task. My man will oversee the assault. You will listen to his orders as if they were coming from me."

The silver-toothed man appears then from the doorway, and his carrying a teddy. It's Rayah's and he hands it to me.

"Your daughter wanted you to have this. To remember her by." The man smiles, and I want to knock his silver teeth out then and there.

Instead, I look into his eyes, and the darkness that passes through my mind, the things that pass between us unsaid wipe that smile from his face.

"I'll do it," I say. "And then we're finished. Got it?"

"Of course." The Duchess lights a cigarette. "Was that so hard?"

*

At the stroke of midnight three carriages roll down the street. We're loaded inside with ten killers, all armed with pistols and close-hand weapons—knives, cudgels, maces, you name it. The other carriages will be full of killers too, and we set off along the streets of the Bronx, headed for the Manhattan bridge.

Images of Rayah pass through my mind. Her voice, laughter, times she cried at night. It all seems so long ago. It seems a lifetime since I'd last held her.

This is why I become a killer. Because of her. I don't want to hold a pistol, not a loaded one, not one intent on murder.

I'm a thief among killers, out of my depth, but then I'd been out of my depth ever since my parents abandoned me on those orphanage steps.

We roll on towards Manhattan, three carriages filled with dark men, intent on dark deeds.

*

We stop outside the House of Two Faces. The three guards standing at the door don't stand a chance. Bullets riddle their bodies, blood splashing back onto the wall, along the pavement. I hang to the back of the group as we storm through the doorway. Pistols flash, screams, men struggle with each other, as blades cut deep into muscle and bone.

My hands shake as I aim the pistol, the man freezes and locks eyes with me. He sees my hesitation and rushes toward me. No-Name appears then, and he shoots the man through the chest, he falls.

"Thank you," I say, but No-Name is turned away, reloading his pistol.

I'm no killer. What am I doing here?

There's a man crawling on the ground. He looks up at me, fear in his eyes.

The Duchess enters the building, two pistols held in her handS, and she blasts the man through the eye. Blood sprays across the side of my face. She points the loaded pistol at me.

"Earn your fucking keep, thief. Up the stairs, now."

She and the silver toothed man follow me up the sweeping stairs. Bodies litter the corridor. There are men and women hiding beside the dice tables, covering their faces, too afraid to face death.

I can't blame them.

We come to the elevator, which is winding back down, the first group have already moved up to the higher floors, and the Duchess follows me inside of it. We stare into each other's eyes as the elevator screeches upwards. I know then and there that I will never see Rayah again. It is written in her eyes, in her expression.

I won't survive this night. But will my daughter?

I shove these thoughts down. I must put my fate with her, or else I have no hope.

More bodies litter the corridors leading up the stairs. Two of the large guards lie dead by the double doors, their dual pistols discarded.

We approach the Ghost's room. Men are battering down the door. The door caves in, and pistol flare from both sides, men fall in the doorway, but more pour in, and the defenders are quickly overpowered. The Ghost still sits behind the screen. His silhouette drips of nonchalance if that can be thought possible. The Duchess enters.

"Ghost, show yourself."

The men rip the screen from between the Duchess and the Ghost. A masked man sits there in an armchair smoking a cigar. His eyes survey the room, and there's something familiar about those pale blue eyes.

The Duchess points her pistol at him. "Take of your mask and tell me your name."

The man smiles as he takes of the mask, and I gasp.

"My name... is Crystallini." His eyes settle on me.

The eyes of my brother.

"No." I point my pistol at the Duchess. She hesitates.

"What do you think you're doing?" There is no confidence in her tone now. Gone is the commanding woman, gone is the lack of fear of death.

For any fool can laugh at death, until its breath is on your neck.

"Point your pistol somewhere else, unless you want your daughter to be tossed out to feed the mutants."

My pistol flashes, and her blood is sprayed across the wall. She drops to the floor, dead.

"Fuck you." I spit on her corpse.

No one threatens my chicken.

*

I run and grab her pistol, but no one is moving, no one is acting. My deed has confounded them. The balance of power has shifted. What seemed like victory moments before is a gaping hole of nothingness now. My eyes shift about the room, looking for the silver toothed man, but he's gone.

"Shit."

I turn and find my brother standing there. He's older, his face gaunt, those eyes that once held wonder when looking up at the stars are filled with a coldness that had not been there before, and I can't help but feel that a part of him must have truly died that day on the Hudson.

"How?" I ask.

"Another time. We must find your daughter first."

"Rayah."

"Yes."

"You know about her?"

"I know more than you could imagine."

"Do you know where she is?"

"I've heard they're keeping her in the top floor of the House of Power, the Duchess's compound."

"Then we need—"

My brother grabs me and pulls me back. "The Bronx won't be safe for you, alone."

"Then come with me! Help me!"

"I can't leave my compound. I step outside of Manhattan and I'm a dead man. But I can send someone along with you."

A woman enters the room.

My world spins.

"Alyssa?"

"Jackson, it's been so long."

The ground comes rushing up to meet me as I faint…

*

I come to in a carriage. Alyssa, Rayah's mother, the woman I loved, the woman I thought dead, is sitting there now in front of me. A hundred questions pass through my mind. Why? How? I thought you were dead.

Instead, I say, "You're a real piece of shit, you know that?"

"I know." She smiles. "You haven't changed a bit, Jackson."

I look around. No-Name and Bella are there, along with five armed men. Bella is throwing shades at Alyssa, and if looks could kill, she'd be a dead woman yesterday. I put my hand on hers and shake my head.

"I didn't want to leave, you know?" says Alyssa.

"Were you even sick, or was that all false? Is your name even Alyssa?"

She nods. "It is."

"Why'd you leave?"

"I was scouting the city out for your brother. Dayton was planning to contact you sooner, but then we had some unforeseen events come up, and he had to go under the radar. I was betrayed by another agent, let's just say it was either leave you and Rayah or risk losing you both."

"So, the Little Diamond is back then, huh?" I shake my head, and I can't look her in the eye just then. I'd never even known her. Everything I'd been told had been a lie.

I'd given Dayton the nickname Diamond when we were youngsters, as his eyes lit up whenever thinking of our next con, sparkling like diamonds.

I slapped my head.

"Crystallini. Latin for diamond." The dots connect. It had been his way of hinting to me he was back.

"So, what's the plan now?" asks No-Name. "We grab Rayah and get the hell outta dodge?"

"We grab Rayah and get the hell out of the Bronx. The four crime-lords are going to war, and it will be bloody." Alyssa picks up her pistol and cocks it. "We're nearly at the House of Power. Stay close to me. Anyone comes at us, put another fucking hole in their face."

The carriage stops and the door is opened. No-Name smiles at me. "I'm starting to see why you like her."

Outside the street is in chaos. Flames are visible from the south-side of the Bronx, figures are running everywhere, carrying their livelihoods on their backs, others are breaking into shops. Not a Warden to be seen, and who could blame them?

We approach the House of Power and there are no guards outside. Shouting can be heard as we push through the front doors. The guards inside see us and throw down their weapons. We pass them by and climb the stairs. The dice tables are empty, as is the bar.

We enter the library where I first met the Duchess. The man in the pinstripe suit is sitting there. Alyssa points her pistol at him, and he lifts his hands in submission.

"Take whatever you want, I mean you no—"

The pistol flashes and the ball rips through the man's eye socket. Alyssa walks on. The elevator is out, the men who normally push the wheel in the basement have abandoned their post. We must take the stairs. Minutes feel like hours as I climb. My weapon is sweaty in my grip.

We find Rayah's crumpled body in the room. Her dress is covered in blood, throat ripped open. I fall to my knees, because the act of standing beneath this weight is just too much, tears flow down my face. My beautiful little girl, left alone to die in some forsaken shithole.

"No... Please, God, no."

Sobs rack my chest. Is this what madness feels like? My hands shake as I press them against her cheek. My vision vibrates, my head buzzes, I feel like passing out. I kiss her cheek, clutch her against me, just like I done when she was small. I keep her safe pressed against me.

My little chicken. How has daddy let you down so bad?

"Jackson," says Bella, putting her hand on my shoulder. I look up and see Alyssa behind her, her face pale. "Jackson, that's not Rayah."

"What?"

I look again, and she's right. They look so alike, but I open the girl's eyes and see blue. Not Rayah's warm brown. "It can't be."

"It's not your daughter, honey." Bella squeezes my shoulder. "Let her go."

I lift the body of the girl. What if it had been my Rayah? I wasn't leaving someone's little world here alone. No. "Where's Rayah?" I say.

63

No-Name appears in the doorway holding a piece of paper. His face is pale.

"What does it say?" I ask.

"He's taken her. That silver-toothed fuck took Rayah. Says he wants ten million dollars by next month or else he'll leave her body floating in the Hudson."

I nod. "He'll get his money. And more."

Alyssa kisses me on the cheek, and I let her. "I thought it was her too. It's been years since I saw her."

I look down at the girl in my arms, and now that I'm not controlled by panic and grief, I do see the slight differences, no dimples, this girl has a button nose.

My Rayah was still alive, and she needed her daddy. I would do whatever it took to get her back, even if I had to tear the city apart.

And the devil help anyone who stood in my way.

Part 2

"Its' better to do something than live with the fear of it" – Joe

Abercrombie

Chapter 5: The Heist

If you've never lost a daughter, then I can't explain to you the hell I'm in right now. Every day is torture. I spend each waking second wondering what she's going through, what she's thinking, where she is, is she safe?

So, when No-Name says, "You're not going to pay, are you?"

I say, "Of course I am. What else can I do?"

"You got ten million stashed away somewhere?" And he's got me there. I've about two hundred thousand put away for a rainy day, and this was more like a damn hurricane.

Alyssa enters carrying a bag. She spills it on the table and its full of notes. "I've three hundred."

"Still a long way off."

"It's better than nothing."

"We'll get the rest," I say.

"How honey?" ask Bella.

"How we always get it. We steal."

*

When going for the kill, you're best off aiming for the jugular. One swipe and you bring down your prey. This is the way my mind was turning. I needed to aim high, higher than ever before.

That meant one thing only. I needed to steal from the wealthiest people in New York, and that meant the most dangerous.

We sit in the courtyard, and Gamma sets out four files.

"OK, so we have the four bosses left of the city. Crystal is off limits, being your brother."

"No one is off limits," I say.

Alyssa looks at me. "He'll help you, Jackson. He's your brother."

I clench my fist. "If he won't, then I'll take him for everything he's got. Brother or not."

Gamma nods. "After Manhattan, Brooklyn is the most powerful. We'd best start there." She opens a file and spreads it out. It's an overview of Brooklyn, showing the streets, and the safehouses of the gang that rules it, at least the ones we know about. "Brooklyn mobsters hold their wealth in two places that I know of. In their main stronghold, which we don't know where it is, and the Brooklyn bank."

I sit up and point my finger at the bank. "Then we do both, at once."

No-Name laughs. "And why not walk on water while you're at it."

Gamma slaps him into the back of the head. "Shut it."

"Sorry."

"He's right. We wouldn't be able to pull it off with just the five of us."

"Four," says Bella.

"What?"

"Chameleon has gone AWOL since the shit hit the fan. Probably on his way to Boston by now." Bella lights up a cigarette and blows the smoke into No-Names face. "Don't tell me you hadn't considered it. He's mutant chow by now."

"Well good-riddance," says No-Name. "He was just a hang-on anyway."

"We're down to four. We need another four, at least. Gamma, can you get your ear to the street and find us some prospects?"

"Already on it," she smiles. She takes out a folder from inside her coat and hands it to me.

I flip through it.

"We need two guns for hire for the bank." I pick out two files. Orson Coates and Patrick Leeway. "These seem to fit the bill."

"We'll need a getaway driver for the bank." No-Name goes and pours us out each a drink of whiskey. I nod my thanks. Something to kill the pain.

"Here, Henry Chillings. Ex-racer at JFK."

JFK airport had been turned into a horse racetrack by the Brooklyn mob. I'd spent many happy days there pissing away a small fortune.

"Sounds like the man for the job," Bella inhales deeply, crushes the cigarette out on the table.

"And this guy. Ace Holden. He's a specialist." I place the file on the table. The picture is of a tall man in a sharp suit, his flat cap peaked, and he drips of criminality.

"A specialist? I didn't know they still existed," says Alyssa.

A specialist is what you used when the shit hits the fan. Imagine a hitman, now multiply that by ten and you still weren't there. They didn't come cheap, but when your back was up against the wall, which mine was, they were the best option. "He'll run the stronghold job. Him and you, No-Name."

"Two men against a fortress. Great." No-Name knocks back his whiskey.

"It'll be like those westerns you're always yapping on about," says Bella. "An old-style shoot 'em up. High noon, and all that shit."

"Fuck yourself, Bella, and the horse you rode in on. I don't want to be turned into no corpse, and that sure as shit will happen if I go in there blazing."

"Look, you're the best-shot this side of the Hudson, No-Name. Don't give me that smirk, you know it as well as I do—you're the man for the job." I flip the folder closed. "Anyway, once we hit the bank, the safehouse will be practically empty of gangsters. It'll be a walk in the park for you two."

"So, it's decided," says Gamma. "We hit the Brooklyn bank, and then once the safehouse clears of men, No-Name and this Ace will rob it."

Bella sighs. "If only it was ever that easy."

*

Ace Holden was not a nice guy. And he went out of his way to make sure that you knew it.

How do I know this? Because the first time I met him he was holding a man over the side of a high-rise, seven stories up.

"This a bad time?" I say.

Ace smiles and lets the man go, and his screams fall, fall away, followed by a *splat,* and then silence.

Ace sticks out his hand. "It's never a bad time for business." I shake it. "How'd you find me?"

"Gamma recommended you for a job."

"Ah, Gamma, and how is the little pixie?" Ace takes out a cigar and lights it.

"She's good." I stick my head over the side of the building, the ground far below is stained with blood. "Better than some."

"He was an informant." Ace shrugs. "Rats don't last long in the city."

"No, anyway. I'm here to offer you a job, like I said." I take out a flask of whiskey and take a sip. Don't look at me like that, I know I've been drinking more and more since they took Rayah. But a man has his vices. And I haven't gone back to the cards or dice yet. I offer the flask to ace, and he takes a sip.

"What's the job?"

"Hundred grand. For one day's work."

"Sounds promising. And what's a guy gotta do to make a hundred grand in one day?"

"Rob the Brooklyn mob."

"You're kidding, right?" Ace lifts a brow. "You crazy?"

"As crazy as a donkey chewing its own ass."

"Right."

"So, you in?"

Ace chews on the end of his cigar, taking a moment to think. He nods. "I want half up front."

"Done."

Ace smiles and places his hand on my shoulder. "I've got a good feelin' about you."

And the ace was in the hole.

*

The other three recruits were easier to track down, and they almost took the hand off me at the offered job. Since the death of the Duchess most criminals were keeping their heads down, and there was little dishonest work going around now.The men were hired, all that was left now was to do the leg work. As usual, Gamma worked out the kinks, planning the routes, while No-Name took care of the firearms and the disguises.

As for myself, me and Alyssa spent the day watching the bank, working out the timing of the heist. The tellers came in at nine, accompanied by four armed men in trench coats. I enter the bank, pretending we're a couple looking to open an account. There's two men to either side of the desk, with a heavy grate behind it, one door leading to another metal one. Two sets of keys, then. And then there was the safe. But that's where my skills came in, as I spent my idle youth learning how to crack them.

I follow the head teller after the bank closes, and he enters a local watering hole. Inside I sit beside him at the bar, my hat pulled low and order a drink. I wait until closing time, biding my drinks, staying silent.

I follow him outside, along the street. Alyssa comes out of a side street and bumps into the teller.

"Excuse me," she smiles, and I can't help but think how beautiful that smile is and so like Rayah's.

The teller nods and wipes himself down, then stumbles on about his business.

"What are you doing?" I ask her. "I was going to get his keys."

Alyssa takes a set of keys from her pocket and swings them around on her finger. "These keys?"

"You're a pickpocket as well as a liar?" I can't stifle the scorn in my tone.

"Look, I never lied to you. I did love you, Jackson. I still do."

I shake my head. "Fool me once."

We head back toward the safe house in the Bronx.

The getaway driver, Henry, is there, along with the two gunmen. No-Name has sorted out matching outfits, grey boiler suits with bandannas.

"Always the cowboy, eh No-Name?" I say, holding the bandanna in my hand.

"You know me, pilgrim."

That night we're sat around the table, the whole gang is there. I stand and lift my glass.

73

"To the job and may thieves rein."

"May thieves rein." We all drink.

Gamma is a great cook. Have I told you that?

On the table is a feast. Turkey, ham, raised on the farms north of the Bronx. But it tastes like lead in my mouth, for all I can think about is that what is Rayah doing now? Is she hungry?

Alyssa seems to read my thoughts and she places her hand on mine. I'm urged to move it away, but instead I fold my hand over hers and squeeze it.

If anything, I need her in this. I need to support her, as she's Rayah's mother, even if she disappeared on us.

After dinner, we smoke cigars on the roof, watching the sun dip down on the horizon, casting a dozen different shades of crimson on the skyscrapers dotted across the landscape. The gang play cards on the table by the air duct, leaving me and Alyssa alone. I put my arm around her.

"She's going to be OK."

"How do you know?"

"I just know. It's a father's place to know these things."

"I've been a bad mother." Alyssa has tears in her eyes. "I ran out on you both when you needed me most."

I wipe the tears from her eyes. We share a smile. "There's still time," I say. "You can still be the mother you want."

"I'd like that."

And I would too.

*

Intel comes in the next day. Gamma has found out where the Brooklyn mob's main stronghold is. The plan is in motion.

*

The day of the heist comes around too fast. We dress in the boiler suits and don our bandannas, then fit into the carriage.

"Mind you don't shoot yourselves in the foot," No-Name says to Orson and Patrick, the two guns for hire.

"I'll make sure to remember that" says Orson, rubbing his waxed moustache. "When I'm standing over your corpse." They look like a pair of thugs straight out of some movie. If movies still existed. Orson is blonde and broad of shoulder, with bright blue eyes that look like they wouldn't harm a fly. Patrick on the other hand is gaunt, hungered looking, with a gold tooth and a toothpick always in his mouth. They both check their weapons, and we silently approach Brooklyn.

No-Name and Ace jump out of the carriage at the bridge, they head toward the safehouse, where they will wait nearby until the gangsters inside leave, drawn to the bank because of the heist.

We stop around the corner from the bank and wait. I check my pocket watch. It's five minutes until opening time.

I peek out the window, and see the tellers being escorted by the four guards in trench coats. Bella is on the far side of the street, arranging the distraction.

After all, the first rule of a con is distraction.

The loaded carriage rolls down the street, doused with flammable liquids, it's on fire. The four guards turn and pull out their pistols, aiming at the carriage. The mules pulling it panic, buck, and the carriage rolls by. We're already out and moving, guns drawn.

I'm not a killer, so I aim my pistol and shoot the nearest guard through the leg. He collapses, but Orson and Patrick hold no qualms and their shots are fatal. Three guards are down, and the fourth tosses his pistol, holds up his hands. Orson butts him across the head and knocks him unconscious.

"Get the door open!" I shout at the head teller. The other two tellers with him look panicked, they have their hands up. The head teller shakes his head, so Patrick sticks his pistol in his face.

"The boss said get that fucking door open, sharpish!"

The teller nods. He must hear the killer in the voice.

Inside, we truss up the two tellers and I get the head teller to let me into the safe. Patrick has his pistol trained on the two trussed up

76

tellers, Orson keeps his on the head teller. I take the roll of tools from inside my coat and set to work on cracking it.

It'll take me, what, five, six minutes to whisper this baby open. But in that time the situation goes from bad to worse.

Two Wardens stroll into the bank. This isn't a two-bit joke like you hear in a bar. They really walked in, holding their batons, ready to fight. Patrick shoots one, and the other tussles with him. Orson goes to help, and the head teller tries to make a break for it. I run after him, grab him by the collar and slam his head off the desk.

"And just where do you think you're going?"

The teller whimpers and lets me drag him back inside the safe room. I peer through the window, and I see more Wardens outside the building.

Shit.

The distraction worked too well and gained the attention of the Wardens nearby.

But that couldn't be possible, as Gamma paid off the Brooklyn Chief Warden, and there wasn't supposed to be any in the area.

What the hell was happening?

Orson and Patrick have subdued the Warden.

"Stay the fuck outside or your buddy gets another hole to breathe through!" Orson shouts through the door, then shuts it. "That should buy us a few minutes.

I focus on the safe. That's my main priority right now. I push out the thoughts of Rayah, of getting caught and being beaten to an inch of my life to the back of my mind.

The safe clicks. The door swings open, and I've never seen so much money in my life. I grab three bags and call Patrick to begin helping me load them with cash. I count the time out in my mind, two minutes, three. The bags are full. We shoulder them and I grab the head teller, then back out the rear door. There's Warden's in the back street.

"Stay back!" I shout, keeping my gun trained on the teller. The getaway carriage comes thundering down the street, and Henry's driving it like a champion, tearing past the Wardens and making them jump aside. I push the head teller inside and we jump in, then the carriage pulls off and turns left. Pistols flash and bullets rip through the inside of the carriage, we duck down. Orson sticks his pistol out the window and lets off a shot.

A rogue bullet catches him in the shoulder, and he drops to the floor.

"Fuck." He clutches at the wound.

"Get us the fuck outta Brooklyn," I scream out the window.

78

"Working on it," Henry shouts back. He takes another left, down a side-street, and we've lost the Wardens, as thankfully none of them are mounted. The Brooklyn bridge comes into view. We're nearly there!

But one of the wheels decides it's had enough. The damn thing falls off and the carriage skids sideways. The horses panic and stop. There shouts in the street behind us. The Wardens are near.

"Move!" I shout. We all jump out and run into the alley, the teller in hand. He's dragging his feet, so I smack him across the face.

I've a rough idea where we are, and the mob's safehouse is nearby. I stop at the end of the alley and stick my head out. I swing it back in just as quickly, as horses come galloping down the street, ten or twelve of them, all mounted with mobsters carrying pistols. They pass by, and I say a silent prayer.

Outside of the safehouse I hear pistol shots inside, we storm in through the front door, I step over the two bodies strewn there with bullet holes in the middle of their foreheads. Blood pools on the floor and I leave a trail of red footprints as I enter. I see Ace in the middle of the room, he's fighting two men at once, No-Name is slouched against the wall, holding his gut. Blood leaks out between his fingers.

Shit.

I point my pistol at the two men, shoot, and the bullet takes the tall one through the chest. Ace sticks a blade between the last man's ribs and floors him.

No-Name stumbles past. We all know where the rich room is, the room where the gang keep their wealth. But how the hell are we supposed to carry anything? No-Name is wounded, and me and the two gunmen are already tied down with heavy bags of cash. There's Henry and Ace, but just two men to carry who knew how much…

And then I see a carriage pull up outside the back window.

A young man comes running inside the building, not noticing me until the last second.

I point my unloaded pistol at him and cock it.

"Don't shoot."

"That depends on your next move."

"You can take her! I never wanted to kidnap her in the first place!"

My heart skips a beat. Rayah? They have my chicken?

"Where is she?" I say.

The young man takes us to a room, and inside is a woman tied to a chair. My heart sinks.

"What the hell is this?" shouts No-Name. "Who is she?"

The young man looks confused. And then smiles. "You've no idea, do you?" He shakes his head. "This is the daughter of the richest man in Boston."

I look at the woman, her mouth is gagged, but her eyes are trained on me. They seem to hold a plea.

Help me.

"Untie her," I say to Orson, and he cuts the woman free. She stands up and takes out the gag, winces. Then goes to the young man and slaps him across the face. "You can come with us," I say to her. I look at No-Name and give him the nod. He aims his pistol at the back of the young man's head and paints the wall with his brains.

We can't leave witnesses. He's seen our faces.

A thief's life is no park of roses.

*

The helps us carry the gold bars we find in the rich room, along with two stacks of cash. How much is it all worth? What's my name, Gamma?

We take the carriage back towards the Bronx, Henry's driving. I tell him to take it easy, don't draw attention. Relief floods through me as we reach the bridge.

It worked. It bloody well worked.

And I was one step closer to getting my Rayah back.

81

Chapter 6: Sunset

I have a road that leads in two directions. And either one might end with the death of my daughter.

So, which one do I pick? Let's back up and I'll tell you what happened.

We got back to the safehouse in the Bronx. Bella was there and I hugged her, glad she was safe. We let the woman have a room and left her to wash up, Bella gave her some fresh clean clothes. We place all the loot on the table, and Gamma is the counter. She adds up the cash. There's over two million there, between the take from the bank and the Brooklyn safehouse, and she estimates another five hundred thousand in gold.

Nice, that brings us up to three million. Not quite there, but slowly I was beginning to see the light at the end of the tunnel. We could do this. I still had three weeks left. Plenty of time.

The woman enters the courtyard and looks at us. There's no fear in her eyes, and I respect her for that, because we don't cut the cheese as the most respectable looking bunch.

"My name is Isabella." She lifts her chin, as if one of us might deny it. "Isabelle Prout." She waits. No one says anything. "You might have heard of my father. Jedediah Prout?"

Patrick inhales deeply, spits his toothpick out. "No shit?"

Isabelle smiles. "No shit."

"Who?" I ask.

"He's only the bloody ringleader of the most notorious gang in Boston. The Waterfront Boys."

I nod then. Of course, I'd heard of *them*.

I stand and offer Isabelle my seat. "Well, don't you worry. We'll keep you safe until your father can sort out you some transport home."

Isabelle nods and thanks me, then sits. "He'll compensate you for your hospitality."

I check on No-Name who's in his room. We've called in a doctor to fix him up. The doctor looks troubled.

"What is it?" I ask.

"The bullet hit his liver. I'm afraid it's only a matter of time."

I nod and thank him, pay him his due and go in to see No-Name, who's clutching a bottle of whiskey. His face is pale.

"What's the word, boss man?" he says.

I smile and sit beside him. He passes me the drink.

"That bad, eh?"

83

"A man's gotta go when a man's gotta go."

"And ain't that the truth of it, brother."

I take a swig and we share a moment of silence.

"I never liked you, Jackson."

"I'm not a likable type of guy."

"But from one thief to another, you're not the worst of them."

"Is that a compliment?"

"The hell it is. Hah! Ah, don't make me laugh."

"I never knew I had a sense of humour. Guess a guy can steal all sorts of things when he's not looking for them."

Another moment passes. I'm just about to say something, when No-Name says, "I had a family once, you know?"

"Yeah?"

I listen closely. No-Name has made a point of it to never talk about his past. And I've made it a point to never pry.

"Yeah. Up in Detroit. We used to grow crops on a plantation."

"You telling me you were farmer?"

"Of sorts. Guess I wasn't always shitting you about being a cowboy, huh?"

"I guess not."

"The guys that run the city wanted my land. I wouldn't sell though. They murdered my family right in front of me, burnt my house to the ground. Told me if I ever showed my face around Detroit again,

they'd skin me alive. Made an example outta me." He sniffs then, and I

pass back the drink. He takes a big swig, and I can feel his pain, as I

know what it's like to wash away your troubles with the bottle.

"I'm sorry to hear that, No-Name."

"Guess a dead man should have a name." No-Name looks at me.

"You think so?"

"Sounds like a good idea. Unless you want your epitaph to say,

'Here lies No-Name, a man without a clue.'"

"Hmmph. I kinda like the sound of that." He shrugs. "My names

Clarence. Clarence Mills. My wife was Cynthia, and my little boy

Terry. They're buried in Detroit." He bites his lip, tears in his eyes. I

look away.

"Life is funny," I say.

"Sure is." A moment passes. "Hey, Jackson. You do me a

favour?"

"Depends."

"If you're ever up by Detroit, leave some flowers by their grave

for me? Might even tell them how I made a life for myself here."

"I think I can do that... Clarence."

"Feels weird." He smiles, and I think it's the first real one I've

ever seen him wear. "Someone saying your name. Feels like someone walking over your grave. I guess when you're dead for so long on the inside, it takes dying to make you feel alive again."

I nod.

What does a man say when faced with death? You can only share the burden so far, and that extends as far as keeping death company.

"Hey, Jackson?"

"Yeah?"

"You take me… up to the roof? I wanna see the sunset one more time."

"Of course."

I help him up and together we climb the stairs. We sit on the sofa on the roof. The sun is setting, throwing up one final wave of warmth, before it dips down below the horizon, and sinks below.

I go to say something to Clarence. But he's already gone. I close his eyes and take a drink.

*

I'm at a crossroads. Not literally.

In one direction I can do as this Isabella Prout is asking me, and I can escort her to Boston. Or I can wait it out and try to steal the other seven million. But New York is learning about me. My name is being whispered around the five boroughs, and the small-time Jackson I guess is as dead as poor Clarence.

86

The gang have all agreed to come with me. Except Gamma, of course, but she'll organize getting us some honest type goons to help get Isabella to Boston, without selling her to the highest bidder.

I take a minute to consider the odds. Spoken like a true gambler, huh?

On one hand, the danger of each heist and con was mounting. It was a fool's bet to remain in New York and keep pissing in the wind. Better to move elsewhere, at least for the time being, and see if this Jedidiah might offer us some chance at making money.

That night I receive a note from my brother. I haven't really thought about him since I've learned he's alive. I guess Rayah has taken up all the space inside of me, and there's no room left for anyone else. I go take a horse and head over to Manhattan.

Once up in the House of Two Faces, I sit down with Dayton and we share a drink and a cigar.

"I hear you might be heading down to Boston?" says Dayton.

"Guess Alyssa's been talking to you?"

Derrick smiles. "She loves you; you know."

"So she says."

"And she's Rayah's mother. You need to give her a chance."

"I'm expected to welcome you both back into my life with open arms?"

87

"I know."

"How did you survive? Where did you go? Why didn't you let me know sooner that you were alive?" I toss back my drink and pour another. "I guess it doesn't matter now, does it?"

"No, you're right. I owe you an explanation." Dayton takes a long pull on his cigar. He's normally piercing gaze clouds as he recalls ghosts of the past.

"That day we stole the diamonds, we made a big mistake. We crossed a gangster, an up-and-coming monster by the name of Freddy Peaks."

"I've heard of him."

"Damn right you did. Everyone heard of him. He was the name on everyone's lips back then. Well, they were his diamonds we pulled off that jeweller. I washed up down shore, on Staten Island, and it just happened to be Freddy's gang's territory. I got picked up by the Wardens and Freddy soon put two and two together. He gave me an option, either me or you would be killed for the act of stealing from him, and the other would from henceforth pay him twenty points of whatever they made. I couldn't allow him to harm you, Jackson. No matter what you might think of me, you're still my brother, and I love you. I said he could kill me, but he wouldn't be troubling you ever again. I think I impressed him because he gave me a third alternative. I

88

would come and work for him, under a new alias, and leave everything behind. That meant you also. He said that it would be a crueller fate to take the only family I had left in the world from me for what I had done, and that the lesson would never be forgotten. So, I began working the streets of Staten Island. Then as the years went by and I rose in Freddy's organization, I made a name for myself."

"Crystallini?"

"Yes. After a decade, I was just as much respected and feared as Freddy was, and he was paranoid that I would usurp him as the leader of the gang. Well, he was right, as I had been chipping away at his foundation, bringing his top boys into the fold one at a time. He placed me on a carriage and sent me west, to California."

"California? Why not just slit your throat and be done with you?"

"Because I'd become like a son to him. When I learned that the Duchess had slew him in a gang war, I made it my business to come back here and even the score."

"You killed her son."

"An eye for an eye. I took something from her. And you helped me."

"I didn't kill her for you."

"I know."

"I did it for Rayah."

"I know that Jackson. I'd been keeping an eye on you ever since I got here. Even took out a hitman that was hired on you after you swapped that bullion of silver. Which I might add was a great con."

"I guess that means I owe you?"

"No, you don't owe me anything. But there is something you can do for me?"

"Maybe, but no promises."

"I need you to talk to this Jedidiah Prout for me. I have means to tobacco, whiskey, guns. Set up a business between us and I'll make it lucrative for you."

"All I want is my daughter."

"And I would help if I could. I have every one of my men on alert in case that silver toothed fucker turns up."

I nod. "I appreciate it." I refill my drink, it's good whiskey. Any whiskey that numbs the pain is good whiskey.

"So can we shake hands on it?"

"Sure." We do.

And my road is decided. I'm on my way to Boston.

*

I'm packing my things in my room when there's a knock on the door. It's Belladonna.

"What's up?" I ask her. She looks troubled, there's tears in her eyes.

"I can't do it, Jackson."

"Do what, Bella?"

"I can't come to Boston with you."

"Why?"

"I'm a small-time con woman, honey. I'm not made for this shit." She wipes a tear from her eye.

"I understand. If the matter of Rayah's life didn't rest in the balance, then I wouldn't be doing any of this either."

"I understand why you have to do it, Jackson."

"Look, it's fine. Stay in New York."

"That's the thing. I think things are just going to get worse here. I think I'm better off heading west."

"What, Detroit?"

She shakes her head. "No, I was thinking of California."

I put my hand on her shoulder. "I wish I could go with you, Bel'."

She nods. "Maybe when everything is done and over with you and Rayah can come visit?"

I nod. "Maybe."

"You sure you don't mind me splitting from the gang?"

I inhale deeply. "No, Bella. I don't mind."

"I love you, Jackson. Not like that, mind you, but like a brother. Take care of yourself, OK?"

I hug her. "You too, Bel'. And I'll see you on the other side."

*

I feel like I'm betraying Rayah by leaving New York, it feels like I'm running away from her. But I know I won't get the money I need by staying, so I ready the gang and we set sail, heading south, for Boston.

I watch as the New York skyline recedes on the horizon, and I just hope that I'm not leaving my chicken in the past too.

Chapter 7: Boston

"I'm home," Isabella says as Boston harbour comes into view. The wind hasn't been favourable, and it has been six hours since setting sail. The light is fading. There's a lone ship in the bay, and it trains its cannons on us as we approach, but thankfully doesn't open fire.

The port is quiet, not the bustling place of business that you read about in books. It is dour, the houses cramped together between the shells of the towers, where many of the poor have chosen to inhabit, and watchers in the windows shut the shutters as we pass by. It is not a welcoming city.

It, like New York, is walled, with the north sector being ran by the Waterfront Boys, and the south side of the city ran by two smaller gangs. These, Isabella informs us, are the Hatchet Gang and the Top Hats.

We make our way through the city, heading north, approaching a walled manor house. The guards at the gate take one look at Isabella and pull aside the gate, nodding respectively. The walk up the drive is bordered by trees, and there are snipers on the roof of the manor house, aiming their rifles at us.

So much for a warm welcome.

A man stands at the front door, watching our approach. He must have recognized Isabella, as he runs down the steps and embraces her in his arms.

"Daniel!" she says, as he picks her up in his arms and swings her around.

"Isabella! I thought I'd never see you again."

"I thought I'd never step foot back in Boston," smiles Isabella. "Let me introduce you to some people." She holds out her hand towards me. "These are the people who saved me."

This Daniel must be her brother, as they both share the same smile, the same bright green eyes, wavy blonde hair. I nod my greetings. After all, I don't much like people knowing more about me than there needs to be. When he offers hishand, I shake it but don't introduce myself. After all, my business here is with their father, not them.

We enter the manor house; its entry hall would fit mine and Rayah's rooms comfortably inside of it. We're shown into a living room, or I guess these people might call it a drawing room, or the like. They stink of wealth, and I won't deny the scene looks prospecting for me.

"Isabella?" A man enters. His features are like those of the other two, but his eyes are those of a criminal, sharp and intent. His eyes go from his daughter to his son, and he smiles. "How?" He looks at us and his expression grows sombre. No, fuck sombre, it is blatant accusation.

"These people saved me, father." Isabella stands between us, as if to take on the mantle of his anger.

"I guess they're seeking some payment or other?" Jedidiah can't help but sneer, and I find myself longing for the feel of a pistol in my hand right then. Show him what a New Yorker is capable of.

"We're not seeking compensation," I say instead. "But there is an offer of business a would like to discuss."

"Business. And what *business* would I have with some two-bit hustlers?"

"We've been sent along with an offer from New York's top boss, Crytallini."

His tone of voice changes then. "Really?" He rubs his hands together, nods. "I guess we can discuss business, then. Please, Daniel, show Mr…" He pauses.

I sigh. Why does everyone always want to know my name? I'm starting to understand why No-Name kept to himself. "Jackson."

"Mr. Jackson… Not the same Jackson who shot the Duke?"

"Duchess," I say. Jedidiah frowns. "The Duke was a woman."

"Ah, how very… New York." He waves at his son. "Please take Mr. Jackson's companions and show them to their rooms." He looks at me. "Care for a drink before we discuss business?"

"Depends on what you got."

"Only the best." He goes to a globe and pulls it open, inside are bottles of spirits. He pours both of us a drink and offers me a cigar. I take it and light it with his gold gas lighter.

"A man could get used to this." I taste the thick vapours, followed by the sweet burn of the whiskey. It might just be the best thing I've ever tasted.

Jedidiah looks at me closely. "So, who exactly *are* you, besides a crime boss killer?"

"I'm a con man and a thief, but an honest one."

"An honest con man? I'd never heard the like."

"Well, your daughter was a show of good faith. We could have ransomed her."

"Yes. So why didn't you?"

"As I said," I tap the cigar ash into a gold ashtray. "I've business between you and Crystallini."

"And what does the most notorious mobster in New York want with a simple businessman like me?"

"Come now, let's not play coy, Jedidiah. You run this city."

"Perhaps."

"And there's always a demand in a city like this for more of everything."

"True."

"Crystallini wants to begin sending you commodities."

"Such as?"

"Whiskey, not as good as this, mind you, but good enough for the masses. Tobacco, grown in California. Firearms made in Detroit."

Jedidiah nods. "And in exchange?"

"Since the downfall of the Duke there's been a blockage in supply for certain things."

"Such as?"

"Cocaine, specifically."

"Ah."

"Crystallini knows you're getting supplies from Mexico. He wants you to set up an account with your supplier for him."

"An agreeable arrangement." Jedidiah considers the deal. "On three conditions."

"Which are?"

"One, he gives me ten percent of what he makes for the first year. A setting up fee, let's call it."

"I'm sure that would be acceptable. And the second condition?"

"He marries my daughter, Isabella. I think it would be a good show of faith and a bonding of both our organizations."

I smile, seeing the look on my brother's face already.

"I'm sure he would be only happy to. And the final condition?"

"I need help from New York, to wipe out these two rabble gangs in the south of Boston. So far, we're at a deadlock, but now I hear that both opposing gangs are in talks to work against me. Ask your brother to send men, at least twenty gunmen, all ready to go to war."

"I will ask him."

Jedidiah lifts his drink. "Then to future relationships."

"And to making a shit ton of cash," I toss my drink back.

"Yes, and that too."

"I'll set sail in the morning and relay your conditions." I go to leave, but Jedediah grabs my arm.

"And warn your brother not to fuck me. I'm not a man to be crossed."

How did he know we were brothers? No one knew, except Rayah and Alyssa.

I close my mouth and nod. "And neither is my brother," I say, pulling my arm away. "And you'd do well to remember that."

*

I leave Boston the following day and the wind is still blowing northwards, so we make good time in reaching New York. We debark onto Manhattan and make our way for the House of Two Faces. Once sat down in Derrick's company, I relay Jedediah's conditions and can't help but smile when telling him about the offered marriage proposal.

"I suppose it would do well to have closer bonds with Boston," says Dayton. "And it would seal the deal on this contact from Mexico." He nods. "Tell him I agree to the conditions, on one of my own. That when I finish helping him wipe out these two gangs, the Hatchet Gang and the Top Hats, that he will return the favour and help me take power in all the five boroughs."

"OK." I go to stand up.

"Will you run this job down in Boston for me?"

"I've two weeks to get the rest of the money. I need to be getting paid for my work."

Dayton reaches behind him and pulls out a bag. Inside I see notes.

"There's five hundred grand there. An advance on the work you've been doing. And it's only the start."

"Any news on Rayah's whereabouts?" I ask.

"I've reason to believe that she's in Queens or Brooklyn."

"Great, the largest fucking boroughs. Can't you do anything else?"

"My power in the other boroughs is limited. But I'm trying, Jackson, I really am. I care about Rayah too."

I nod. "Thank you, then, I guess."

"She's my niece, you know. I don't want to see any harm come to her."

I clench my fists. "I'll tear this city apart if anything happens to her. No one will be safe."

Dayton nods. "We'll get there... brother."

I look him in the eye. "I wouldn't ask you if I wasn't desperate, but..." I pause. I can't bring myself to say the words. I'm no beggar. Never have once in my life.

Dayton shakes his head sadly. "I gave you everything I had, Jackson. Right now, all my money's tied up in commodities, the whiskey, tobacco, and guns. You sell them down in Boston and I'll split the earnings with you. How's that?"

"And how much is that we're talking?"

Dayton adds it up. "About one and a half million. Each."

I put out my hand. "You've got your man."

We shake hands.

*

My path had been decided. I would head back to Boston as Dayton kept his ear to the street and watched out for that silver toothed fucker.

Gamma agreed to come down with me to Boston and help plan out our first means of attack. Dayton hired twenty goons and together we boarded another ship and I couldn't deny I had tears in my eyes as I watched New York grow further and further away.

If before I felt like I had been betraying Rayah, now it was a sense of hopelessness that pierced my heart. It was two weeks until he'd kill her. I was still seven million off.

I needed a damn miracle.

*

Gamma spent the afternoon once we arrived back in Boston going over the city charts. I made my way to the local watering hole, on the south boundary with the Hatchet Gang's territory, accompanied by Orson and Patrick, who had decided to stay in my employment as my muscle.

Inside the tavern we sat at a table, and I took in the scene. It was quiet, with only a few patrons occupying the bar, talking amongst themselves. There was a game of blackjack in the corner, but I ignored it, not without a great deal of temptation though.

"Shouldn't we be staying close to the manor house?" Orson asked me.

"I thought we'd get our ear to the street, feel out the city. After all, Gamma is out of her depth here, she doesn't have the contacts like in New York."

101

Patrick nodded, chewing on his toothpick. "Sounds about right."

"Course it does. You know I'm the brains of this operation." I wave down the barman and ask him to leave the bottle of whiskey on the table. He sets it down beside the three glasses. I pour us each a tot and slide their drinks across the rough surface of the table.

"Don't normally drink on the job," says Patrick.

Orson doesn't hold such qualms and tosses back his drink. I pour him another.

"Guess that was before you were with me, then." I toss back mine, pour another. There's an old man wearing a striped suit playing on the piano. The scene reminds me of an old western, and I can't help think of Clarence.

I lift my drink. "For No-Name."

"Ayuh," says Orson. We drink our whiskey and chat about which of the two gun men is the better shot, talk about the women we've loved and lost. The conversation is turning to cards, when the door opens and two men enter. They're wearing trench coats, hatchets brandished on their waist, along with a couple of sharp looking knives.

Orson spots them before Patrick, and his hand goes under the table, slowly. The two men are behind Patrick, who notices Orson's change of posture, and his hand goes under the table too.

102

"Gentlemen," I say to the two men, who are obviously members of the Hatchet Gang and scouting out the area. I stand up and lift the bottle. "Care to join me for a drink?"

"Don't drink with strangers, stranger," says the one with the discoloured eye. His teeth are yellow, and everything about his appearance speaks of violence, the scar running down one side of his cheek, the red bruising on his knuckles. The other man is smaller, quieter, with suspicious eyes, and I think this man the senior member of the gang. His eyes find mine and I smile, no subterfuge in my expression.

"A man can only call himself a man if he can share in his wealth and good fortune with those he meets along the road."

The smaller man thinks for a moment, then nods, and the barman sighs with relief, brings two glasses from behind the counter and places them at the table. Then he slides two chairs to the table and goes back behind the bar. The smaller gangster hasn't blinked in all that time, his eyes locked on mine.

I guess a criminal knows another one when he meets them.

"Please, sit?" I sit down, and my two gun men haven't taken a breath since the two gangsters entered, but as the smaller man smiles, they seem to ease, their hands never leaving the pistols handles though.

The two Hatchet men sit at the table and the scarred man picks up his drink and sniffs it. I lift mine and take a sip, showing that it's safe. The man grunts and tosses it back. The smaller man twirls the glass on the table, he looks from Orson, to Patrick, and back to me.

"You Waterfront Boys?" he asks me, plain and simple, the accusation clear in his voice.

"No, not them." I refill the scarred man's glass. Patrick and Orson haven't touched their drinks.

The scarred man stares at Patrick. "Hey, don't I know you?"

Patrick shakes his head. "'Fraid not."

"Where you boys from then, if not the Waterfront?" asks the small man.

"New York."

"Oh yeah?"

"Yeah."

Silence passes.

"I do know you!" The scarred man points a finger at Patrick. "Fucker killed Lamone after he got caught cheating at poker!" The scarred man stands and pulls out his blade. The two men jump up and snap out their pistols, pointing them at the two Hatchet men.

"Please!" pleads the barman.

"Shut the fuck up!" shouts the small Hatchet man. He looks at me and throws down his blade. "Look, we don't want no trouble. Bjorn here is just a bit hot headed, is all."

"Fuck that, these cunts killed my friend!" shouts the scarred man, Bjorn.

"You sure about that?" I say. Bjorn frowns at me. "A man can get confused sometimes, might think he knows a face, but then aren't faces funny? And one can look like another." I throw back my whiskey.

The two men are outmatched. Bjorn curses and slips his knife back into his belt. He points a finger at Patrick. "This ain't over between you and me!" He turns and storms out, banging the door shut behind him. The smaller man smiles as he backs up to the door, then with a final nod, he turns and flees after his friend.

"We should've killed them," says Patrick.

I shake my head. "We kill them, then the gang will know somethings up." I stand and smile. "Instead, we'll use them."

"Use them how?"

"Simple, by following them. And finding out where they all hang out. Then we hit them, hard and fast. I want this war to be finished by yesterday."

Chapter 8: Truth Hurts

I'm no killer. I've already told you that. So, the next day, after Gamma and I talk to the goons, I wish them luck and watch as they bustle into two armoured carriages and they roll down the driveway, away from the manor house.

I'm a con man, not a gun man.

"I thought your brother put you in charge?" Jedidiah says to me as we stand on the top of the steps. "Shouldn't you be going with them, to make sure everything runs smoothly?"

"A leader leads. A dead man cannot lead." I look at him. "I'll oversee the war between our organizations and these gangs, but I won't put my life in jeopardy. I'm lucky to be alive with what's been happening the past month, and I won't push my luck when I don't have to."

"Spoken like a politician."

"I'm a thief, not a politician."

"What's the difference?"

I smile. "I steal from the rich."

"Indeed." He waves for me to follow him inside. We enter the room, and he pours us drinks. "Tell me, Jackson, what is it that you want?"

"I want my daughter back."

"Yes, Isabella told me about what happened. Terrible business. I would never stoop so low as to target someone's family."

"My brother's keeping an ear to the street. If anyone can find her it's him." I think for a moment. "I can't figure out how you knew we were brothers."

"A man mustn't reveal all his secrets."

"That's kind of what I'm getting at. I never told anyone, except..."

"Rayah." Jedediah nods. "I think your brother isn't telling you everything, Jackson."

"What do you mean?"

Jedidiah smirks, and that really pisses me off. I place my drink down on the table. "Jedidiah," I say. "This might be your city, but if you don't tell me everything you know about my daughter right now, I'll make it my business to make you a fucking pauper before the end of the week." I take a step closer to him, my fist clenching so hard that my knuckles crack. "Or I can make you a dead man. The devil knows

I'm no killer, but you cross me, and my daughter and I can be... I *can* be."

Jedidiah smiles wider. "The man you're looking for goes by the alias of Peakers. He has silver teeth, right?"

"Yeah."

"And a scar across his cheek?"

"That's him."

"He arrived here about two weeks ago."

"He's here?"

"He *was* here."

"Then where is he, now?"

"I don't know. He came here with a girl, your daughter. I hadn't known it at the time, or I would have held her here. I'm not afraid to say that I would have ransomed her back to Crystallini for an extortionate fee."

"You would have what?" I go to take a step closer to him, my fist lifts involuntarily. There's a click. I stop and turn and see Isabella standing there.

"Don't."

I take a step back. "Wouldn't dream of it."

Isabella doesn't aim the pistol away, so I drop my fists.

"Very good," she says.

108

"Look, it's nothing personal, I just would have seen an opportunity against an opponent in a rival city. But now our organizations are to be aligned, I view you as an ally. I want to help, Jackson."

"Then help. Get me my daughter back. Between you and my brother, there must be something you can do."

"New York is a big city, and there's plenty of places to hide."

I sigh. "Well, I have two weeks left to make seven million. I just hope this deal between you and my brother is more lucrative than it seems."

"The whiskey, tobacco and guns have been unloaded," says Jedidiah. "But listen, I'll help you anyway I can. Why don't I give you some of my stock of cocaine. You can sell it in New York and split the profits with me. Call it a show of good faith."

"Why would you give me it? Wouldn't you be leaving yourself short here?"

"Gods, no. I'll give you... say, five kilos. You bring that back and chop it up, sell it off and make... one million off it."

"That doesn't sound like a split down the middle," I say, adding up the sums.

"Well, I have hands to grease here in Boston, officials, inspectors, politicians. It's not like New York here, with each borough bending to their crime lord's will. Here money rules."

"I see. Well then, I'll gladly accept your help. But I won't be able to begin selling it in New York until I'm finished up here in the city."

"True. So why not enjoy yourself while you're here. Eat, drink, make merry."

"Excuse me, Jedidiah, but I'll enjoy myself when I have my daughter back, and not until then."

He nods. "That's understandable. After all, I felt the same way when they'd kidnapped my Isabella."

Isabella nods. The pistol is still trained on me.

"I'm not going to attack your father." I pick back up my drink and toss it back. "At least not while he sticks to his word."

"Of course," smiled Jedidiah. "A man's word is all he has, and he doesn't break it for no one."

*

I step over the body, and into the safe house. The wall is riddled with bullet holes. The fighting had been bloody, but the goons Crystallini had hired had been hardened fighters to a man, and they'd only lost six to the Hatchet Gang's twenty-four. Blood pools on the ground. In the back I find packages wrapped up.

I cut it open and snort it.

Cocaine.

I wave for Orson and Patrick to come over.

"What is it?" asks Orson.

"Get this stacked up in a carriage. I don't want Jedidiah finding

out about it."

"You double-crossing him already?" asks Patrick, twirling the

toothpick in his mouth.

"Why not? It's not like he's helping me out. He's practically

robbing me with the coke deal he's set up. No, I'll take whatever I can

wherever I can get it. So get this shit in the carriage, before his men get

here." I look past the two muscle at the hired goons. "And you can take

whatever you can carry. I hope this buys your silence."

They smile and set to searching through everything, pockets,

drawers, taking the expensive furniture even.

Orson and Patrick enter the carriage with me, and we set off along

the road. The carriage behind us is carrying the cocaine. We head up

the hill, turning right, when a bullet tears through the wall of the

carriage. I duck down and cover my head, as the two men return fire.

The horses panic and flee down the street, more bullets rip through the

wall, one hits Patrick in the leg. He curses and reloads.

The carriage pulls left, hits the curb and the carriage tilts. And I scream as it flips over, spilling the three of us around the wrong way. I hit my head off a beam of wood and the world blurs. There's movement. I look up and see men approaching the carriage. I pull out my pistol and aim it, fire, taking the closest man through the chest. But it doesn't stop them. They reach the carriage and pull open the door. Orson struggles with the man, his blade cuts him across the arm, but the man is joined by two others, and together they overpower Orson. Patrick aims his pistol, he can't stand. The bullet takes the man on the left through the throat. He clutches the wound, blood pouring out through his fingers as he stumbles back a step and drops to his knees.

There are more shots outside, as the goons have heard the commotion and are running up the street. I'm grabbed by a masked man and pulled out of the carriage. Orson is on the ground, being beaten by two men clutching wooden clubs. His face is covered in blood, as is the cobbles beneath him.

"Boss!" screams Patrick, as I'm manhandled across the street, and into another carriage.

The hired goons are streaming up the street now, and the Hatchet Gang crowd around the carriage, bullets rip through the wall and window, I count at least a dozen of the Hatchet Gang, pressed up

112

behind crates on the corner of the street, firing back at the approaching goons.

Then the door shuts, and I'm left inside the carriage with two men, and it rolls off, turning into a side-street, and the sound of firing guns quickly falls into the distance.

I look at the smaller man. It's the man from the bar that day, the one with the suspicious eyes. The scarred man is sat beside me, holding a pistol aimed at my head. What was his name again? Ben? No…

"Bjorn," I say, smiling. "How nice of you to drop by."

Bjorn sneers.

The small man sits forward. "You should have told us you were Crystallini's man. We have business to discuss."

"You could have just sent a message."

"But now Jedidiah has broken the peace. It is war from here on out."

"It would look that way, wouldn't it?"

Bjorn smacks me across the face with the pistol.

He'll come to regret that.

I say, "You and the Top Hats were looking to start a war. He knew you were in meeting to ally against him."

"Well, it's up to you to turn the tide of things," says the small man. "New York must side with us."

"That's not my decision, is it? Do I look like I can change Crystallini's mind? I'm just a con man."

"And I'm a damned ballerina," says the small man. "Look, you need to decide where your allegiances lie. Jedediah is looking to turn this city legit, and that'll never happen, because legit was a thing in the past. Only crime can work these days, as its honest."

I must agree with him there. "What do I call you? Hatchet Man?"

"You can call me Jones. Franklyn Jones. He leans forward and shouts out the window. "Stop the carriage. He's getting off." Jones looks at me. "Think about what I said. New York has more in common with us and the Top Hats than that uppity asshole."

And again, I have to agree with him.

"Alright, I'll consider your offer, but no promises."

Jones smiles crookedly, and I find myself starting to warm to him. "We're criminals, Mr. New York, and what's worth is the word of a criminal?"

"About as much as a whore's sweet nothings," I say.

"So, let me tell you something, Mr. New York."

And then Jones tells me something, and it changes my world, forever.

*

I'm let off deep in the Hatchet Gang's territory, it's mostly tenements and warehouse districts. I'm stopped a couple of times but I don't have any belongings on me, so I'm let go each time. It's late by the time I reach the manor house.

"We were so worried about you," says Isabella.

Gamma shakes her head. "You could drop Jackson into the pits of hell, and he'll be having tea with the devil before lunchtime."

"What happened?" asks Jedediah. We're in the drawing room, he's standing in front of the fire holding a glass of whiskey.

"Is Orson and Patrick, OK?" I ask Gamma. She nods. I look at Jedediah. I pull out my pistol and shoot him through the face, blood spatters the wall behind him.

Isabella screams.

"We're taking over, is what happened."

Daniel comes running in carrying a pistol. He sees his father's corpse and gasps. Then goes to aim at me, but Patrick steps in from nowhere and punches him across the face, rips the pistol from his hand.

"Your father doesn't control Boston anymore." I step over his body. "Neither does the Hatchet Gang or the Top Hats."

"How could you?" Isabella's hands are shaking. She crouches down on the floor and places a hand on her father's shoulder.

"Easy." I pick up the bottle of whiskey and pour myself a drink. "It seems your father and my brother haven't been totally honest with me so far."

Gamma is still staring down at the body. She's no good with violence. Neither am I, to be honest, but when Jones told me what had happened two weeks ago my world had changed.

Gamma looks up at me. "Who are you?"

"I'll tell you who I am," I say, taking a sip of whiskey. "I'm a father at the end of his tether. A man not prone to violence, but hard times make hard men."

Alyssa shakes her head. She looks at me with empty eyes. "Jackson, what are you doing?"

I point a finger at Jedidiah's body. "He and my brother have been lying to me this entire time. This Peakers, that silver toothed fuck that has my daughter, you remember him?"

"What about him?" says Gamma.

"Well, it just so happens that he is employed by my loving brother."

"What?" says Alyssa.

I look at her. "Tell me you didn't know!"

Alyssa blanches. She lifts her hands. "Jackson, I swear, why would I ever work against you or my own daughter?"

"So you had no idea that Dayton was using this Peakers to force me into coming to Boston?" I step closer to Alyssa. There's fear in her eyes. And I know she's close to cracking.

"No…"

"You had no idea that he would take our daughter and use her as leverage, did you?"

"He was just supposed to give you a gentle nudge," she says. I stare down at her. I can't hide the hatred that flames in my eyes, like a tornado whipping across a forest fire, it seethes from me and into her, and her lip begins to tremble. Tears form in her eyes. "I'm so sorry, Jackson."

I turn away from her, stare into the fire. "When we get back to New York, we go our separate ways. You can run back to Crystallini. Tell him I'm coming for him, and everything he's got."

"Jackson, you can't." Alyssa can't hide the desperation in her voice.

"I just realized something." I turn and face her. "You love him, don't you?"

"What?" Horror passes over her face, like some monster peered through the gap in your wardrobe, and the truth was obvious to me then.

"You were in love with both of us. Weren't you?"

"No, Jackson. I only ever loved you."

"Don't lie to me, Alyssa."

"I… Yes. I loved both of you. But I loved you first, Jackson. It's just that you're so alike. It's hard to know where one of you stops and the other begins…"

I nod. "And you have no idea which one of us is the father, do you?"

She bites her lip. Shakes her head.

Gamma growls and rushes at Alyssa, but Patrick gets in the way and holds her back. "I'm going to fucking kill you, whore!" Gamma has a temper, like I already told you.

I put my hand on her shoulder. "Gamma, enough." I look at Alyssa. "Me and you, we're done.But for Rayah's sake, I'll get by with you. You can be her mother if you want. But I'm her father. Not him. He hid away and played his games of being gangster, and now let him hide away in his House of Two Faces and live in fear, because one day I will take everything from him."

"Jackson, please, don't be like that. We both love you. You're his brother."

"The fool of a brother that he let believe was responsible for his death for all those years. And not only did he lie to me about that, he went behind my back and took the woman I loved from me." My hands shook, my guts boiled with anger. "But I won't let him take Rayah. He

can't have her, you hear me?"

Alyssa nods. "I understand."

"You can take the ship in the morning back to New York," I say,

and then I leave the room, walking away from one of two things I have

ever loved in this world.

Chapter 9: Two Bullets

I guess you understand now that Jones told me how this Peakers had come to Boston and sought the help of Jedidiah? He had fled from New York after getting greedy and deciding he really did want the ten million bucks, and Crystallini wasn't happy with him.

But Jedediah hadn't known then that there would've been a profit in holding them both, so had let them leave, and Peakers went to the next most powerful man in Boston, Franklyn Jones, and laid out the whole story to him. But Jones, while a cold-blooded killer, wasn't a child kidnapper or ransomer, and for that he had my thanks.

The following day Alyssa boarded the ship and headed back for New York. I sent word to the boss of the Top Hats and Jones that we should meet up somewhere, at a disclosed location of a random tavern. Random, so none of us could set up the others, and there was to be no hired goons or the like allowed to come along. It was simply the bosses.

That night an armoured carriage comes rattling up the drive and I load into it. The boss of the Top Hats is there, along with Jones.

"I guess you're the man we should thank for ridding the city of that pompous asshole, Jedidiah?" asks the Top Hat. I nod. "I thank you.

My name is Harry Gains. And Prout has been a thorn in my ass since I first moved down here from Detroit."

I take a long hard look at the man, and wonder was this the same gangster that had killed No-Name's family and kicked him out of the city?

Perhaps. But this wasn't the time to exact revenge. Besides, I'd been frisked when climbing into the carriage by the driver and had no pistol.

I kept my face neutral.

"It was my pleasure. I never much liked him anyway." I notice that the windows are blacked out, so none of us know exactly where we're going.

Well, not exactly none of us...

*

Let's back up for a second. Do you really think Gamma would let me get in that carriage with no plan of action? Have you even been paying attention?

OK. So here's the con.

Gamma has been keeping her ear to the street ever since we arrived. She's made connections quickly with a few of the rogues that inhabit Boston, the free agents. When the word comes in that there's gonna be a meet between the three bosses, everyone in the city is on alert.

But it's Gamma who finds out where exactly that the meet will be.

Why is that so important?

*

A bird in hand is worth two in the bush, right? Well, I've never been a believer of that expression. I'd rather the three birds altogether, and whatever you might have in your pocket to boot.

It was with this type of mind frame that I kept silent as the other two chatted amongst themselves in the back of the carriage. They seemed to be well-acquainted and kept glancing at me. I could read the expressions.

They were planning something. And that little voice in the back of my head, the one that's kept me alive since I was abandoned outside an orphanage, screamed.

But I kept my expression unworried, even smiled when they told a joke. And waited.

We came to a halt and the door opened.

Jones climbed down first, me second, and Harry Gains third. We're stood outside a tavern, the cold air whips up the street, and I huddled into my cloak as we step through the door. There are a few people inside, a game of cards, a man playing a lute, all the norm. We take a table by the bar and order drinks.

"Good player," says Jones, looking up at the red-haired kid on the lute.

Gains nods. He looks at me, and smiles, and there's nothing warm or reassuring about it, it seems to me like something a shark would look like if they still existed.

"So, tell me something, Mr. New York." Jones is still looking at the lute player as he talks to me. "Why does this Crystallini want your daughter? What does the most powerful man in New York want with a little girl and a two-bit hustler, no offense."

I smile. "None taken. He's my brother."

"Not a very good one," says Gains. "If he's taken your daughter hostage."

"No." I take a sip of the whiskey. "But I didn't come here to talk about my daughter."

"No?" says Jones.

"Business," says Gains, and I nod.

"Ah," says Jones. "My most favourite subject."

"I think we should discuss territory first," I say.

"We've been considering that in our talks we've been having," says Gains. "I think we would like a quarter of your territory."

I suck my teeth.

"Each," says Jones.

"That would leave me with only the Waterfront," I say.

"But you'd be alive." Gains lights a cigar. "Alive to run it. And we'll help you in this war against New York."

I nod. "I can offer you a fifth of my territory, in exchange for your help."

Jones shakes his head. "This isn't up for negotiation, Mr. New York. This is our city. Since you took down Jedidiah, which we appreciate, by the way, your muscle has halved in number. If you go to war, we'll crush you."

I grimace. It's the truth. Since I decorated the walls in the manor house with Jedidiah's brains and taken his son and daughter hostage, many of the loyal men had crossed sides and swollen the enemy ranks.

"And just for trying to haggle, the number goes up to a third or your territory." Gains taps ash into a tray. "Think before you speak, or else you'll find yourself ruling nothing but the port."

"Or a ship outta here," says Jones.

I frown at him. "And here I thought you a reasonable criminal."

Gains shrugs. "Criminals are prone to greediness."

"It's true," says Jones. He claps as the lute player finishes playing. He looks at me. "You should have stayed in New York, Mr. New York. Leave Boston to the men who know how to run it."

"I guess that means the two of you then?" I sit back and look from one to the other.

"I guess it does. Unless you *do* want a war. And now that you don't have support of your brother, what, you didn't think we knew about that?" smiled Gains. I want to reach across the table right then and there and smack him.

"We know you've lost the support of New York, Mr. New York," says Jones. "You could probably last a week against us, but we'll tear down that manor house and leave your bodies floating in the docks. And then we'll find your daughter, even if we have to pay for it... And the things I'll do to her, you don't even wanna know."

I narrow my eyes at him. I stand up. "I need to take a leek."

Gains stands up and goes to frisk me.

"I've already had him searched," says Jones.

"Still, I'd rather check myself." Gains frisks me and finds nothing. I enter the men's room and wash my face. I enter the stall by the window, inhale deeply and take out the two pistols behind the cistern. I check to make sure they're loaded, but Patrick isn't stupid and has them already loaded and cocked. I slide both beneath my cloak and re-enter the bar.

Gains is chatting to a half-naked woman. Jones looks up at me and his smile falls from his face.

"What did you say about my daughter?"I ask him. He shakes his head.

I whip out both pistols, and Gains makes a break for the door. The bullet catches him in the back. He hits the floor.

Jones lifts his hands, his lips moving but no words are coming out. There's fear in his eyes.

What does a man say when faced with death? You can only share the burden so far, and that extends to keeping death company.

But this time it was different. This time *he* was keeping the company, and I was death.

I pointed my pistol, pressing it against his forehead. He closes his eyes, muttering a prayer perhaps. And who said religion was dead?

"You won't get away with this…"

I pull the trigger and Jones rocks back in his chair, his head blasted back from the power of the bullet tearing through his skull.

I drop both pistols on the floor.

"I already have."

I exit the tavern.

126

*

In four days, I had gone from no one, a rumour in New York, to the most notorious gangster in Boston. I had taken the city in my grip, and wiped out the three ruling gangs' leaders, forming them into one gang, and all bowed before me.

I didn't want power. But if Dayton wanted a war, I would surely give him one.

All I wanted was my Rayah, and I would bring hell upon the Earth to get her back.

And that meant one thing and one thing only. I was heading to New York, with the full weight of Boston behind me. I would rip the city apart and leave nothing left, until there was nowhere for anyone to hide my daughter.

I would become the monster they were forcing me to become with every moment they kept her from me.

Chapter 10: Staten Island

New York. Year of the Thief, a good omen as my ship pulls into the bay. It's New Year's Eve, and fireworks splay over the cityscape, turning the remnant towers and skyscrapers into a canvas of colours. The men aboard the ship sip whiskey and smoke as they watch the show, and I stand back at the stern, looking over the five boroughs, wondering where my little girl is hidden.

I have over four hundred gunmen aboard. All dark men with dark deeds, and each one was ready to kill on my word.

I would overpower each of the five crime lords, leaving my brother until last, letting him know with each one that fell that I was coming for him.

Which one first? Well, that's where Gamma comes in. The little woman stands beside me, and we share in a glass of champagne.

"I think you're the only woman who never fucked me," I say, watching as a blast of bright red sparks showers over the bay.

"You have a funny way of chatting up women, Jackson." Gamma smiles.

"You know what I mean."

"I do."

"I can't believe Alyssa done this to me. I never thought when I was with her…" I shake my head.

"She's lucky Patrick held me back. I would've clawed her face open." Gamma sighs as she takes a sip of the champagne.

"I don't want to hurt her. No matter how much she hurt me, I just can't do it."

Gamma laughs. "No, you just take your anger out on everyone else."

I look at her. "They deserved everything they got. They were gonna do it to me once my back was turned. I just beat them to the punch."

"I never said you were wrong."

"I know."

I put my arm around her. "It's just us left of the old gang now."

"I wonder where Chameleon is?"

"The devil knows."

"He wasn't in Boston anyway."

"Probably took a caravan west, to Detroit or California, or some other shithole backwater town."

"Or got himself eaten by mutants."

"Or that."

"So," Gamma puts her head on my shoulder. "What's our first move?"

"I was hoping you'd tell me?"

"You know as well as I do that it's you running the show now."

It's my turn to sigh. "I never wanted to be the boss, Gamma."

"A man must take the burdens he is given or fall beneath their weight."

"That from something?"

"No, it's just something my pa always said."

"He still alive?"

"No. Died when I was young. My momma brought me here with a caravan. I thought it would be exciting. Then she died when I was sixteen. I had a choice, either become a thief or sell myself."

"Which did you choose?"

She frowns. "Fuck yourself, Jackson."

I laugh. God, it feels like forever since I laughed.

"You know when all this business is over?" she asks me.

"Yeah?"

"What you plan on doing?"

"I just want to find Rayah first. I haven't decided on anything after that."

"You know you can't walk away now?"

130

"What do you mean?"

"I mean," she grabbed the bottle of champagne and filled both our glasses back up. "I mean you are in it for the long haul. These men, these men depend on you now to call the shots. To get them through the shit show that's about to happen."

I look out across the bay at Staten Island. "You think I can do it?"

"I know you can."

"Thanks Gamma."

"No problem, boss."

"Don't call me that. Not you. Ever."

"Sorry."

She follows my gaze. She can almost read my thoughts. "You're planning on attacking Staten Island first?"

I nod. "The Cartel there are weak. We'll blow through them like a forest fire in summer."

"Don't take them lightly."

"I'm not. But if it's Rayah or them, then they haven't a snowballs chance in hell."

"What if you take over the five boroughs, kill your brother, and you still can't find her?"

"Then I'll put the torch to the city, until someone comes up with a location." I look into her eyes, and I see a shred of fear there. I shake

131

my head. "It won't come to that. Dayton will see reason. He's not stupid. A cruel, conniving bastard of a brother perhaps, but he's not stupid."

"He'll never bend the knee."

"You think?"

"Would you, if you were in his shoes?"

"No, I don't think I would."

"Then there's your answer."

We sip. Silence is broken by the occasional firework. The show is petering out.

"I always wanted to see California," she says.

"Yeah?"

"Uh-huh."

"What's stopping you?"

More silence.

"Jackson?"

"Yeah?"

"What would you say if I said it was you stopping me?"

I turn and look at her. I don't think I ever realized just how beautiful she was. Her warm brown eyes twinkle from the lantern bobbing over us. I lean in to kiss her...

"Boss?"

We both open our eyes. She turns away. I look around and see Patrick and Orson standing by the rail.

"What is it?"

"There's someone you probably want to meet."

*

"What did you say your name was again?" I ask, sure I misheard him.

"Freddy Peaks." The man is a shell of who I'd met almost a month ago. He was gaunt in his face, deep shadows around his eyes, but the scar was there, and he had the silver teeth. "Some call me Peakers."

"Peakers?" I grab him by the collar. "Why shouldn't I tie you up somewhere and begin letting my boys pound the living shit out of you?"

Peakers hangs his head. "I never wanted to take your daughter, man. It was all Crystal's idea. He wanted leverage over you."

"Well, now he has it, doesn't he, because of you?" I smack him across the face. I can't stop myself. This was the man partly responsible for Rayah's kidnap. He'd held her ransom, at Crystallini's request, and then decided he wanted more of a cut and hauled ass outta dodge, just so he could fork a little more cash from the job.

I smack him again.

"Where is she?"

"I told your boys already, Crystal put a hit on my head. If I didn't hand her back, I was a dead man."

"So why come here? You should have brought her to *me*." I go to slap him again.

"I don't know what else to do, man!" Peakers breaks down into tears. "I used to run this fucking city almost. Now look at me!"

"Wait..." I stand back. "Did you say your name was Freddy Peaks? *The* Freddy Peaks?"

"Yeah."

"Freddy Peaks is dead." I pull a pistol from one of my men's belt's. I cock it and press it against Peaker's head. "Begin telling me a story, and make it a good one, because it might just save your life..."

*

I exit the room, pull down my sleeves, and see Gamma leaning up against the rail of the ship.

"I guess you heard all that?" I ask.

"I can't believe it. I think half of Staten Island heard it."

"Well. I just had to make sure he was telling the truth." I rub my knuckles, swollen from the interrogation. "I hadn't wanted to do it. But the thing that he told me had set me on edge, and I had to make sure it had been the truth."

"So Chameleon was an inside man the whole time?" Gamma laughs. "I think your brother's been playing you for a fool for years."

"You missed the best part."

"Yeah?"

"Turns out Chameleon was more than an inside man."

"How?"

"Turns out that he was Crystallini's fucking lover."

"No shit?"

"So, now we have leverage. We just need to find Chameleon, then we..." I trail off.

Who better than to find him than our old friend, Ace Holden?

"Ace?" says Gamma. "You sure you want a specialist for such delicate work?"

"Why not?"

"You know specialist's only care about money. Who's to say he won't just sell you out at the first chance he gets?"

"Because I can give him something the others can't."

Gamma laughs. "Yeah, what's that then?"

"Power."

*

Ace Holden was not a nice guy, and he went out of his way to make sure that you knew it. So, it was funny the second time I met him, it was like a case of that thing… what was it called? Oh yeah, de ja vu.

"We've gotta stop meeting like this," smiles Ace, as he holds the man over the side of the building. We're on Staten Island. I've fifty goons downstairs waiting for me. A thief can work alone, but a wanted guy like me had to take precautions.

"You never get sick of this kind of work?" I ask. Gamma is there with me, and she doesn't look like this type of scene appeals to her taste of business.

"Never. Take a hold on this guy, will you?"

I step up and grab the man by the arm and leg. He looks up at me with wide eyes. Ace reaches in and takes out a cigar, lights it with one hand. "Thanks, buddy."

"Please, help me!" shouts the man I'm holding.

"Shut up," we both say in unison.

"I heard you were back in town," says Ace.

"Yeah, I missed the weather."

Ace shrugs. "I've never noticed. Still, I guess there is something beautiful about the city this close to winter." Ace looks up at the Manhattan skyline across the river. Dark clouds brew on the horizon, promising a storm within the day.

136

"Not much of one for architecture," I say, and my heart pangs as I say it. "Though my daughter was. Is."

Ace nods. "I heard about that."

"Yeah?"

"It's all over the city. Your brother has your daughter as prisoner and wants ten mil' within the week or else."

"Well, that's where you're wrong," says Gamma.

"Is that so?" Ace looks her up and down.

"Yeah, 'cos we're gonna be running this city before he gets the chance."

"Hmmph." Ace chews on his cigar. He looks from Gamma to me, and back again. "What can I do for you?"

"Please, pull me back up! I swear I never took that money!" shouts the man.

"Shut up!" we shout in unison once more.

"I've gotta job," I say.

"Kinda job that pays hundred grand a day?" says Ace.

"Kinda job that will set you up for life, so you won't have to be hanging unfortunate fools off the side of buildings anymore."

"That so?"

Ace chews for another moment, then pulls the man back over the side of the building. He wipes down the man's clothing, fixes his collar. "Guess it's your lucky day, mister."

The man is unsteady on his feet, and who could blame him?

Ace points at me. "You see this man right here?"

The man stares with wide eyes. He nods.

"Well, this man just saved your life. His name is Jackson. Don't you forget it."

"Thank you, Jackson. T-Thank you!" The man shakes my hand and stumbles along the rooftop, down the steps.

Gamma watches him go and shakes her head. "Do we wanna even ask what all that was about?"

"He's a doorman for the Staten Island cartel. Got caught doing a number on one of their takes, skimming notes off the top. Boss wanted me to make an example for the other workers."

"Why the change of heart?" I ask.

"Well, since you're going to be taking over Staten Island and the rest of the city within the week, I don't see no need to set an example."

"You sound sure of yourself," smiles Gamma.

Ace smiles back and places his hand on my shoulder. "It's 'cos I've got a good feelin' 'bout you."

*

138

We left Ace to set about the task of finding Chameleon. Easier said than done, as that was one slippery son of a bitch, but I had faith. We headed back towards the ship, escorted by my retinue of goons, and we made quite the picture. I'm sure the cartel had knowledge of my presence, but I moved fast and got the carriage rolling before any ambushes could be set.

We made it back to the ship without trouble, which was nice for once.

Now all that was left was to finish planning our hit on the Staten Island cartel leader.

Easy.

*

You're probably wondering why hadn't I just hired Ace to take out the leader of the cartel? Well, my priority was Rayah. I had a fair idea that Dayton wouldn't have it in him to kill his own niece. But I wasn't putting it past him.

I knew if I moved on Manhattan too early that he might be forced to act, and that meant putting her life in jeopardy. My current plan of action was to knock each family off their pedestal and take control. Then when I had the four boroughs in hand, I would offer Dayton a chance at peace. I would offer him a way out. And when I had my Rayah back, I would crush him.

Ace Holden was a wildcard. A long shot odds, and if it worked, then I could use Chameleon as leverage to get Rayah back.

*

So how do you take down a cartel leader? It goes without saying that we needed to watch him. The next day myself, Patrick and Orson head into Staten Island. Gamma has given us three addresses where the leader might be holding up. As I said before, the crime-bosses don't share there aliases easily. Crystallini made it a point of fact to share who he was because he wanted everyone to know his name. We heard rumours of the Duke from Gamma, but even then, it could have been one of a dozen gangsters who *really* ran the Bronx.

It was Gamma's job to figure out the who. We just needed to figure out the where. We spent an hour watching each safe house, marking down the comings and goings of gangsters, and it seemed there was most activity at the second safe house. We headed back and got a drink at a tavern around the corner. Inside we sat at the bar and ordered drinks. There was a card game, and I sat down at it, leaving the two muscle to watch the room.

It had been too long since I'd played my hand at cards or dice. I'd promised myself that I wouldn't ever play cards after Rayah was born but seeing as Dayton probably wouldn't hand her over even if I offered him money, then I saw no point in biding my time. I played a few hands of poker, losing some money, but I cleaned them up on the fifth

hand when I got four aces on the river turn. I laughed as the old timers

cursed me for a huckster. The dealer thanked me after I flipped him a

fifty and went back to the bar.

"What's the plan, boss man?" says Orson. "We head back to the

ship?"

"No… I have an idea."

Patrick bristles. "I don't like that look in your eye, boss."

"Stick with me. I won't steer you wrong." We leave the bar and I

head around the corner, approach the safe house, and am stopped at the

door by four men toting pistols on their belts.

"Fuck you want?" says the man with the cockeye.

"I want to speak to your boss." I scribble my name down on a

piece of paper. "Give him this. He'll be expecting me, perhaps."

Moments pass after the man enters the building. He comes back

out and nods. "Only you, your two boyfriends can wait outside."

Orson and Patrick look glum at the thought or me entering alone,

but I give them a wink and enter the building. Four more guards sit at a

table inside playing dice. They stare at me as I walk past and follow the

guard up a flight of stairs. We walk down a corridor, and he knocks on

a door. The sound of latches being pulled aside sounds behind the door, then it opens. Smoke wafts out, along with classical music. I think it's

Satie, but I'm not sure, Rayah was always better at telling them apart.

I enter the room and a fat man sits behind an enormous desk. On it

is a pistol, cocked and most probably loaded. "A brave man, to enter

here alone."

"Not bravery," I say. "I just like to gamble."

"Huh."

"You like to gamble, Mr...?"

Silence. "Call me Mr. Sykes."

"Sykes."

"What can I do for you, Duke Killer?"

"I want Staten Island."

"Is that so?"

"Yeah. But I don't want to kill anyone who hasn't it coming. I

never had any problems with you. So, how about a gamble?"

The man sits forward, and the light from the desk lamp hits his

face. His heavily wrinkled, advanced in age, but it doesn't show in his

voice when he talks. "What kind of gamble?"

"A game of chance. Between you and I."

Sykes chews his lip. Then lifts his pistol and aims it at me. "Tell

me why I shouldn't just put lead between your eyes right this

moment?"

"Because I've four hundred armed men who want to tear this island apart, and you to go along with it. I don't want a bloodbath. I avoided a major war in Boston, you might have heard about it?"

Sykes nods. "Everyone heard how you crushed them fools in Boston. But this isn't Boston. You're in my territory now."

"OK. So how about I even the odds. I win, I get Staten Island, and you come work for me. I'll set you up somewhere, Detroit, California, you won't be outta the business. You'll still be running where you're at, but answering to me. I have stakes in both cities now, and you can have a piece."

Sykes considers this. "And if I win?"

"You can have Boston. All of it. You won't be the weakest gangster crime lord in New York. You'll be set up, and ready to take on the other crime lords on an even keel."

"Hah. You're a mad man."

"Some call it madness, some call it genius. Me? I call it being lucky. You think you're lucky, Mr. Sykes?"

Sykes taps his fingers on the desk with his free hand, then puts down the pistol. He waves his hand, and the cockeyed man pulls up a chair. I sit down.

"OK. You know what, I'm interested. Drink?"

"Like a fish."

Sykes pours both of us a drink. I take a sip. It's good.

"What's the game? Cards, dice?"

I shake my head. "Oh, a much more dangerous game than that, Mr. Sykes."

He stares into my eyes. "You really are a mad man, aren't you, Duke Killer?"

"As I said, I guess I'm just lucky."

Chapter 11: Blind Man's Bluff

The game was set. We'd meet up on the ship the next day, at dusk, as the game being played wasn't legal and we didn't want the Wardens breaking it up. My goons would wait offshore, along with Mr. Sykes's men.

It was stated by both of us that no matter who won the other man's goons wouldn't retaliate, under oath of the criminal law. All had agreed, and the dead man's men were free to go or stay as they pleased.

The rumours of the game spread throughout the city and everyone was betting on who would walk away first, or who would bite the bullet.

What's the game we're playing?

Why, haven't you ever heard of Blind Man's Bluff?

*

I sit on one side of the table. Mr. Sykes on the other. Orson and Patrick stand behind me. Bjorn, the scarred man, and the cockeyed guard stand behind Mr. Sykes. We're sat on the deck of my ship, and there's five flintlock pistols on the table.

One of these is loaded.

The referee has seen to the loading of the pistols, and the placement, and only he knows which is which.

"Now, gentlemen. Before we begin, I must tell you the rules."

I take off my coat and fold it over the back of the chair. Patrick pours me a whiskey. Orson crosses his arms and stares at the pistols.

"First," continues the referee, "Once the pistol is picked up, the holder must shoot. If he is to forfeit, it is to be before he picks up the pistol. If he does not shoot, the other man has the option to take a shot at twenty paces. The forfeiter must not move until the shot is taken. If he should duck or try to dodge, he will be hung as a coward. Is this understood?"

I nod, as does Sykes.

"Second, the first shooter is decided by a coin toss. The winner of the coin toss shall decide who will go first, and the other man will go second if the shot shall not be fatal.

"Lastly, and I need not remind gentleman such as yourselves, if you should turn and try to shoot your opponent, you *will* be executed in the most torturous manner thought possible." The referee looks from myself to Sykes. "Do both men agree to the terms?"

"I do," I say.

"I do also." Sykes looks calm and collected.

The referee points at me. "You will be heads." He flips the coin. Tails. Tough luck.

Sykes smiles. "It seems luck is favouring me. I will go first." He leans forward and his hand glides over the five pistols. He watches the referee, but the man has been chosen for his poker face and gives nothing away. Sykes' hand stops over the third pistol and picks it up. He presses the end of it against the side of his head.

"Here goes nothing."

He pulls the trigger.

It clicks harmlessly.

Sykes replaces the pistol in its position. Now it's my turn.

My hand goes from the first to the fifth, without shaking, I might add. I choose the second pistol. I put it against the side of my head.

An image of Rayah passes through my mind.

I'm sorry my chicken, but I didn't know how else to get you back. Please forgive daddy...

I pull down on the trigger, and it clicks.

The silence that follows is deafening. And I'm not sure if it blasted the side of my head open, and now I'm simply dead. But no, I hear someone sigh in relief, and I open my eyes. Sykes frowns down at the pistols. His odds of survival have just dropped drastically.

Down to one in three, precisely.

147

Sykes laughs. "A mad man!" He slaps his knee. "A drink, before we go any further?"

Sykes picks up his whiskey, as do I. We toast.

"May thieves rein," says Sykes.

I lift my drink in salute. "May thieves rein." I toss it back.

Sykes lifts the fourth pistol and shoves the end of it under his chin. "Arghh!" he growls, then pulls down on the trigger.

It clicks once again.

Shit.

I have one of two pistols left in front of me. And one of them means getting Rayah back, but the other one means death. Which do I choose?

"Decisions, decisions," smiles Sykes.

"Care for another drink," I say. Sykes nods.

"I love drinking with dead men. It makes me feel… alive." Sykes looks like he's enjoying himself.

I didn't know whether I loved or hated this asshole.

Patrick poured me another tot of whiskey, filling it up to the brim, I might add. A good man is Patrick.

I look over the rail of the ship and who do I see there but Alyssa. I think it's damned sweet of her to come and watch the father of her child blow his head off.

That's if I am the damned father...

No, it doesn't matter if he... if he gave the seed. I'm Rayah's
father. I held her hair back when she was sick. I helped break her fevers
and held her close those nights she cried for her mother.

I look away from Alyssa, fighting the stinging in my eyes. I toss
back the whiskey, the whole nine yards, as they used to say, and it
burns beautifully going down.

A dead man has no fear.

No fear.

I lift the fifth pistol and put it against the side of my head.

"I'm so sorry Rayah."

My entire life flashes before my eyes. Of Alyssa, naked on the
bed. Of her swollen stomach, her morning sickness. Of her vanishing
act, of a lone crib in the apartment and Rayah's heart-breaking crying.
Of the years that followed, of Rayah learning to walk and talk, of small
hands in mine growing larger, of teeth falling out and regrowing.

A life's worth of memories in a moment to ponder.

I think of Dayton then, and anger bubbles up in my chest. Would I
let him take away the one thing precious left in my world? He took the
woman I loved. He would *not* take my chicken.

149

The trigger slowly pulls inwards, and my heart beats in my chest, and I inhale deeply, and a lungful of air never tasted as sweet as your last.

But the pistol clicks harmlessly.

There are cheers from the crowd below the ship. I replace the pistol on the table.

"Sudden death," says the referee. "I've never seen it before. But what normally happens here is you each take twenty paces from the pistol, and on the count of three, you both turn and run for the pistol. Whoever reaches the pistol first, if the shot shall not be fatal, it is a fight to the death."

The referee looks from myself to Sykes. He is much older than me, not as fast. We both know he would lose in a fight. Sykes nods. "So be it."

I hold up my hand. "One more drink."

We both sit close to the table, and Sykes has madness dancing in his eyes.

"You don't have to do this," I tell him.

"I do. Jackson. I don't want to be number three, or number two anymore. You know what it's like living in the shade of those above you your entire life?" Sykes wipes sweat from his brow. I look out over the crowd. They're still taking bets; the odds have changed in my favour.

"I know what's it's like to be ruled by fear." I shake my head. "Join me, Sykes. You can have a good life, out in California, growing tobacco, or running guns in Detroit, it all depends on what *you* want. Just don't do this. You won't win."

"You don't think I could beat you?" Sykes smiles.

"I don't think you want to take that chance."

"Maybe. Maybe not..." Sykes sighs. He tosses back his drink. "But then if we never try, we'll never know, right?"

I shake my head. "You're making a mistake."

Sykes stands up and pushes away his chair.

I stand up and do also. I take twenty paces away from the chair.

"One."

I can't believe this is happening. I don't want to be responsible for his murder.

"Two."

I've tried my hardest since I've been forced on this path to save lives where I can. I'm not a perfect man, the devil knows, but I'm not evil.

"Three."

I turn, as does Sykes, and we both run toward the table. Everything moves in slow motion, as adrenaline courses through my body. Three steps, four steps, and Sykes is reaching out, but I'm faster, I knew this would happen.

I reach the table and grab the pistol. The handle is sure and steady in my grip. I kick the table forward and it collides against Sykes's knee. The fat man stumbles, falls, and hits the table face-first. The table buckles beneath his weight. He hits the floor.

I aim the pistol down at his face, and he smiles up at me.

I look up. It's a fight to the death. Everyone knows that. I can't walk away, or they'll hang us both as cowards. I look back down at Sykes, and nod.

What does a man say when faced with death? You can only share the burden so far, and that extends to keeping death company.

But this time it was different. I had no want in the part in this task that was to be played. Still, a man is better off doing a task than living with the fear of it.

I close my eyes, and I pull the trigger.

*

Click!

I lift the pistol and re-cock it, then point it to Sykes once more and pull the trigger. The pistol clicks harmlessly. I turn to see the referee jumping over the railing of the ship.

"What in the..." I back away from Sykes, sure this is some ploy, that I'm being betrayed somehow, but he looks just as confused as I do.

"What's going on?" he asks. "Why don't I have another hole to breathe through right now?"

I check my pistol. "It wasn't loaded." I go the rail and watch as the referee swims away. Men and women on the dock are fuming. They are running up the gangplank, pistols and knives in hand, and the referee fades into the darkness just in time, as men and women fire into the water at random.

"Stop!" I shout.

Gamma is there beside me. "Why?" she asks. There's that temper of hers.

"Because I want to know what the fuck is going on," I say calmly. "And I can't interrogate a man who's lying on the bottom of the bay, now, can I?"

"Good point. Men, women, hold your fire!" Gamma walks through the crowd, explaining that they needed to catch the referee and not turn him into a human lead ball.

"What's going on?" It's Alyssa.

153

"I don't know," I say, and turn away from her.

I stare out into the darkness.

What in the hell just happened?

*

"We caught him on the far side of the bay." Patrick twirls the toothpick in his mouth.

Orson is more forthcoming. "Says he will only talk to you, boss."

I enter below deck of the ship, not my ship, mind you, and enter a cabin where they're holding the referee. They searched the entire bay with lanterns until they'd found him half a mile from where we'd played the Blind Man's Bluff.

And since the referee had taken a hiatus, the match had gone to me, since I would have had the finishing blow.

Staten Island was mine, but right now what I was more interested in was who in the hell this referee was and what he thought he was playing at exactly.

He was pretty beat up by the look of him, the boys had begun interrogations already, and I told them to take a hike. They waited outside, leaving me alone with the ref.

"And just who in the name of the devil are you?" I ask him.

"Don't you recognize an old friend?"

The man looks up. And there is something about his eyes. I pull at the beard and moustache, and they both come away, revealing the gaunt face of Chameleon.

"You look like shit," I tell him.

"Hah, tell me about it. I've been in hiding from Crystallini and you since I left the gang."

"Hiding from him? I thought you were lovers?"

"Yeah, so did I. But he's changed, Jackson. He's not the man I fell in love with."

"How so?"

"He's paranoid. Thinks I'm going to betray him. The fuck I would."

"I know you wouldn't. That's why you're going to help me get back my Rayah."

"He won't go for it. You have him terrified. He doesn't even leave the House of Two Faces anymore. He has Rayah locked away on the top floor. She's impossible to get to without an army."

"Well, that's just what I'm building now, isn't it?"

"Set up a meet, Jackson. He still loves you."

"Loves me?" I laugh. "He's fucked me over every chance he's gotten. You wanna know who I was talking to?"

"Who?"

"Freddy Peaks."

"Shit."

"Yeah, shit."

"So, you know?"

"I know it all. I know that Dayton didn't really play the caring brother. No. He chose to abandon me. He chose a life with this fucking Peakers, living it up with a gang rather than support his only fucking blood left in this world."

"I'm sorry Jackson. That must have been hard to hear."

"You think?" I seethe. I want to hurt this man, because he means something to Crysyallini, and that means I will be evening the score. But instead, I say, "I was abandoned by my parents, by my brother, by my wife, if I could have called her that, and now I've had my daughter ripped from me by that same brother, and my world turned upside down. So, you'll understand if I'm not exactly in a forgiving mood right about now..."

"I don't want your forgiveness, Jackson. I don't need it because I never betrayed you."

"You were working for Crystallini the whole time."

"We all were."

"What?"

"Me, No-Name, Alyssa, and even your untouchable Gamma."

"Don't you fucking lie!"

"I'm not. Ask her. She hasn't worked for him in years, but she did once."

"Why? Why were you all working for him? Against me?"

Chameleon shakes his head. "You don't get it, do you? We weren't spying on you. Dayton hired the best of the best to keep you *safe*."

"Bullshit. He just wanted to keep tabs on me at all times."

"That too. He feared you, Jackson. He still does. And could you blame him?"

"You think he's scared now?" I smile, and there's nothing nice about it. It is a smile reserved for butcher's blocks, for death row inmates. It was a smile of a man too far gone.

"I think he's still your brother, and I think there's a part of you in there that still loves him."

"Love." I laugh. "And what good is love, when all it does it give people a weapon to turn against you?"

Chameleon shakes his head. "I don't have all the answers, Jackson. I'm just a man."

I leave Chameleon inside to ponder our next conversation. I tell the boys not to touch him, after all, I don't have anything I need from him yet.

"Orson," I say.

"Boss?"

"Get word on the street. We have Crystallini's lover in custody. He has one month to vacate Manhattan and never set foot in New York again."

"OK, boss. I'll get working on that right away." Orson goes to get to it.

Gamma looks at me. "You sure about this? It might piss him off."

I look up at the Empire State building, knowing now where my little Rayah was.

"I'm hoping on it."

Chapter 12: The Gloves Are Off

Sykes left that night, on a ship bound for Boston. He said he wanted to go see Mexico, so I allowed him. He'd stop off on the way in Boston and bring a bulk of guns down to Mexico for me. I wouldn't be cutting him on the coke deal though. As that would give him an opportunity to gain a foothold of power. No, he could have a small-time gig for the foreseeable future, until I could trust him not to fuck me, which might just be never, but for now he seemed content on just traveling, so I let him.

"Duke Killer," Sykes greets me on the dock. I've hired a schooner to take him down the coast. It doesn't have any cannon on board, but he'll have no need for it.

"You know the other guys call me boss, right?"

"Huh. Guess you want everyone licking your boots?"

I shake my head. "You know, I'm glad that pistol wasn't loaded."

"Yeah? Why's that?"

"I don't want your blood on my hands." I offer him my hand then, and he takes it in his. I pull him close. "But I won't be so amiable if you decide you want a bigger piece of my organization. You just remember who won that game, alright?"

Sykes nods. "You know something?"

"What?"

Sykes smiles. "I feel like a free man. I thought it would be the end of my world, losing everything. But it feels more like... More like I've gained something, rather than lost. You know?"

I think of the enormous burden of leadership pressing down on me. The unfathomable amount of weight on my conscience that is the loss of Rayah. I nod. I can understand. A part of me wishes our situations were reversed.

But a wish isn't worth the paper it's written on. I watch him climb the gangplank and board the ship. He has a big grin on his face as the anchor's raised and they lower the sails.

I watch as it fades away into the distance.

*

With Staten Island under my belt my sights turned to the Bronx. I knew Brooklyn and Queens were ready for war since I arrived, and I also knew that a war with one would only work in the others favour by depleting my manpower and exposing me for attack.

But the Bronx was still divided. It had been in conflict since I blew the Duchess's brains out what seemed a lifetime ago. My ranks had swelled to just over six hundred from taking over the Staten Island cartel, with half that number of lower rank employees, such as drivers, doormen, watchmen, and more importantly, spies.

Spies would win me this war.

Gamma had her old network of agents up and running, and now with a score of spies on the street her power grew exponentially. I hadn't discussed with her what Chameleon told me about her being in Crystallini's employment at the beginning. I didn't want a rift between us because I needed her.

I also was wary of my affection for her and realized it could be exploited by Crystallini or the other crime lords. I kept her on the ship, with fifty men armed with flintlock rifles and pistols. A floating fortress.

Chameleon was still locked away on board too. I had put the word out that I had him, but Dayton had yet to respond. It was only a matter of time until he responded, I knew.

So, the Bronx. How best to take over? We could have wiped out the gangs one at a time or all at once. They were small-time, fighting over street corners while I was controlling boroughs and cities. I had twice their combined numbers so even if they did join forces, which they wouldn't, they still wouldn't win. But I didn't want a war. I wanted to take over in a fashion that would only serve to intimidate the other crime-lords.

161

This is where Ace Holden came in. He had returned after hearing

Chameleon had been caught. He was eager to prove to me that he was a

man of his worth. I set him loose on the streets of the Bronx, telling

him I wanted the leaders of each gang made an example out of. I

wanted their heads left out in the open for all to see. I wanted them to

know that *anyone* was touchable in the Bronx.

The word came back by midnight that the heads of the leaders of

the four gangs controlling the Bronx had been found in their respective

territories. Within the hour word was put out that the four gangs would

bend the knee and allow me to rule the Bronx, on the condition that the

four gangs still be allowed to run their territories, while cutting me in

on fifty points of their take of course.

I agreed.

In the space of a few hours and without getting my hands dirty I

had taken over the borough that I had called home my entire life, the

place I had squabbled a measly living as a small-time con man.

There was still three days left until the deadline for Rayah's

murder. It was like a game of poker, both myself and Dayton holding

our cards close, waiting for the other to give away what we had. But I

would not break, my poker face would hold strong, and now I had

leverage in case he decided he wanted to make an example out of me

by hurting Rayah.

162

That left Queens and Brooklyn to take over. I knew they would be far harder to control, I knew that to take them nothing less than all-out-war was needed…

*

I am not a killer. This I have told you again and again. But I needed to show my men that I wasn't afraid to go to war. So the next day when my men were loading onto ships and carriages to attack Brooklyn from two directions, I joined the carriage in the middle of the convoy. There was a rifleman on the front and back of the carriage, along with Patrick, Orson and two other muscle men inside with me.

Gamma had marked maps of the enemy's safe house locations and handed them to the Capo's of my gang. Each Capo controlled thirty men, with the orders coming from me specifically, or if the chain of command got disrupted, the commands would then come from my underboss, namely Gamma.

We rolled along the bridge and down into Brooklyn. The tenements made for ideal ambush locations, but we went by untroubled. There were three hundred men in my convoy, with another three hundred attacking from the east, coming in by ship and sweeping the streets.

We were passing by a market when the shit hit the fan.

A flaming carriage came hurtling out of an alleyway, straight for my carriage. The riflemen riddled the driver with two shots, he fell off the carriage, but it still came straight for us. It collided against the side of our carriage and sent us reeling over sideways, but we didn't go fully over, and we jumped out the other side. Shots were coming from everywhere. They picked their location perfectly. It was at an overpass of a crumbling highway, with cramped market stalls beneath offering plenty of cover.

I whipped out my pistol and shot at a man behind a stack of crates. It missed.

"Shit," I growled, ducking down and reloading my pistol. A bullet struck the carriage to my left. Patrick grabbed me and forced me back inside the carriage, which was not a great idea, as it was catching light on the other side. He jumped in with me. The air was smoky. Patrick aimed and shot, his bullet catching a goon in the shoulder.

I reloaded my pistol and aimed, this shot was deadlier, catching a man in the right eye.

I had been practicing.

Orson was outside the carriage. He was in a scuffle with a tall man carrying a cleaver. Orson whipped out his stiletto blade and shoved it up beneath the man's ribs.

"We need to get fucking moving!" I shouted. I pushed my way past Patrick and outside, grabbing Orson by the shoulder and dragging him behind me. Patrick was following closely behind. We made it to the next carriage, which men were shooting from inside. I pulled open the door and shoved both my muscle men inside, then jumped in after them.

"Pass the word along!" I shouted out the window. "Get fucking moving!" The carriages began to roll, the shots falling away behind us as we passed deeper into Brooklyn.

"Snipers!" someone screamed, as a flintlock rifle peeled through the silence. I peered out the window to see a figure up in the abandoned buildings above us. Then another shot from the other side.

We were surrounded by snipers!

A shot hit one of the drivers, because we rolled to a stop again. Shots were exchanged, but my men were coming off worse, as the men outside on the carriages had no cover and it was like shooting fish in a damned coffee can.

I pushed my way out of the carriage. Patrick and Orson filed out behind me, shouting what in the hell I thought I was doing. I was moving up the convoy, but there was a sniper! And I jumped back just in time because a bullet hit the ground where I'd just been standing.

Patrick and Orson were capable shots and returned fire with their

pistols, but the distance was much too far.

I reached the carriage that had been holding up the convoy and

pulled the dead driver off. Patrick sat up alongside me, Orson on the

back. I whipped the horses, and we began rolling away, a final shot hit

the carriage just behind me, and we were rolling downhill, thankfully

out of range of the damned snipers. We were nearing the middle of

Brooklyn now, approaching the first safe house. Thankfully they hadn't

known which route exactly we'd be taking, and the opposition so far

while challenging hadn't been crippling. I pulled up behind the carriage

in front of me and jumped off. There was men on top of the safe house,

and my men were taking cover behind their carriages, firing up at the

snipers up on the roof.

Where was No-Name when you needed him?

But a man must make way with the tools he is given. I spotted

Ace Holden among the press of men. I grabbed him.

"You're a good shot, right?"

"Yeah."

"Right. Patrick, Orson, Ace, get three rifles each and get on top of

this carriage. I don't care where you get them. You, and you, get this

fucking carriage rolling closer."

My three best gun men climbed on top of the carriage and two goons rolled it closer.

Shots were exchanged, but the return fire allowed the footmen to approach the safe house without sniper fire. There were still shots coming from the windows though, but there was nothing I could do about that. The front door was barred.

Shit.

"Get the damned dynamite!" I shouted.

Ace comes running up the steps, bundle of red sticks in hand and he sets to work wiring it up and spooling it down the steps. We stand behind the carriage as the door is blasted apart and the ground shakes like an earthquake. Damned dynamite cost me a pretty penny.

Men swarm in from the street beside us, and it takes me a moment of horror to realize that it's the other half of my men, coming in from the east. Well thank the devil for that. They look pretty beat up, so more than likely the boss of Brooklyn thought I was putting my full weight of my attack from the water, as only a madman would have attacked from land.

Well, I guess I am a mad man then.

*

Danny Gloves was an eighteen-year-old small-time gun for hire who'd been orphaned in Boston and grew up never tasting a silver spoon in his

167

life, even via crime. When he'd been given the chance of leaving the

Top Hats, an organization he never liked as he didn't believe in their

twenty-point tax system and was given the chance to join this New

York gangster, Jackson, in a quest for revenge, it seemed like

something straight out of one of those paperback books he liked to

read.

They climbed down into the boat, him, twenty-nine other soldiers,

and their Capo, a grease-ball by the name of Charlie Fitz, who had a

stammer, but his hand never shook when holding a blade.

They, like the other ten or so boats, pushed off from the ship and

oared their way towards the docks. That's when the shit had hit the fan.

As soon as they neared the docks the shots had begun to ring out.

The ship behind them opened fire with its cannon, ripping the

tenements by the docks apart. The snipers there were many, at least

thirty by the number of smoke plumes appearing from the windows.

They were like sitting ducks as they reached the docks and began to

climb onto the jetty. Danny only had a fucking long knife and a cudgel,

how the hell was he supposed to take on long-range opponents?

One of the soldiers beside him got hit in the arm as he reached up

onto the boardwalk. Danny ignored him and ran on. It was every man

for himself. Another bullet hit the water mere paces away and Danny

zig zagged as he reached dry ground. Another bullet hit a crate right beside him and he ducked down, letting the cannon fire rip the fuckers

apart. He wasn't playing as anyone's target practice.

A minute passed by, and Fitz appeared beside him, snarling over

the noise of the cannons and the shots. "I said get fucking moving!"

Fitz grabbed Danny and pushed him on, and Danny stumbled along

behind the other fools. A man got hit in front of him and blood

splattered across Danny's face.

"Fuck," he wiped the blood off and spat. The man had a pistol on

his belt. Danny reached down and snatched it off. He wouldn't be

needing it anymore.

Danny checked the man's pockets and took the ammo pouch and

powder. Then he ran after the rest of the men as they reached the

laneways. The plan had been told to them on the ship. Run like fuck

and head west, and until you ran into friendly faces, stab the fuck out of

anyone you met.

A man came screaming from a doorway to Danny's left. He was

wearing the red shirt that marked him as a Brooklyn mobster. Danny

aimed his pistol and shot. The fucking thing missed the man's face and

hit the wall behind him. He wasn't exactly a marksman, after all.

Danny clutched the pistol like a club and drew his blade, and the

man came at him carrying a mace. Danny ducked the mace and drove

his blade up into the man's gut, opening his innards to the cold air. The man screamed as he fell. Danny clubbed him over the head with the pistol, then after the man stopped screaming, he reloaded.

A man appeared behind him. A friendly. They nodded to eachother as he passed, the man was younger than Danny, not sixteen if he was a day. A sniper leaned over the edge of the building above them and opened fire. Danny only knew this after the fact, as the bullet ripped through the young man's face like a mallet through snow. Blood splattered across the side of Danny's face and the ground. Danny jumped back against the building and pointed his pistol, well not his pistol, up at the roof in case anyone else thought about shooting. He edged around the corner and legged it. A bullet ripped into the ground two paces to his left, and he ducked right, another bullet bit into the wall in front of him. He ducked around the corner of the laneway and found himself on a road. There were bodies splayed on ground here and there, some wearing red shirts, others not.

A cannon ball ripped through the building to his right, sending debris flying. He ducked down as chunks of mortar and brick went tumbling around him.

Fitz stumbled from the laneway covered in dust. Danny grabbed him and dragged him out of the road as footsteps approached. About ten men in red shirts passed by carrying swords and axes.

"Holy fuck," said Danny. "Which way is fucking west?" He pulled his leather gloves tight, the knuckles on the gloves were studded with metal.

"I-I think it's this way?" Fits led them through the maze of lanes and alleys, until they came to another road. There were a few men there, four in total, all friendlies. Danny waved at a man he recognized as from his group. There was no sign of the others though. Fitz was the Capo so they followed him along the road. A red shirt came stumbling from a burning building and Dannyshot him through the chest. Fuck you.

Danny reloaded. He's the only one with a pistol. Fitz has lost his and looks like he's thinking of taking it from him, but he looks at Fitz, challenging him to fucking try it, and he turns away.

They creep onwards through the street. The cannon fire is still ongoing, ripping the tenements behind them to shreds, filling the air with dust. Danny wraps his bandanna around his face to keep it from choking him, as do the others. They turn a corner and what do they walk straight into? But a group of damned red shirts all standing over bodies, picking their pockets. Danny quickly counts seven. They could fight, six against seven, but he's never one for even odds, and prefers them in his favour, so he turns and runs, and he's not the only one.

Fitz is right behind him.

"Oh fuck, oh fuck, oh fuck," Danny's muttering, as they head

what Danny thinks is west but might as well be fucking to China for all

he knew. Buildings pass him by in a blur. Fitz is lagging, and Danny

shouts for him to hurry it the fuck up. It wouldn't do to have another

Capo take his place. Fitz might be an asshole, but at least he let them

keep the loot they found to themselves and didn't tax them like some of

these fuckers.

A man appears on the steps of the building to his right toting dual

pistols. He's tall, broad of shoulder, with sharp blue eyes. Danny eases

as he's not wearing a red shirt.

A door bursts open to Danny's left, and he pauses as the sight of

red comes through the door. Two of them, carrying pistols.

"Shit," Danny mutters.

*

We run in as the dust settles after the dynamite blasts the door open.

"Jackson, get the hell back!" shouts Ace, as he runs inside the

building. I follow him inside and Patrick and Orson are there beside

me. I see a discarded pistol on the ground and pick it up. Two is always

better than one.

Men flood in through the doorway, men are up on top of the

stairs, and Ace is there, he aims his pistol and the crack splits through

the room, smoke spitting around him. The bullet catches a man upstairs

172

and he falls through the railing, down, hits the floor and blood pools beneath him. Pistols are no good in here. The fighting is close pressed, and I keep to the back of the fighting. I'm no good with a blade.

A man comes screaming out of a secret compartment in the wall. He's holding a spiked mace and he comes straight at me. I act on instinct alone.

I aim, shoot, and catch the man in his red shirt. The shot takes him through the heart, and blood splatters back across my face. I wipe it off, aim the next pistol at a man coming down the stairs, fire. The shot takes him in the leg, and he rolls down the steps. One of the men finish him off with a coup de grace.

Men are running through the safe house now, and the red shirts are fleeing.

I walk out the back of the building. Two men appear to my left. They're with us. A door opens to my right and two men step out carrying pistols, wearing red shirts. I aim both pistols. I know they're unloaded.

"Drop 'em!" I shout. Both men see the stream of bodies pouring out behind me. They're outnumbered ten to one. They toss their weapons. One of the men run and pick up both pistols, shoves them in his belt. I nod to him.

I aim my weapon against one of the red shirts' foreheads. "Where is your boss?"

He turns and points up at a tenement further along the street. Red shirts, at least fifty of them, are fleeing up the street and hiding behind stacked bags of what I guess is sand. "I need a name?"

"Valez," says the red shirt. "Justine Valez."

I falter. "A woman?"

He nods.

"I want you to take her a message." I cock back the pistol. "Make sure you don't fuck it up."

"I won't."

"Tell her she has one chance to save her men. Lay down your arms, or I'll rip your gang apart and leave nothing left but carrion. Got it?"

"She won't like that," says the other red shirt. The young man with the three pistols smacks the red shirt across the face.

"What'd you fucking say?" he growls, sticking the pistol into the red shirt's face. The man wisely shakes his head and holds up his hands.

"Go," I say. "Tell her she has until dusk to come out and surrender."

The two men run up the street.

174

The young man aims his pistol and fires, taking down the one of the red shirts, the one who spoke back.

I look at him, he shrugs.

"Only takes one to carry a message."

His eyes snap up to the building behind me. He jumps, knocking me aside as a shot splinters through the air. I hit the ground and there's yelling. Men turn and fire up to the roof.

"Sniper!" someone shouts.

I look. The man has been shot through the chest. I crouch down beside him and staunch the wound.

"Get this man help," I tell Ace, who nods and goes to fetch a doctor. I look back down at the young man. "What's your name, son?"

"Danny Gloves. Friends just call me Gloves."

I nod. "Well, Gloves, I'm your friend now. You just saved my life, and that means your set up for good, so don't you go dying on me, OK?"

Gloves smiles. "I don't plan on it." He looks at the men gathering around me. "W-What's your name?" he asks.

"Call me Jackson."

His eyes widen. "No shit."

"No shit."He passes out.

Chapter 13: The Pragmatist

As dusk settles, Justine Valez appears from the tenement, escorted by two tall men wearing bandoliers and bandannas, with machetes jingling from their belts. It's like a scene straight from a western novel, and I know No-Name would have shit himself to be here right now.

Valez is beautiful, but not in a feminine way. Everything about her shouts she's a hard woman in a man's world. Her eyes are steel cold blue, her hair black as coal, her stature tall and broad as a backroom brawler's, with two golden pistols on her belt. She has a hat cocked on her head, with a playing card shoved into the fold. I think it's an ace of spades.

"You Jackson?" she asks me. I nod.

"The last time I checked."

"Hmm. You want me to lay down my weapons and hand over Brooklyn to you?"

"That's what I want, yes."

"You crazy?"

"So I've been told."

"You're pretty, guess you could come and work for me, how about that? You could fold my linens, empty my pisspot, warm my bed." She folds her arms, the muscles bulge beneath the skin.

"I appreciate the offer, but I've bigger aspirations than being your bitch."

"Aww, you're breaking a little girl's heart." Valez spits onto the ground. She reaches into her pocket and Patrick aims his rifle at her. "Ah, ah, ah!" She takes out a pouch of what I suspect is chewing tobacco. Yup. This woman is a cliche.

She sticks in a wad of tobacco. "So, you think you can take on my boys?" She looks behind her, at the tenement, at the figures behind the sacks of sand, and on the roof, and in the windows. There's about two hundred, I'd wager. Maybe more.

"You're outnumbered and outgunned. I can rip these tenements apart with my ship's cannons." I reach inside my coat, and the two guards standing behind Valez move for their machetes. I take out a cigar, light it with my gold gas lighter. I blow the smoke at Valez.

"Tell you what," says Valez. "I'll flip you for it."

"What?" I frown. I must have heard that wrong. "I could have sworn you just said you'd flip me for it?"

"Uh-huh. That's right."

"And the stakes?"

"I win," says Valez, "You boys turn around, fuck back to Boston and leave the city to me." She looks at me then, and there's a hunger in her eyes. "But *you* have to stay and be my bitch."

I laugh. I'm beginning to like this girl. "And if I win?"

"I'll give you Brooklyn."

"And you'll be *my* bitch?" I can't fight the humour in my voice.

"Maybe, if you treat me right." She shrugs. "So, what's it gonna be?"

"Seems like the pay-out favours you," I say. "You get all of what I've taken so far, against what, one borough?"

"Brooklyn is the heart of New York, daddy. You take her you can access any borough you want with ease. Queens will be a walk in the park."

I chew on my cigar.

"One condition," I say.

"What's that?"

"I get to choose the side."

"Done." She takes out a coin. "I have a coin right here."

"Mind if I have a look?"

"Aren't we the suspicious type?"

"No offense, I just don't trust anyone."

She offers me the coin. I check it. There are two different sides.

OK, then. Which do I choose?

"Heads or tails?" Valez asks me.

"Heads."

She flips the coin and the sound of hundreds of men breathing in fast sounds through street. The coin spins up through the air as if wading through water, then back down, it hits the ground and spins a couple of times before coming to a rest.

"Heads." She looks up at me. "Guess that means you win."

"Guess it does."

She laughs. Then her face empties of humour. She kicks dirt in my face and turns, flees back towards the tenement. Her two escorts look as confused as I'm feeling right now, but they have the presence of mind to get in the way as Patrick and Orson go to take a shot at her back.

"No!" I shout. They look at me. "Save your ammo… I'll let the cannons do the work."

*

The next day the cannons rip the tenements in the way to pieces, bringing them down to rubble. Men exchange half-hearted shots from the rooftops. I watch from the ship with Gamma.

"This Valez sounds… interesting." Gamma looks at me sideways.

"You know you're the only girl for me, Gamma."

"Huh."

Another blast tears chunks off the roof of the tenement. They're sitting ducks. And I have all day to bring their stronghold to the ground.

"She sounds ambitious. You sure you want to take her into the fold?"

"If I didn't know you better, I'd say you were jealous." I take out my flask and take a sip of whiskey, then offer it to Gamma.

"Me? Nah. I just don't want you surrounding yourself with zealots."

"What are we, then?"

She shrugs. "Opportunists."

"I think we passed that hurdle a long time ago."

She laughs. "A long time ago, huh? This time two months ago you were a nobody con man living in the back ass of the Bronx."

I nod. "And I'd give it all away just to be back there."

"Yeah?"

"Yeah, of course. I miss the old gang. The old cons."

"Me too, I guess." Gamma's jaw juts out as she takes a swig of the flask. She has something she wants to tell me; I can feel it. "I know you know," she looks at me sideways.

"Know what, Gamma?"

"I know you know I was working for Crystallini."

"And?"

"And… And I'm sorry, I guess. I didn't think I'd grow so attached to you. We all did, me, No-Name, Chameleon and Bella."

"And you were all working behind my back with my brother."

"Yeah, but I stopped. I stopped taking his money."

"Why?"

"If you have to ask me that, Jackson, then you're not as sharp as I'd thought."

I turn and face her. The cannons roar below on deck, shredding the tenement's eastern walls apart.

"Tell me then. Or don't you have the balls to say it?"

She frowns. "I… I lo—"

"Boss?" It's Orson.

"Devil's balls, man, don't you know when not to interrupt me?"

"Sorry boss, but word has come in that Valez wants to talk."

"Then bring her here, unarmed."

"Got it, boss." He looks from Gamma to me. "And, sorry."

"What were you saying?" I ask Gamma.

"Nothing." She chews her lip as a final cannon blast rips another chunk out of the wall. I call a stop to the demolition.

"Well, if you ever want to let me know, I'm here." I walk away.

*

Valez sits on one side of the table. I sit on the other. There's a bottle of whiskey on the table. Valez looks worse for wear. She's covered in dust, with scratch marks across her face and upper arms.

"You're a real piece of shit, you know that?" she says, reaching over and grabbing the bottle.

"So I've been told."

"Huh. I lost a lot of good men from your damned cannons."

"You could have surrendered yesterday."

"And lost the respect of my men?"

I shrug. I can understand her predicament.

She shakes her head. "Damn place was a mess. Bodies everywhere. Men crying. Fuck…" She takes a long swig from the bottle.

"I'm sorry it had to come to that," I say, and I mean it. And I think she can hear it in my voice, as she frowns at me.

"Who in the hell are you, Jackson?"

"Just a man trying to get his daughter back."

"And you'll tear the whole of New York apart to get it?"

I reach across the table, and she hands me the bottle. I nod as I drink. "I would raise Heaven and Earth for my girl."

She reaches into her pocket and takes out her chewing tobacco. "I guess I can respect that." She pops a wad of it into her mouth. "So what now? I've to suck your cock, I guess? Be your bitch."

"You have a way with words, Valez."

"Thanks. Poppa always told me my mouth would get me into trouble one day. That's when he wasn't busy beating the shitoutta momma." She spits onto the floor. "Guess my mouth could do me some good for once."

"Your mouth will stay firmly free of cock's for as long as you wish, don't you worry."

She lifts her chin. "So what do you want?"

"I want you and you're men to join me. Same deal as the gangs in the Bronx got. You keep your territory but kick up a percentage to me."

"Sounds reasonable... Too reasonable."

"I don't want to wreak havoc. I am taking over New York, but I would rather have something to rule by the end of it."

Valez looks up at the tenements, or where the tenements used to be. "You've a funny way of looking at things, mister."

"Call me a pragmatist."

"A what?"

"Nevermind."

"Guess I could live with myself if I called you boss every once in a while."

"There would be more to it than that." I hand her back the bottle. She looks at me filled with suspicion.

"Like?"

Gamma clears her throat. "Like taking out the boss's enemies, dip-shit."

Valez looks Gamma up and down. "Well fuck me sideways, it talks."

"It also bites." Gamma can stare down the best of them, and the air between the two women fizzes with electricity, enough to make your teeth buzz.

"Ladies," I say, spreading my hands. "We're all on the same side."

"So you want me to help you take Queens?" asks Valez, not breaking eye contact with Gamma.

"Yes," I say.

"And Manhattan," adds Gamma.

"Hmm. Manhattan will be a shit ton harder than Queens. Crystallini has hired every two-bit goon in the city. I say his numbers are up over a thousand soldiers on the street. You think you can take that on?" Valez breaks eye contact and looks at me.

"I think I can handle it."

"Well then," Valez sits forward. She slaps her hand down on the table. "You've got your woman."

We shake hands. And Brooklyn was in the bag.

*

I check on the young man who saved my life. Gloves. I've hired the best doctor to fix him up, and thankfully it's good news.

"The bullet went straight through," says the doc'.

I pay the man and enter the room.

Gloves is lying on the bed, clutching a bottle of whiskey, and it's a scene of de ja vu if ever there was one.

"How'd things go with Valez?" asks Gloves.

"She had no other choice but to join."

"That woman's a viper. Watch your back with her."

I take the offered bottle.

"I watch my back with everyone."

"You don't trust me, then? Even after taking a bullet for you."

"There's only one person I trust in this world, and it's not you I'm afraid to say."

"Y'know, I heard the guys talking about you."

I hand back the bottle. "Is that right?"

"Yeah. They say this Crystallini is a brother of yours."

185

"Guess everyone knows that these days."

"So why you want to take him down?"

"You mean besides him kidnapping my daughter?"

Gloves thinks for a moment. "I thought family was supposed to mean something. I guess I wouldn't know, being an orphan."

I laugh. "I guess we share something in common, then."

"You were an orphan?"

"Yeah."

"Guess you think you did pretty well for yourself, considering?"

"Can't complain."

There's a knock on the door. Gamma enters.

"Just wanted to check up on the man who saved the boss's life." Gamma sits down beside me. Pushes back a strand of hair. She's let it grow and the red locks suit her. Suit her bright brown eyes.

She catches me staring. I look away.

"And I guess you must be Gamma?" says Gloves.

"Guilty as charged."

"You know the boys have a bet on how long it'll take you guys to hook up." Gloves hits the nail right on the head.

I shrug. "Gamma only loves thievery. And subterfuge."

"And whiskey," she smiles, and Gloves offers her the bottle.

"Guess there's worse things a gal can love." Gloves has a roguish smile, and I find myself warming to him.

"Such as?" Gamma pushes back her hair.

"Such as a man who won't return her love, for one," Gloves looks at me and back to her.

"You a psychiatrist or a two-bit gangster?" asks Gamma.

"Guess I've just got a sharp eye and a bigger mouth."

I take the bottle from Gamma. "Don't let me stand in your way of happiness, Gamma."

"Who says I need a man to be happy?" She sticks her fingers to her mouth, spreads them licks between them. "Perhaps I bark up the other side of the tree?"

We laugh, and it feels good.

It feels like I can take a moment and just breathe. I could see the finish line now, and I didn't know what waited behind it, but it had to be better than not having my little chicken around.

"Penny for your thoughts?" Gamma says.

"Just wondering how Rayah's doing."

"Rayah is your daughter?" asks Gloves. I nod.

"Yeah."

"She's a strong little woman," says Gamma. "She'll be doing just fine."

"A daughter needs her father," says Gloves, and I nod. "I guess I couldn't forgive my brother either, if he did something like that."

I hand Gloves the bottle. "He's times coming, don't you worry about that."

Gamma puts her hand on my shoulder. "We'll make him pay; don't you think otherwise."

I just hoped that I could see into the future. I just wished that I could see what the path held ahead.

I just wanted to hold my little girl, and I would trade it all away for it. But I couldn't give in to Dayton's demands, when they did come. I had to stay strong.

Or else it would all crumble beneath me. My Empire of Sin.

Chapter 14: Three's a Crowd

How do I topple Queens?

I don't offer them a coin flip. I don't offer them a chance of taking what's mine. I've more than half the city in my grip and I'm not losing it now, not when the end is so near.

I take a warehouse of empty thick glass sphere's, and I take another warehouse with flammable liquids, and I put two and two together. I fill the glass spheres with the flammable liquid, and I load them onto the ship.

I send word to the mob ruling Queens that they have until nightfall before I set the borough aflame.

It's a bluff, don't worry. I'm not that cruel-hearted. But I tell the cannon crews to aim at an abandoned tower and I set it alight. It burns as a warning to all in the borough. The mob get back to me within the hour with their answer.

"A race?" I say.

"Yeah," says Orson. "They said they want to race you for the borough. You win, they kick up fifty points like everyone else and they work for you."

"And if I lose?"

"They just have to kick up five points a year, incrementing by five points every five years until it reaches twenty points, and it stays there."

"Good. They have sense at least," I look at Valez, who narrows her eyes at me.

"What's your answer?"

"Send word down to Boston. Tell them to send their best racing horse. I want it here by dawn." I take out my flask and take a sip.

Orson nods and goes to relay the message.

"What about the racer?" asks Gamma.

"Why, our old friend Henry will surely help us out."

You remember Henry, right? From the bank heist, he was the getaway driver. He would be my jockey.

Gloves is standing behind me, beside Patrick. He's been taken on as my third inner circle of muscle. Gloves says, "Why not just burn them to the ground anyway? Show them who's boss."

I offer my flask to the kid. He takes a sip. "Because you rule by fear through the threat of pain and loss, not by its infliction." The kid hands it back.

"I guess that's why you're the boss."

Patrick twirls the toothpick in his mouth. "Can we bet on the race?"

"Sure," I say, "As long as you bet on me to win."

"Wouldn't think otherwise."

Gamma walks over and whispers in my ear. I nod.

"Of course. Get it done."

And the wheels are set in motion.

*

I read once that JFK had been an airport, that hundreds of thousands of people flew through there each year. It was hard to imagine that amount of people. Today, it was used as a racetrack. The Queens mob ran the track and earned a killing from it.

Word was put on the street that I was to be made untouchable when I entered Queens, but the convoy I travelled with would put fear in the heart of the most brave of hitmen. I had no doubt about my safety. Gamma was with me, with Gloves, Patrick and Orson, even the beautiful Valez had decided to join us, and it made me laugh when she said no one else would kill me except her.

I think she was taking a liking to me.

The horse was in a horse-carriage just behind us, and it was a majestic creature, big as a house, with muscles that even made Valez jealous.

"What we gonna call it?" asked Gamma.

I smile. "Crystallini."

"You're kidding," she says.

"Why not?" says Gloves. "It's a good name for a beast."

"Because it will only work to aggravate him," says Gamma.

"That's what I'm intent on. It will be a clear 'Fuck you'." I light a cigar.

"You do remember he has your daughter?" asks Gamma.

"I know he won't do anything once I have Chameleon in my possession. This will just rattle his cage a bit."

We approach the old airport, and the crowds begin to thicken, and the carriages force their way through the press. I stick my head to the window and there's a few cheers, a kid is running alongside the carriage, and I wave at him. He smiles widely and is lost in the crowd.

I think about my Rayah, and how much she'd like to be coming with me, how much she'd enjoy riding a horse, feeding it. How much has changed since the last time I'd set eyes on her. I wondered would she even recognize the man I'd become in so little time. Then another part of me wondered how much she had changed.

Would it be the same little girl that was so curious about everything? The same little girl who read poetry to ravens and tucked her teddy in at night?

I chewed on my cigar and forced away the tears.

We entered through a checkpoint with armed men. They waved us through, and we pulled alongside a high stand where the rich and the powerful would watch the race from. The rest of humanity was crowded around the old airfield, the track closed off by fences.

Oh yeah, there's one more thing I should tell you. Races today weren't like the races back then. Nowadays you were allowed a baton, and you could beat your opponents with it and try to get them knocked off. Deaths weren't unknown to happen.

But Henry was a natural. I'd seen him race a few times back before Rayah was born. He would have no problem staying in the saddle.

Not to mention the juice I had a doctor inject into my horse. Damn thing cost over a hundred grand. That would surely help. Not like they tested the damned animals anymore.

Hey, I am a thief at heart after all. I told you not to trust me.

*

I approach Henry as his donning the colours, my colours, black tunic with a white helm, the colours of the grim reaper, Gamma called it. For death was coming to Crystallini, and this was one way to let him know.

"You ready?" I ask him.

"Ready as I'll ever be," he grins.

"You're gonna have competition out there."

193

"Don't I know it."

"But you have allies too."

"Huh?"

"I greased the palms of two of the other jockeys, they'll be on your side."

"I wonder how many of the other twelve the Queens mob have?"

I put my hand on his shoulder. "You just use that baton well and club the shit outta anyone that comes near you, got it?"

He nods.

I take my hand away. "And don't you fall."

"Oh, I never fall. Not once in my entire life."

"That's what I like to hear."

I leave Henry as he mounts up. I climb the steps and take my seat between Gamma and Valez. They have a bottle of champagne and Gamma pours me a glass.

"To Crystallini!" says Gamma.

"And may he not be as big a bastard as his namesake!" I laugh. We clink glasses and drink.

The jockeys are cantering their horses to the starting booth. I roughly estimate about twenty hurdles placed in sporadic locations around the track. I just hope the horse is good at jumping as they raced her on flat ground down in Boston.

"You nervous?" asks Gamma.

"About the race?" I say.

"About what comes after."

"You a fortune teller?"

"No."

"Then how do you know what comes after?"

"I guess it's open for discussion."

Henry is in the booth now and the flagman is readying up. The fifteen horses are ready and loaded.

The flag lifts, then drops, and the booths pop open. The horses come flying out of the stalls. Not too fast, as they won't kick in their heels until the final hurdle.

"I don't know what to think," I tell Gamma.

"You're going to kill him, right?" says Valez. Her eyes follow the horses as they canter along the track. No one has gotten close to Henry yet, but it's only a matter of time.

"I am." I think of Dayton and all those times we spent together as young kids. Could I really bring myself to kill him? After all he done to me. I didn't know. But I had to sound sure to my people.

"Don't you think forgiveness might be the better path to take?" says Gamma.

"Forgiveness?" says Valez, "Forgiveness is for pussy's and fools."
She places a hand on my knee. "Neither of which is my Jackson."

"Your Jackson?" Gamma shifts closer. She puts her arm around
me and whispers in my ear. "I think she likes you."

"You hear that, Valez?"

"Hmm?"

"Gamma here thinks you like me."

"What's not to like?"

Her hand inches upwards.

Gamma reaches over and slaps her hand off. "Ah, ah, ah! Hands
off the boss."

"Oh, you're no fun, Gamma." Valez lets back her drink and pours
another. I look away from her ice cool blue eyes as they watch me
closely, and I see Henry is approaching the second hurdle. He's in
second place when the first jockey comes at him from behind. The
baton smacks against the back of his ribs, making him lose the rhythm
with the horse for a moment. He turns and smacks his own baton
against the jockey's forehead, and the jockey tumbles from the horse,
unconscious, his foot getting caught in the stirrup and he's dragged
behind, until they reach the hurdle, and he smacks against it, and his
foot comes loose. The crowd goes wild.

"That's one to us!" shouts Gloves, who's sitting between Orson and Patrick in front of us.

"So Gamma," says Valez, scorn thick in her voice. "Have you told Jackson that you love him yet?"

I choke on my drink.

"Fuck yourself, Valez." Gamma takes her arm from around me.

"Everyone can see it. Except him, of course."

I look Valez in the eye, and my dark expression makes her playful attitude crumble. "That's enough."

"What? You guys haven't fucked yet, have you? What are you waiting for? Instructions?"

"Valez."

Valez smiles and looks away. She's a piece of work, is that woman. Gloves was right about the viper.

I put my hand on Gamma's, and she looks across at me.

"Do you?" I ask her.

There's a cheer from the crowd. I don't look, but by the shouts of Gloves and the others below, one of the jockey's I'd bribed had taken a fall.

"Does it matter, Jackson?" Gamma says.

"It matters to me, yeah."

Gamma inhales deeply. A feeling bubbles up in my chest as she

goes to say something, it feels like I'm standing at the edge of a great

drop.

"Yes. I do." She smiles. I lean in then and kiss her.

There's laughter below and whooping but I ignore the halfwits

and put my hand behind her neck, pulling her into me. She feels like

fresh wind to a man imprisoned. She tastes like rain to a man dying in

the desert. We pull apart and smile at each other. I feel a hand grab me

from behind, grab the back of my head, and Valez turn me to face her,

then leans in and kisses me.

Where Gamma is warm and soft, Valez is rough and cool, her

tongue presses against mine, our teeth knock together as she bites down

on my lip, licks my lips, and backs away, smiling across at Gamma.

"Yum," says Valez. "You don't mind sharing, do you, Gamma?"

I turn to expect Gamma's fist come blurring past my face, but I

see a hunger in Gamma's eyes. She leans forward and grabs Valez by

the hair, and I think she's going to headbutt her, but instead she pulls

Valezclose, and I can't believe my eyes as they kiss each other.

There's cheering. I look past Gamma and see Henry battling

against another opponent, no, two opponents. Then the other jockey I'd

bribed comes in from behind and smacks his baton against the back of

one of the opponents' heads. The man goes down like a sack of horseshit. Henry overpowers the other opponent, and then focuses on the hurdle coming up, and they soar over it, that's the... seventh hurdle.

The girls break apart, and Gamma looks at me. "Did you like that?"

I smile. "This has got to be the best race ever."

I put my arms around both women and they sling an arm around each of my shoulders. Valez leans in and kisses me on the cheek. She whispers in my ear. "Told you you'd be my bitch."

Gamma lifts my glass and I let her pour some Champagne into my mouth.

Henry is in the lead, he's on the final stretch now, and there's only one jockey behind him, but the bastard is closing in. Henry turns and glances back, then kicks in his heels, and Crystallini soars over the final hurdle, landing as smooth as fucking peanut butter.

The opponent lands just behind him, and they tear up the final stretch, both jockeys in perfect rhythm with their horses, both up on their stirrups, and they've abandoned their batons now, and it's an old-fashioned sprint to the finish. Henry is paces in front, as they reach the last hundred yards, and as the opponent goes to overtake Henry, he lashes out with the side of his fist and smashes it into the other jockey's face. The poor man collapses off the horse and tumbles away through the dirt.

199

Hey. We don't play fair.

I jump up and cheer as Crystallini tears through the final yard and brings it home.

The odds were three to one on my horse to win.

I'd stuck my entire fortune on it. Twelve million at three to one.

You do the math.

*

That night Gamma and Valez pay a visit to my cabin in the ship. The two guards outside my door smile at me as I shut the door closed.

Gamma is wearing a full body leather coat. Valez is wearing her usual outfit, leather armor, with dual golden pistols.

"What can I do for you ladies?" I ask them. I go and pour us each a drink of whiskey.

When I turn back around, Gamma opens her leather coat. Beneath it she's wearing a tight red brasserie and thong, with red fishnet tights and a smile. Valez is standing behind her and takes her coat, tossing it onto a chair. Gamma walks around Valez, her eyes on me the entire time, as she pops off Valez's hat, tosses it aside, then unbuttons her leather jacket, reaching her arms around from behind. She pulls it open and Valez shuts her eyes and tilts back her head as Gamma pulls it off her arms, then tossing it too aside, she begins unbuttoning her pants.

I abandon the drinks, walk over and kiss Valez's neck. She moans as I nibble on her earlobe. Valez reaches down and begins unbuttoning my pants, she's between me and Gamma, wearing nothing but the skin she was born in.

I lead Valez to the bed, and Gamma is right behind us. I lay her down and begin unbuttoning my shirt. Gamma begins kissing Valez's stomach, the muscles expanding and retracting as she breathes in and out. I climb onto the bed and pull Valez's legs apart. Her pubic hair is cut into a diamond shape, I kiss it, moving slowly downwards, as Gamma moves upwards, licking her nipple, pulling at the other with her fingers.

I slip my tongue around Valez's clitoris, press gently against it, and move my tongue around. She sighs deeply and grabs the silk sheets between her fingers. I move down slowly, entering her, then back out and back in, making her moan. Gamma sits up and undoes her bra, and her petite breasts swell and fall with her quick breathing, her nipples erect, as am I. I take myself in my hand and enter Valez, and she moans louder. Valez sucks on Gamma's nipples, her fingers working between Gamma's legs. I suck on Valez's nipples as I slide inside of her and back out, slowly, gently.

She reaches up and grabs me by the hair.

"I thought… You wanted to fuck me?" she says, throat husky in her throat.

"I do."

"Then fuck me like a gangster, and not a lover."

I do.

Sweat beads along my spine as I look into her eyes. Gamma tilts back my head and licks my throat, moving up, then kisses me on the mouth, sliding her tongue across my teeth, my lips. She bends down and bites my nipple, and oh god, it feels so nice.

Valez is moaning louder now, the sound of our flesh smacking together echoed by the sound of her wet fingers working back and forth between Gamma's legs.

Valez reaches up and smacks Gamma across the face, hard.

"Smack me harder," Gamma moans. "Oh, faster."

"Sit on my face, you ginger bitch," snarls Valez, smacking her across the face once more. Gamma moves and spreads her legs, placing herself onto Valez's mouth, and I lean forward, biting Gamma's ass cheek, while I'm still working myself in and out of Valez.

"Go faster, boss," says Valez. "Oh, god, faster."

Gamma looks back at me. Her hair is sweaty, spine sticking out on her back, as she moves her crotch back and forth on Valez's face.

Valez moans louder, and I pick up the pace, and she reaches up and grabs Gamma's ass with two hands and squeezes them, leaving red fingerprints on the cheeks, along with my teeth marks.

Valez and I come together, and I sag on top of her, trailing kisses down along Gamma's spine.

Gamma giggles then and moves off of Valez. She kisses her on the lips, and then reaches over and kisses me too.

I sit back, reach across the floor, and pick up a packet of cigarettes. I light one up, take a drag and pass it to Valez. I look at Gamma, then growl playfully as I jump up onto the bed and fling her down onto her back.

I take both her legs in mine, and she kicks at with a smile.

I smile back. "And just where did you think you were going?" I ask, as I move down to kiss her.

Chapter 15: The End

I awake with light spilling through the curtains. My head is pounding, as we drank to excess, and for a moment I think it was all just a dream, but nope, Gamma is on one side of me, Valez on the other, and I slowly move off the bed and begin dressing. I shut the door quietly behind me. Gloves is standing guard outside with Patrick and Orson. The three of them smile.

"Good night?" says Patrick.

"Can't complain. You?"

"Alright."

Gloves smacks me on the shoulder, his grin infectious.

"What the hell are you so happy about?" I ask.

"I had a bet on with these two dipshits that the three of you would hook up together." Gloves reaches in and takes out a wad of cash rolled up with a bit of string.

"You guys need help," I say.

"A man's gotta find means of entertainment somewhere." Orson crosses his arms. "Can't all have beautiful women fawning over us all the time."

I clap Orson on the shoulder. "Well, if you weren't so damn ugly I'm sure you would too."

"Huh."

"Any word from Crystallini?" I ask.

"Still quiet," says Patrick. "But it's only a matter of time. He can see the ship clear as day."

I'd anchored the ship on the western side of Manhattan. I put word on the street that I would reduce the buildings around Crystallini's safehouse to rubble until they handed him over.

I thought it would instil fear and disloyalty among his men.

I had arranged for Valez and the other gang leaders to set up road blocks on the bridges. There would be no escape for my brother. Over a thousand gangsters were ready to invade Manhattan and fight for my girl. Most of Crystallini's men were mercenaries, hired goons, my people knew to fear me, and wouldn't back out of the fight.

"We've given him enough time. Tell him to arrive within the hour at the docks with my daughter to exchange prisoners or I turn his city to ash and rubble."

Orson nods. "I'll get right on it."

He goes to send the message.

We go below deck and enter the cabin where I'm keeping

Chameleon prisoner. I've been treating him well, with food and fresh

clothing, books, I'm not an animal.

"It's almost time," I say.

He sighs. "You gonna kill me if he doesn't play ball?"

"Just might. Nothings impossible at the moment."

"I never thought it would come to this, Jackson" Chameleon looks

up at me. "Never thought you and me would end up on opposite sides."

"Guess that's what happens when you double cross someone."

"Guess so."

I leave him alone to brew on his thoughts.

Minutes feel like hours as I wait up on deck. Gamma joins me.

"Any news?"

I shake my head.

She catches one of the men grinning at her.

"What the fuck are you so happy about?" she shouts.

The man's smile drops faster than a whore's pants on payday. "N-

Nothing!"

"Better fucking not be! Get to work, shit-for-brains." Gamma has

a small smile touching the edge of her lips as she looks back at me. I

think her temper is beginning to thaw somewhat.

"You enjoying yourself?"

Gamma shrugs. "Can't let them think I'm some piece of ass for the boss. They need to remember the pecking order."

"My girl."

She goes on her tip toes and kisses me.

Valez walks up onto the deck. She's buckling on her belt and spits over the side of the railing, then sticks a wad of tobacco in her mouth. I tell her there's no news before she asks.

"Fucking coward."

"A man bides his time when faced with no escape," says Patrick.

Gloves looks up at the towering House of Two Faces. I follow his gaze. "He's gotta be shitting a brick."

"He should be." I light a cigarette. "I've the whole four boroughs turned against him. I've his world crashing down around his ears, just like what he done for me."

"You can't storm his safehouse," says Gamma.

I nod. "I know that. He'd slid her throat and toss her off the top of the building if I got the better of him."

"So what do you do, boss?" says Patrick.

"The hell if I know."

Valez clears her throat and I look at her. "You duel him."

"What?"

"Challenge him to a duel."

"He won't accept that."

Valez puts her hands on her pistols. "You challenge him, he can't refuse. He refuses and he loses face with his men. His men think him a coward, then they slowly begin to look for new horizons."

"You think?"

Valez laughs. "Those men he has working for him, they aren't men. They're rogues, cutthroats, bandits, men with no loyalty, no honour. Not like my men." She spits over the side of the railing. "One of my men could kill three of theirs."

I suck my teeth. "A duel, eh?"

"Or Blind Man's Bluff?" says Gloves.

I shake my head. "Once was enough for me." I sigh. "Alright. Send word. I challenge him to a duel at dusk. Winner takes all."

The challenge was made. And I only had to risk my life one more time to finally get my daughter back.

I prayed that luck would be on my side.

*

Word came in within the hour. Crystallini accepted my challenge.

*

We travel through the streets of Manhattan, people throw black roses on the road in front of my carriage. I can't help but feel the breath of death blowing against my neck.

We're all there, the whole gang. Gamma reaches over and places her hand on mine.

"You're going to do it," she says. I nod.

I look out the window. "It's a fine day to kill the only blood you've left in the world."

Gloves takes out a cigarette and lights it, hands it to me. I thank him and take a drag.

I don't want to kill Dayton. I don't want to do it, simple as that, but it's too late to turn back now. The task has been set in stone, as sure as the day you were born, one of us was going to die today.

Please, God, if you are real, guide my hand today. Make steady my aim. Make strong my back and let it not crumble beneath these burdens you have place upon my shoulders.

We arrive outside the House of Two Faces. The street is filled with people. People wave and cheer. The doors open and Crystallini steps out, he's dressed in a black overcoat, with a flat peak cap pulled low, and his cold blue eyes lock on mine.

Ace pushes back the people as I step closer to my brother. He offers me his hand, and I turn away and spit on the ground. He takes his hand away.

"Brother." He smiles. There' movement behind him. My breath catches in my throat. It's Rayah.

209

I push past Crystallini, and crouch down as she wraps her arms around me.

"Daddy!" she cries, tears in her eyes.

She's so beautiful that the ball of dread wrapped in my chest like a cannon ball of fire melts, and it feels like sunshine spreading across my face as I take in the sight of her, drink in all her innocence and love.

"Daddy loves you, chicken." I kiss her cheek.

"I missed you."

"And I you. But Daddy's got to do one more thing before we can go home. OK?"

She nods. Gamma steps in. Takes Rayah's hand. She leans in close. "I'll keep her busy inside until… until you take care of it."

I nod. Gamma takes Rayah inside of the building.

I turn and face Crystallini once more. He's taken off his overcoat and hat, hands them to an attendant. We walk out onto the road, the street fills with silence. The windows of the buildings are filled with faces. A man awaits us, holding a black box. He opens it. Inside are two silver pistols.

"You can choose first," says Crystallini. I step up and take the one on top. We stand back-to-back. I look across and see them all there, Valez, her eyes shining bright, she nods. Gloves, he tips his hat to me,

Patrick and Orson, both as stern and unflinching as ever, and Ace, who takes off his peaked flat cap and holds it to his chest.

"Gentlemen, take twenty paces and wait. When I say turn, you shall turn and fire. If neither shot shall prove fatal, then both pistols shall be reloaded, and the duel will begin once more until a winner is decided. Do not, and I repeat, do *not* turn until I give the order. To do so would be forfeiting the duel, and the other man shall be entitled to take a shot at his leisure at ten paces. Is this understood."

I nod.

"Twenty paces, gentlemen."

I begin walking.

The walk of a dead man, perhaps. Leaving a trail of nothing but empty promises behind and empty hearts.

Have I been a good man?

Have I been a good father?

I never thought myself evil, but now that I brush with death, I can't help but consider my own mortality. I think back to the past and think back to the mistakes I've made. I see Alyssa in the crowd. She's standing on my side. I can't help but think is this symbolic? Has she chosen me over my brother?

Can she love a dead man?

I'm at ten paces.

211

I think about what Rayah will grow up to be like. I imagine life without her Daddy. Of birthdays gone by with an empty seat where once a man who loved her sat.

Fifteen paces.

A tear falls down my cheek, and I don't wipe it away. In it are a lifetime of woes. A lifetime of what ifs? And the next that falls is filled with promises of forget-me-nots, as their faces flash through my mind.

Twenty paces. I stop.

What does a man say when faced with death? A man can only share the burden so far, and that extends to keeping death company.

But this time it was different. This time I walked alongside death, holding its hand, embracing it, if it's what God had planned for me.

I was never a religious man, but I swear on my word that if I should survive this day, I would be a *better* man.

A better father. A better lover.

"Turn and fire!"

I spin around!

The scene blurs, the motion moves as if through water, the pistol steady in my hand, my heartbeat loud in my ears, as loud as a cannon roar.

My pistol flashes, the shot rips through Crystallini's shoulder, blood splatters back behind him, and he stumbles back a step.

My shot hasn't been fatal…

Crystallini stands back up. He smiles, and there is no remnant of my brother in those eyes. This is a shell of a man.

He lifts his pistol. The muzzle flashes, all I hear are screams and silence, and my world goes dark…

*

"No!" screams Valez.

She runs out onto the road, the smoke from the pistols still wafting along the cracking surface. She checks his pulse.

But he's gone. Jackson is dead.

Chapter 16: One Year

One year later...

Ace Holden was not a nice guy, and he went out of his way to make sure you knew it. So when Danny Gloves walked into the bar and saw him sitting there bouncing a small little girl on his knee, it made a man wonder what really went on inside people's minds.

Here was a cold-blooded killer with the heart of a stone, and the mind of a shark, and here he was making funny faces and fart noises, to make the girl laugh.

"Ace," says Gloves. "You going to get working on loading those crates or are you gonna shoot the shit with your girl all day?"

Ace frowns. "Hey, watch your French around my girl."

"Sorry, but that shipment of whiskey aintgonna load itself."

Ace nods and puts his daughter down, then stands up and goes to unload the cart of crates of whiskey Gloves had just brought down from the docks. Gloves worked his horse and cart all over the city, transporting goods. He'd had enough crime and death to last him a lifetime.

Boston was cold this time of year, and Gloves warmed his hands up by the fire. He went to the bar and nodded to Valez.

"Hey beautiful. How about a drink?"

"Fuck yourself. Aint getting no more liquor until I see some green."

"I ever tell you I just love a woman with an attitude?"

"Only about twelve times a day." Valez blows into the glass she's holding and wipes it with the cloth. "How's the boys doing?"

"Ah, they're OK. Orson got himself a new wife."

"No shit? What's that, three now?"

"Yup. They're thinking of moving up to Detroit once the weather thaws."

"Hows Patrick? Heard he got himself beat up pretty bad."

"He'll never change. Man's a goon 'til the day he dies."

"Guess we all can't change our ways."

"Guess not."

Valez sighs and pours a glass of whiskey, slides it across the counter.

Gloves winks at her. "I know you love me, deep inside."

"Must be deeper than the goddamn ocean."

"As is my love for you."

Someone enters through the door. Gloves glances back, and who does he see but the one and only Daniel Prout, the most notorious gangster in Boston. This wasn't good news.

Prout approaches the bar and tosses his gloves onto the counter. Valez's lip involuntarily lifts in disgust, but thankfully Prout is staring up at the picture hanging behind the bar.

"Thought I told you to take that down the last time I was in this shithole." Prout leans against the bar.

Gloves looks up at the photo of Jackson, taken on the ship, it had the whole gang surrounding Jackson on both sides. Gloves stifled a sigh. A part of him missed those days.

Valez lifts a bottle of whiskey and pours Prout a glass. She slides it across, and the man goes to pay, but she holds up her hands. "It's on the house."

"Thanks. But still, take that down. You know I don't want to be looking at that fuckerevery time I come in here."

Prout takes a sip. Fucking dandy. Gloves knocks his back.

Wasn't the only thing he'd like to knock, but a man can't have everything.

"What you staring at, boy?" Prout looks across at Gloves, who looks away.

Valez takes down the picture and slides it out of view. She opens the till and takes out notes, then hands them to Prout. Prout slips them into his pocket.

"A drink and some cash," says Prout. "Guess a blowjob's outta the question?"

"Ace hears you talking like that, and you won't have legs left to stand on."

"Where is the old huckster anyway?" Prout leans back. "Hey! You old fuck! Get in here."

Ace comes in carrying a crate and places it on the counter beside the till.

"Daniel, that time of the week already?"

"Sure is. Just telling Valez here how nice her mouth looks."

Ace frowns. "We don't need any more trouble than we already got, Prout. You have your money, so be gone."

"Alright, alright, I know where I'm not wanted." He lifts his gloves from the counter and smacks them against it. He looks at Valez. "You think about that other thing I was talking about, if you ever get sick of cleaning glasses."

Proutlifts up the crate of bottles and exits the tavern.

"I wish Jackson would'a put a bullet in that fucker like he did his father." Ace watches the door as it swings shut.

217

Valez turns away, goes to clean more glasses, but Gloves saw the tears in her eyes. He couldn't blame her.

It was one year since the day they'd duelled in the streets of Manhattan. One year since Crystallini took control of New York and had been ruling it with an iron grip since. Boston had returned to war, and Daniel Prout pretty much controlled all of it.

He hadn't heard what became of Rayah, only that Crystallini hadn't let her leave the House of Two Faces, and had kept her on as a prisoner in case any of the old gang thought about kicking up a fuss over Jackson.

Ace pours them both a drink, then replaces the picture on the wall, fixing it so it hangs slightly crooked, a nod to their crooked past.

Ace lifts his glass. "To Jackson, one year since you bit the bullet, my friend, and a better thief there hasn't been seen since the day you left us."

Gloves clinks glasses with Ace, and they drink.

"I still remember it like it was yesterday." He looks down at his hands, remembering the blood, so much blood from one man. The bullet had caught him in the face and ripped half it off. It had been a real shame, as Gloves had taken a real liking to the guy.

Valez rubs her eyes and turns to face me. "You like digging up the past? You like twisting old wounds?"

"I'm sorry, Valez, I didn't mean to… I just guess I miss him. Man had balls. Gotta respect that." Gloves slides his glass back across the table. "Well, I'd best be getting on. Cargo ain'tgonna load itself."

"Give my best to the guys," says Ace. Gloves nods. He turns and leaves, his heart as cold as the Boston winter that waited for him.

*

Rayah finished feeding Edgar the raven and shut the cage. She blew him a kiss, knowing all too well what it felt like to be caged up for most your life, for the outside world to seem like it was on a distant planet. Like those people that walked the streets below her window were figures from a different world, characters from some story book.

She met Gamma outside in the drawing room. Gamma was sitting by the window, staring out at the falling snow. She looked up and smiled as Rayah entered.

"Hey, chicken."

Rayah goes and sits down beside her, wraps her in a hug. The fire is crackling, logs splitting loudly, throwing out a wave of warmth that Rayah couldn't enjoy.

One year.

A full year of an empty chair where once her father had sat. A full year of imprisonment, of a life of luxury, but even golden bars offered no sense of freedom.

219

"I miss him too, sweetheart." Gamma can almost read her thoughts. Of course, she remembers today, it was the man she loved. Gone in an instant, the sound of a gunshot ripping through your heart like a summer's breeze to autumn leaves. But her heart was trapped in winter. And no tide of tears, no matter how many, would ever thaw the coldness that grew within her with each passing year.

Rayah felt she should cry, but that part of herself that showed emotion had been damaged. Taken away.

"You look in deep thought, Rayah. It's not well to ponder the past." Gamma puts an arm around her.

Rayah gives her a hug, and then goes out into the corridor.

Two guards follow her as she enters the elevator and they begin descending, the chains grinding as they are lowered floor by floor.

They exit out of the elevator and enter the gaming hall. It's filled with players, sitting at card tables, roulette, dice, you name it, it's there. Rayah has been learning the ropes from her uncle. Crystallini, Rayah refused to call him by his name even though it irritated him, was bent on her taking over some of the responsibilities of the House of Two Faces when she came of age.

A part of her wished Crystal would offer her freedom for her birthday. To go explore the city, or what lay beyond the walls that enclosed it.

Her world was a world explored by books, a world long dead, more than a thousand years, and the world that existed today was as alien as the love her uncle held for her.

"Rayah," Crystal greets her from behind. And she can recognize his presence even before he speaks, as it sets her teeth on edge and her fists clench. A year hadn't thawed the hatred she felt for this man.

"Crystal."

"I'm so glad you chose to join us."

Us was the other people sitting at the table with him playing in a game of cards.

"Not like I have anything better to do, uncle."

"Come now, let's not be like that. Sit down, show everyone how much you've learned this past year."

Rayah sat down. It wouldn't do to push his patience any further. Crystal had a dark side that few people ever got to see, and even fewer people saw twice.

The dealer dealt her in. She picked up her cards and checked them.

A five of hearts and a ten of clubs. Shit hand.

She pushed forward a thousand, raising the stakes. Crystal lit a cigarette, his eyes bright behind his golden mask of a skull. The celebrations of his victory went on until the early hours. Marking the death of her father.

"So, tell me," Crystal said through a cloud of smoke. "How is our red-haired friend with the foul temper? Is she well?"

Rayah bets another two thousand as there was a ten on the flop. She nods. "You should go up and see her some time. I'm sure you have much in common."

"Hmm. Always the feisty one, aren't we?" smiles a woman in a mask. Rayah recognizes her by face, but she can't be bothered remembering these people's names, as they are nothing but simple cardboard cut-outs, two dimensional and false. Dulled mirrors placed around Crystal to reflect his own terminal vanity.

"I guess." Rayah bets five thousand on the turn. She's one card away from a ten-high straight. "But then I've had a good tutor." She flashes a smile at Crystal, and it's filled with as much loathing as she can muster.

Mind you, she doesn't always give him a hard time. But today wasn't any day. Today was a raw reminder of just how much this monster had taken from her.

"Manners, Rayah." Crystal crushes out his cigarette. His smile is as false as the friends he clings around him, like fungi to a rotten trunk, nothing grew there but parasitic life.

Rayah bet her whole chunk of cash the dealer had given her, ten

thousand in all, and only one person matched her bet. Crystal watched

with hungry eyes as the cards were shown. The last card was turned.

And she got the straight on the river.

*

Call me Mors. Mors Lament. I am a man with many paths ahead of me.

I have journeyed across the plains, from New York to Detroit to

California. Let me tell you my story…

I leave the Gate of No Return, the main gateway in and out of

New York City and we strike out west, me and my companion. We

huddle beneath our cloaks, pistols securely fastened to our belts, and

lean into the cold wind that bites from the north. The gale breathes

through the silver mask I wear on my face. The ground rolls by beneath

us, my horse sure and steady in his gait. The hills are covered in scrub,

and empty shells of farmhouses and their silos pass us by, forgone

human way markers that mark our progress.

The land is riddled with radiation, but we have taken our pills to

keep healthy on the journey, and this close to the city is patrolled by the

gangs who run it, keeping the mutants at bay. But it won't be long until

we come across one.

That night we camp in a crop of trees, hitching my horse to a

towering elm, I set down my bedroll and my companion sets to making a fire. He puts in a few chunks of the dried meat and vegetables we carry. The stew releases odours that soon make my stomach grumble, and I nod my thanks as he hands me my bowl. I eat.

My past is shrouded in mystery, alas, and I cannot explain any of it to you, for to do so would be exposing myself to retribution and rebuke.

Let us just say that I am not a bad man, and I have tried to do good in this world so corrupted by evil.

The next day we break camp and set off west once more. At midday we come across a patrol of six horsemen, all armed with sabres, pistols, and rifles. But my companion and I show them our papers.

"Just the two of you heading to Detroit?" asks the leader. He is young, younger than some of the posse behind him, and he must be prone to violence to have risen in his ranks so fast. I keep my tone even.

"We're merchants without merchandise, men finding greener pastures to the west. California, specifically."

"Well, I'll be surprised if you even make it to Detroit. You should have hired guards."

I shrug my shoulders. "Don't have the coin, friend. I guess we must put our fate into luck's hands."

The young man nods. "Better you than me." He hands back our documents. They watch us as we breast the hill and disappear from view. No doubt thinking they would never see us again.

That was OK. I had my doubts also. But I had to make it.

I had to.

The days pass by in a steady rhythm of watering and feeding the horses, setting camp, cooking, eating, sleeping, waking, breaking camp, riding, and all over again.

It was on the fifth day that the mutants attacked.

I was setting my bedroll down when I heard movement behind me. My pistol was still on the saddle. Foolish me. A man out here on the plains shouldn't be ever more than reaching distance from his weapon, but I guess I had grown too confident in the lack of mutants so far. I turn, slowly, and my companion is crouched by the fire, his eyes wide as they stare at me.

There's one mutant crawling through the brush behind him. They are sneaky.

My companion nods, probably goodbye, and spins, drawing his pistol from his waist in one fluid motion.

The mutant erupts from the brush. Its ribs stick out like tree roots over a cliff's edge, its hair matted and tangled, eyes bloodshot and bulging, teeth yellow, sharp.

225

The pistol shot takes the mutant through the eye. My companion is a good shot. The mutant collapses, dead.

But there are more moving through the brush now, further back, but running, as the game has been given away and their surprise attack has been blown.

I run to my saddle and rip both pistols from it. I cock them both back as three mutants come tearing from the trees.

I shoot, my shot rips through the front runner's chest, and it goes down in a pool of dark, congealed blood.

Two more are coming at us, fast. My last shot takes the next one through the stomach. Damn it! I've been lacking in my marksmanship.

My companion wrestles with the mutant that pounces onto him. Trying to grip his other pistol on the back of his belt. But it's no good. The mutant bites into him, tearing a chunk from his neck.

I pull out my sabre from my saddle and take stance as the other mutant pounces. It's long, dirty, sharp nails flash, and they bounce off my mask harmlessly.

I slash the mutant across the stomach, and stinking entrails spill out across the floor. But the mutant is nonplussed and comes at me again. Its nails dig into my arm, slitting through the woollen fabric with ease and tearing the skin.

I jump back and lash out again, and the blow catches the mutant across the jaw, ripping its face open. The mutant stays coming, more congealed blood running out from the gaping wound, black tongue waggling from the open maw that was itsmouth.

I strike a final time and bring it down.

My companion is on the ground, the mutant clinging onto him, clawing at him. I take the top of its head off with my blade, and it collapses.

My companion is still alive.

I quickly staunch and bandage my companion's neck, then we decide to break camp and find a better place to sleep.

"They must have been tracking us." This is the first thing my companion has said since we left New York. I nod. He speaks the truth. Mutants are known to group up when ambushing travellers on the road.

I just hoped they wouldn't try again this night.

*

It's three more days of hard traveling before we reach Detroit. The horses are tired, as am I. We check into the gate, paying the toll, and enter the city. We find a tavern with a stable, where we leave our horses to rest, and enter the tavern.

Inside are a few men playing dice. A few at the bar. None pay us any heed as we sit at the bar and order drinks.

227

I drink. Then leave my companion to go about some business in the city.

The next two days we rest and on the third we take our horses, and head west once more. It will be two weeks before we reach California. Two weeks of bandit and mutant riddled terrain.

I checked my pistols and nodded to my companion.

I was ready.

*

Life on the road is a hard life. A life of solitude, even when traveling with a companion. None can take the burden of the world on their shoulders, for it must be mounted alone.

We rode for three days west, with shuffling noises coming from the trees around us on the third night, but it must have been a lone mutant because it did not attack. I was glad for my companion's company then, as surely if I had been alone, I would be vulnerable to these lone harbingers of death, unable to take turns at taking watch, afraid that they would tear out your throat in your sleep.

The next day we come upon a walled town, and refresh ourselves inside, replenish our stores of dried meat and grain for the horses, and purchase two flintlock rifles. The next leg of our journey was known for its disappearances.

We paid the tax for passing through the town. Money was getting low. We struck off west, with little over a week of hard traveling left between us and California.

*

On the fourth day after leaving the walled town we noticed the bandits on the horizon. Like a storm cloud of dust, their horses kicked up dirt and sand in their wake.

"Quickly now," I say. I dig in my heels, and we set off at a gallop, but the bandits seemed to have seen us as they follow our direction as we veer south then west. They are gaining on us. An hour passes, and the horses are tiring, the bandits' mere minutes behind us.

We come to a hollow before a rising hill, where a dead fallen tree lies. This is good ground for ambushing.

We hitch our horses behind the dead tree, take cover, our rifles and pistols already loaded. We aim.

I count ten bandits coming over the ridge. They each have a spare mount, so it was no wonder they were gaining on us, as they could swap back and forth and let their horse's rest.

"Wait," I say. I let them come closer, down into the hollow, and climbing the hill.

I pull my trigger. The bullet catches the bandit in the front, right through the chest. He falls, dead. I had hoped that if I killed their leader that they would break and scatter, but they don't. They dig in their

heels and come screaming up the hill. My companion's shot takes the

next bandit through the head.

I'm reloading. I manage one more shot before they reach the

breast of the hill, and it takes one of the bandits through the throat.

We pull out our pistols and fire.

One of my shots takes a horse in the neck, and it bucks the rider

off. My next shot is fatal, taking the bandit through his left eye.

My companion is a better shot than I. Both of his are on the mark.

Headshots.

Six dead and one down. The three bandits come around the tree in

a circle and let off their shots. One hits the tree by my head, one hits the

dirt in front of my companion, but one finds it's mark and hits me in

the arm.

Luckily it is not my sword arm.

I parry the thrust as one of the mounted bandits comes at me with

his sword. I crouch and slice my sabre through the horse's flank, and it

buckles. I finish the rider off as he is trapped beneath the horse.

There is no honour in these types of fights.

My companion is parrying one of the bandit's blows. The final

bandit comes at him from behind, fifty paces away, sword lifted to

strike.

I reload, taking my time not to drop the power of bullet. I aim. My bullet takes the bandit through the heart, one of my best shots, if I do say so myself.

My companion overpowers the bandit and has him down on the ground, then inflicts the coup de grace.

There is one left. He is down on the ground, a hundred paces below the dead tree. As I step closer, I see his leg is shattered, turned around the wrong way. He is only a boy. Thirteen years old if a day.

"Please, don't. My mother... Please!" The boy pleads.

I slice open his neck.

There is no honour in this land.

*

We make it to California, where we meet a contact who exchanges new identities for us. We spend an entire year there, pulling jobs until I make myself enough money. And then it was time to leave, as I have business elsewhere, and it cannot wait.

We strike out south. To Mexico.

*

Sykes finished loading the guns onto the truck and waved off the driver. The men were loading the cocaine onto the ship, and he would be bound for Boston within the hour, then on to New York.

The two men leaned against the fence, watching as they loaded the crates.

"Got names?" asked Sykes.

The masked man seemed to smile, or his eyes did, for his face was hidden behind a silver mask. Thing gave him the heebiejeebies.

"You can call me Mors. All my friends call me Mors." The mask man shakes Sykes's hand.

Sykes smiled. There was something about this guy he liked from the get-go. "We friends now, mister?"

"I guess. A man can never have too many friends."

"Where were you before Mexico?"

Mors sucks his teeth. "Everywhere. I was in Detroit, then California. Now I'm here." He reaches into his coat, pulls out the wad of cash and hands it to Sykes. Sykes nods and slips it inside his coat.

"Right, you can come with me to New York, but either of you begin getting sick on my boat and I'll toss you right off. Got it?"

Mors nods. They climb aboard, he and his silent companion, and soon the ship sets sail, leaving Mexico in its wake.

Chapter 17: Stomping Ground

Gloves finished loading the crates onto the cart and wiped the sweat from his brow. How he missed a dishonest day's work. How can a man truly be a man if he must earn the bread he eats by the strength in his back and not using the mind God gave him? Or the pistol he invented?

He was tired. Tired of breaking his back for a living. But he wasn't going to return to old habits. No.

As he finished up his day's work dropping off the cargo to a local warehouse, he headed to Valez's tavern to wet his beak. Inside he placed a wad of tens on the counter, and Valez feigned that she was about to faint.

"Is this money I see before me?" she says. "Surely it can't be Gloves, parting with actual cash?"

"Get bent, I pay my tabs. Where's Ace?"

"Brought Ellen down to the docks to go fishing."

Ellen was Ace's daughter. He'd surprised them all when they turned up in Boston not long after Jackson died, looking for honest work. Valez had had money stashed away, as everything that they couldn't grab and run with Crystallini had taken from them. Valez had opened this tavern in Boston out of her money, and because of her links with Jackson, Prout was giving her a hard time, increasing his taxes every year, threatening to burn down the tavern if she didn't pay on time.

Valez had taken on Ace as help around the tavern, not to mention as added muscle. Like she needed any.

"That's nice."

Valez stopped polishing the counter and her eyes narrowed. "I know that look."

"What?"

"That look!"

"What look?"

"The look you get every time your feet get itchy, and you need to go traveling to scratch them."

"I'm just tired, Val'."

"Well don't you be bringing no trouble around here with whatever plan you're cooking up. We've enough of it already."

"I wouldn't dream of it."

With what was left of Gloves's cash he decided to play a few games of cards with. They were playing Blackjack, and within the space of an hour he'd doubled his money. He'd always done OK with cards.

Gloves looked up as someone stepped through the door. It was a woman. There was something recognizable about her, and it didn't take him two seconds to put a name to the face.

"Isabella Prout," says Valez, placing a wine glass onto the counter and pouring the woman a glass. Isabella sits.

"Do I know you?" says Isabella.

"No, but your reputation proceeds you. Not to mention there's a striking resemblance to your brother."

Gloves folds his hand and collects his cash. He wants to get a clearer view of the woman. He'd never seen her, as she was always holed up in that fancy manor house. Some said she was as ugly as sin to be hiding away like that, but Gloves thought she looked mighty fine.

"What brings you down to this part of the city?" asks Valez.

"My business is my own."

"Fair enough. Don't mean to pry. Just peculiar you being here is all. Your brother now, he's like a piece of the furniture, or a bad smell that we just can't rid of."

"I'll make sure to tell him."

Valez smiled crookedly. "Ah, now, there's no harm in a bit of jesting, is there?"

"I guess not."

"Tell you what, since you're practically family, how about this drink's on the house?"

"That's very kind of you, thanks." Isabella huddled into her coat. It's not cold inside so Gloves figures it's either nerves or she's coming down with a dose of the chills. Gloves slides over onto the seat next to her as Valez's back is turned.

"Name's Gloves," he says. Isabella doesn't look across at him, instead she twirls her drink.

"Funny name."

"Ain't names just funny anyway?"

"I don't think so."

Gloves sighs. He's never had much luck with the ladies. "No, me neither."

He goes to move away, sit beside the fire for a minute before he heads home, but Isabella's hand snatches out and grips onto his wrist.

"Don't leave."

"Excuse me?"

"Stay, please, keep me company. It's been so long since I've sat and talked with someone other than my brother."

Gloves sits back down. "Guess that can't be much fun conversation, seeing…"

"Seeing what?"

236

"Seeing as he's a Grade A prick, no offense."

Isabella smiles. "None taken. He is a prick." Her smile fades. "A mean, nasty, cold, lying, cheating bastard whore mongering fuck of a prick…"

Gloves is impressed. "Quite a mouth on you there."

"Sorry."

"Didn't say it was a bad thing. Just not used to hearing ladies speak like that. Now, Valez," Valez turns at the mention and her eyes widen at seeing them talking to each other. "Valez cusses like drunk sailor caught with his prick in the zip."

"What do you think you're doing?" asks Valez, not at all happy. Gloves shrugs.

"Just shooting the shit."

Isabella smiles again. "He's fine. I'm enjoying the company."

Valez lifts a brow. "Then lady, you need your head checked. Only company Gloves keeps is with his mule, and that old girl has all the brains of the operation, not to mention the looks."

"Fuck yourself, Val'."

Valez laughs and walks to the other end of the bar to serve someone.

"So, how did you end up with a name like Gloves? What's your surname, boots?"

237

"Heh. No, it's a long story. But you see these here gloves," Gloves clenches his knuckles, and the metal studs of his gloves bulge. "These babies won me more brawls than a sharp right hook. People in the orphanage picked on me so I learned to fight young, you see?"

"You were an orphan?"

Gloves blushes. He's said too much. The damned drink made his tongue loose.

"It's nothing to be ashamed of." Isabella rubs the back of his hand. He moves it away.

"Ain't nothing to be proud of either though."

Silence passes for a few moments, and Gloves thinks it's time to go, when the woman looks up at the picture hanging on the wall.

"Did you know Jackson?" she says.

Gloves feels his balls shrink. "No, not really. Why?"

"He... He killed my father. Just that you know Valez, I thought you might have known him."

"I... I didn't know him, no." Gloves stands up, and it's about time he was going. Isabella sips the last of her wine and looks at him.

"You going?"

"Mule ain'tgonna work itself, even if Valez thinks it's got half a brain in its head."

"Hmm. Can I talk to you again?" Isabella looks away. "I've…
I've liked our chat. It feels so fresh, compared to the politics and
business my brother bores me with."

Gloves sticks on his flat cap and pulls it down tight. He offers her
his hand, and she takes it. He lifts it and kisses it. "It would be my
pleasure, madam."

Isabella bursts out laughing, and it sends tingles up Gloves's
spine.

"Sorry, cheesy. Something I read in a book." Gloves blushes,
thinking he's made a fool of himself right when he was getting
somewhere.

"It wasn't cheesy."

"No?"

"No. It was beautiful."

"I dunno about that now."

"Until next time, Mr. Gloves." Isabella stands and heads towards
the door. Gloves watches her as she pushes through the doors and out
into the night.

*

Daniel Prout was not an evil man. Not a man prone to flights of
violence, like his father, nor fits of depression like his mother. He was
not a man to be crossed, but he was a fair man.

But when he saw his sister exiting the tavern, that rat-hole infested shit-den, he saw red. He pushed her up against the corner of the building.

"And just where do you think you're going?" he hisses into her face.

Her face falls, and she tries to look away, but he grips her jaw in his free hand and makes her look at him.

"You don't leave the manor. Ever. Are you trying to get me killed? Do you want to be kidnapped?"

"I'm sorry, Daniel. I just wanted to talk to someone who—"

"Talk? What do you have to say to people like them? They're nothing. Worthless."

"I'm going crazy up in the house alone. With nothing but hired hoodlums to keep me company. I want to be free, Daniel."

Daniel growls, pulls back his hand and slaps her across the face. "Free? *Free?* You know how much I've sacrificed for you? How much I've done? Bad things, things I didn't want to do, but I did it for us."

His breathing grows heavy as he feels her against him. The alleyway is dark.

"Tell me you love me."

"Daniel, no…"

"Tell... me... you... love me!" He slaps her across the face again, then tears open her cloak, rifling through her drawers. She fights him, and he slaps her across the face again. He grabs her by the hair.

"You want to speak with dogs? You want to *lay* with dogs? OK then. I'll do you like a dog."

He forces her around, and she cries as he snatches up her dress, pulls down her pants and is about to force himself inside her when there's movement behind him.

He turns, pants down around his ankles, and a fist comes flashing straight at him. It catches him right in the side of the head, and his thrashed against the wall. As he slides down against the wall, and his world turns black, he hears his sister say one word.

"Gloves..."

*

Gloves stomps the fucker into the face. The woman pushes him away with one arm, fixing her clothes with the other.

"What?" he cries. "He was trying to fucking *rape* you!" Gloves goes to get back to work with his boots, but Isabella pushes him back once more.

"I... said... no!"

"Why?"

"Because... Because he's my *brother*!"

241

Gloves takes a second to realize the full implications of what she's saying. "You're brother... Not the same brother as..."

"That runs Boston? Yes!"

Gloves looks down at the unconscious man.

"Oh, fuck."

*

Call me Mors. I am a man with two faces, but you will never see my real one. I hide my past behind this mask of silver, I hide my pain behind these eyes, for the world does not deserve to look upon it.

The ship pulls into Boston Harbour and the ship idle in the bay trains it's cannons on us. But it doesn't open fire. I tell the man Sykes, that I wish to go ashore, and he tells me to be back within the hour or he's leaving without me.

The city is cold this time of year, a shock to the nerves after California and Mexico. It feels good, but the icy wind that blows through my long hair does little to dampen the rage the dwells within me.

I enter the bar. It's called *The Diamond in the Rough*.

A familiar face cleans the counter.

I sit at the bar. She slides a whiskey onto the counter. I pay and take a sip.

"That's a fine mask you've got there," she says.

"ThanksValez." I let back the drink.

She frowns. "I know you?"

"Not recognize an old flame?"

"Can't say your face rings a bell, what being made of silver and all."

"Guess time has a funny way of blurring faces."

Valez frowns deeper. "I do know you."

"Can I tell you a story?"

"If you buy me a drink, I'm all ears."

I reach inside my coat pocket and take out a wallet, pull out an inch thick stack of tens. "This should do for a time."

Valez snatches the notes and shoves them in the till, then refills my glass. "Shoot away."

*

Once upon a time, there were two men. One was a man made of disguises. A man who could fit in anywhere and no one could ever recall what he looked like. He called himself the Chameleon.

The Chameleon was a man without a past, a man who had left it all behind and only looked to the future. A man who had no identity, so filled the shoes of ghosts to become a person.

The other was a man of action. A man prone to anger and would destroy the world to gain the safety of his daughter. That man is the same man you have hanging on your wall there.

Yes, Jackson.

Now let me tell you a little story about these two men.

One was a prisoner. Chameleon was on a ship, surrounded by enemies, until Jackson, knowing he was walking to his death, or his redemption, decided that he was done with being a bad man. So, he let his prisoner go, secreting him out the back of the ship on a boat and letting him loose in the city.

Then came a road of black roses. Jackson duelled against the notorious Crystallini and lost.

But this isn't where our story ends…

*

"That right?" says Valez, refilling their drinks. "You gonna just tell me things I already know?"

There was movement behind me, and I don't turn and look but I know who had just walked through the door.

The man sits at the bar and orders a drink.

"Mors," he greets me.

I look at him. His eyes are the only thing I recognize.

"You gonna finish the story?" says Valez.

I nod to the man.

"The Chameleon hurries into the streets of Manhattan," says the man who has just entered. "He finds a man with a case. Inside are two loaded silver pistols. The Chameleon kills the man and dons his outfit. He goes to a house with two faces and waits..."

*

"What does a man say when faced with death? A man can only share the burden so far, and that extends to keeping death company.

"But *this* time, this time it was different..."

*

Valez stares at me with wide eyes. Her hand shakes as she takes the bottle and drinks down a mouthful.

"I only ever knew one guy who said that..."

I take my hand and lift my silver mask.

Valez inhales deeply.

"No... Jackson?"

I place the mask on the counter, and smile.

"Hello, Valez. It's been too long."

Ace walks in then and he smiles at Valez but seeing her expression his face hardens.

"And what in the hell is going on..." He pauses as he steps forward, his face pales as he recognizes the killer in my eyes.

245

Gone is the con man. Long gone is the Jackson these people

knew. For I have walked the plains this past year as a ghost in hiding,

biding my time.

"How?" says Ace.

"How does a man cheat death?" I say. I shake my head. "One

word, revenge."

The Chameleon smiles. Reaches inside of his coat and takes out a

cigar, lights it and hands it to me.

"You're dead." Valez is shaking. "I saw the bullet tear your face

apart, you died!"

"Yes." I put my hand on the Chameleon's shoulder. "But I learned

a man can die and come back again. This man here saved me."

Chameleon nods. "I secreted Jackson into a carriage after the

duel, once Crystallini was satified he was dead he left me to take the

body. I shot Jackson with a syringe of adrenaline and done CPR until I

got him to a certain doctor."

I smile, and it feels like it has been too long since I have smiled, a

year and counting. "A certain doctor who specializes in bringing people

back from the dead, who aren't long gone, mind you, and this doctor

also has a penchant for facial reconstruction."

Valez leans over the counter and takes my hand, kisses it. "I can't

believe it."

246

I lift the mask and slip it back over my face, hidden once more.

"You'd best believe it. And I'm coming for Crystallini and everything he's got."

"How?" says Ace. "He has an army behind him now, thousands, and you, no offense, haven't."

"I'm not going to fight him. I'm not going to even let him know I'm alive. I'm going to do the one thing I know how to do better than anything else."

I knock back my drink.

"I'm going to steal."

*

So what? You thought I was dead? That's OK. So did everyone else. But now I'm back.

I had travelled the land as Mors Lament, and spent a year pulling jobs, cons, with Belladonna in California.

I paid a certain grave a visit too in Detroit, mind you. I don't forget promises made to friends. I left flowers by No-Name's family's grave and told them how much of a good man he was, of how he'd made a life for himself, living every day like it was his last.

So now I was back, under the alias of Mors.

Don't know what it means?

It's Latin for death.

247

But I wasn't intent on Crystallini's murder. I wanted to kill him on the inside, take everything he had and leave him a broken shell of a man.

Word was that Crystallini was celebrating the one-year anniversary of his success over me with a tournament. A high stakes tournament, winner takes all.

And I was planning on it.

*

I would love to say that the old gang got together. But that isn't true. Gamma, Valez told me, had stayed in New York to keep an eye on Rayah.

Valez couldn't just sell her stake in the tavern, so she was out, as was Ace, who had chosen to stay in Boston with his daughter. And I could respect that.

Anyhow, I wouldn't need Ace's skillsets.

I needed con men. Thieves. And who better to help me find them than my dear old Belladonna.

What, you think she stayed in California? Do you even know her?

*

Gloves peeked out through the window. It had been two days since he stomped the most powerful man in Boston into the pavement. Two days of fear, not knowing if you'd last out the day.

Isabella had secreted him away in this warehouse, which was located in a remote sector of the city. Only she knew where he was hiding out. Only she could save him now.

There was a knock on the back door. Gloves went and opened it to see three hooded figures, and his heart sank. But then Isabella's voice rang out through the cold wind, and he eased.

"It's me."

"Thank the devil. What took you?"

Isabella looked to the other two men. "I bumped into an old friend of yours."

Gloves moved aside as the three figures entered.

One had a silver mask on he saw as they moved into the light.

"Not recognize the face of an old friend?"

Gloves knew that voice.

"You saved my life once, kid. Now it's time to return the favour."

The man lifted off the mask, and there was Jackson, with longer hair and scars running across the side of his face, from his left temple to below the jaw, but the eyes. They were colder, harder, hungrier.

"You're dead." Gloves looked from Isabella and back to Jackson. "I saw you go down, even checked your pulse myself."

"Guess I'm just lucky when it comes to dying." Jackson smiled, but it didn't reach his eyes.

Gloves looked at Isabella. "I thought you hated him? He killed your pa?"

"My scumbag of a father deserved it. My brother deserves it too, as he's just like him. The same..." Her voice hardens, and she stands up a bit straighter. "I'm not like them. Valez introduced us to eachother. Told me if I wanted a way out of Boston then Jackson was it. I guess that means you too."

Gloves looks at the other man, who's shrouded in darkness. "Who's this?"

"The Chameleon saved my life, he's OK," says Jackson. Gloves nods.

Gloves goes to the window and peers out. "So, where we headed boss?"

Jackson smiles. "Why, back to the streets of New York, of course..."

Chapter 18: The Bull

So the four of us climb aboard Sykes' ship, he doesn't know who I am by the way, and head north, and by the time the sun has dipped down below the horizon, we're entering New York. My eyes are drawn to the towering House of Two Faces.

The tournament was in two weeks' time. There was an entry fee of five million per player. I had two million on person, and another five hundred stashed away in New York.

I was already halfway there. Gloves said he wanted in on the game and was looking to enter the tournament himself. Well good luck with that kid.

All I had to do now was find myself a mark willing to part way with their funds.

In a city of fools, how hard could that be?

*

We enter our old safe house, the one in the Bronx. It feels like a lifetime since I set foot here. I walk into Rayah's room and my heart is beating in my chest. Nothing has changed.

Everything has changed.

I sit on her bed, and I'm not ashamed to admit a tear comes to my eye, the first one since that day I took a face full of lead.

My baby. One year since Daddy held you in his arms. And she didn't even know I was alive.

My thoughts turned to Gamma.

I could do with her help, but how the hell was I supposed to get word to her that I was back?

I couldn't. I wanted to, the devil knows I did, but to risk exposing myself, to risk letting Crystallini know I was still alive…

No, I had to do these cons without the help of my brains of operation.

I had the kid, Danny Gloves, a good fighter. I might be able to use him.

Belladonna was of course an asset. She was the best Beguiler in the business.

As was Chameleon, no better man to wear a disguise.

Isabella had decided to stay in a local tavern and would stay in contact. I think Gloves has a thing for her.

I couldn't trust anyone, not without Gamma's resources. I couldn't work with people I didn't know.

So, the four of us against the city. I liked my odds.

"Gloves," I say, they're sitting in the courtyard. "You feel like you could win a fight?"

Gloves cracks his knuckles. "I'm not bad in a scrap. But I don't have the cash to ante up."

"I'll cover it. Chameleon, get your ear to the street, find out who's taking on fights."

Chameleon nodded.

"What about me?" asks Bella.

"I need to use the time I've got wisely. We've only two weeks to get the money. And if the kid wants in, that means an extra five mil'."

Gloves sighs. "Look, I know you're doing this for your daughter, Jackson. I don't want to step in your way just 'cos I want to play a game of cards."

"Thanks, Gloves. But we'll see what we can do. I wouldn't mind having a wing man in the House of Two Faces. You think you can win a fight?"

Gloves smiles. "I know it."

I nod. "OK, we'll start off small. I'll get you a fight and bet small, and you prove yourself, then we aim higher. Your fists just might be the answer to all our problems."

*

Fighting is a risk. I would use half my money to bet on the kid, and the other half to invest in setting up the ultimate con, which had yet to show itself. That was a one and a quarter mil' split even between both.

Chameleon came back that night with four fights happening in the next few days. Me and the kid looked them over and decided on an old bruiser named Gerry "Bull" Riggs. I found a respectable bookie and placed a bet of a half million on the fight for the kid to win. The odds against the kid were two-to-one, the old timer was a veteran and the favourite despite his age.

The next day Belladonna came in and said she'd been chatted up by a sailor just back from Boston. Says that a special passenger on board had been escorted by six armed guards. That this man had a briefcase chained onto his wrist, and hell or high noon couldn't part them. I told Bella to do a bit more digging, as it sounded promising.

The wheels of fortune were slowly turning, and there was never a sweeter sound in all the world.

How I had missed being a thief.

*

Gloves was working on a heavy bag I'd gotten him the night before. That kid could throw a punch, I tell you. The fight was that evening in Brooklyn.

I was watching the kid pummel the shit out of the bag when Belladonna came through the door.

"I've got word."

"What?"

"About the man with the briefcase. Turns out there's a big diamond deal going down somewhere in New York in the next few days."

"That it? Not a lot to go on." I chew on my cigar.

"Yeah, I miss Gamma."

"Well, keep at it. Something might turn up."

Belladonna went to wash up and change into fresh clothes, as she was scouting out every tavern in New York for information. Subtly, of course, we're not idiots.

The devil knew where Chameleon was.

It was just me and the kid heading down to Brooklyn.

*

We approached a three floored tavern by the name of *The Bloody Nose* and nodded to the doormen. The place was packed. A rough ring had been made, a wooden platform about three feet off the ground surrounded by a rope. Not exactly professional standard, but there you go.

The kid was buzzing.Gloves swung his arms back and forth.

255

"You ready for this?" I ask him.

"Ready as I'll ever be."

Gloves looks across the crowd and his face pales somewhat. I follow his gaze, and there pushing his way through the crowd is one of the biggest, ugliest bastards I've ever seen, and I've seen a few. He must have been born with a crooked nose, as that thing on his face had more angles than a con man's alibi. His torso was covered with scars, a large tattoo of a bulldog across his chest, and a massive bright gold hoop hanging from his ear.

He was an intimidating cunt, I'd give him that.

I slap Gloves on the back. "And here I thought you were gonna have trouble." I need to sound sure, to be confident, even though I think the kid has as much chance as a donkey fucking a monkey. Up a tree.

The Bull stepped into the ring and began circling it, then when he reached our side, he sliced his thumb across his neck at the kid.

Gloves, and I'll give him credit for it, didn't seem bothered. He was loosening up, then looked at me and winked.

The bastard winked at me.

Gloves pulls off his tunic then, and I stare at the scars running down his chest, up his arms. He is covered from waist to neck in tattoos. An upside down cross on his chest, demons faces across his back, names crossed out on his wrist. The devil's own was this kid.

256

Gloves bends down and steps beneath the rope, entering the ring.

The Bull is in the far corner, waving to a big titted blonde woman who was in jeopardy of her nipples slipping out at any moment, who was blowing the big man kisses. The referee appeared and stepped into the ring.

"Ladies and gentlemen!" he shouts, and his crisp, deep voice cuts over the noise of the crowd. "And all you other fucking miscreants!"

He gets some laughter.

"Tonight, for your simple-minded amusement, we bring you a fight of all fights, a battle of David and Goliaths!"

The crowd roar, and most are cheering for the Bull.

The Bull throws up his fists, soaking it all in.

"So, get your drinks drank, your piss pissed, because once this baby starts you won't wanna move!"

The referee went over to a man in the crowd, a bookie no doubt, and waited while the final bets were being made. The Bull looks over at Gloves, and laughs. A full bellied laughter, and the crowd laugh with him.

A minute passes. The bookie leans over as another bookie whispers something in his ear, then nods to the ref.

The ref goes to the middle of the ring and waves both men over to him.

257

"Right, I wan't a dirty, ass-clenching, shit-heeling fight that will drive the crowd crazy. There are two simple rules. No biting, Bull, I'm looking at you. And no kicking if the other man's down. You do them while they're on the deck, you're out! Got it?"

Gloves nods. Bull just smiles a gap-toothed smile.

The ref pushes both men apart, then takes out a red bandanna.

"As soon as this touches the floor the fight will start. There are no breaks, no stops, not until the fight is done. Best of luck, gentlemen." He lifts the bandanna high over his head, then let's go, turns, and flees the stage.

I take in a deep breath.

The bandanna hits the ground, and Bull comes rushing at Gloves, arms spread akimbo, muscles clenching like a bear.

Gloves ducks and dives, circles him around to the other side of the ring. He's fast, I'll give him that.

He would need to be.

Bull lunges in and takes a roundhouse swipe at Gloves, who ducks it just in time to avoid serious brain damage. The big man is caught off guard, but Gloves doesn't step in and hit him, instead he lunges to the side, spins, and drives his boot down into the side of Bull's knee. The big man screams and there's a splintering *crunch!*

"Yes, fucking yes!" I can't help myself, I'm having a good time. I light a cigar.

Gloves backs away into the corner from the limping Bull, a smile touching his lips, and it only seems to spur on the big man, who growls and lunges at him once more, favouring his better leg, as he punches out with a left jab, fast for a big man, and the swipe clips my man on the side of the ribs. Gloves stumbles to his right, winded, and the big man is behind him. Bull wraps Gloves around in a bear hug and lifts him up, swinging him this way and that like a rag doll on strings.

"Get out!" I scream, my cigar burning into a woman's arm beside me, but I couldn't care less.

Gloves is red in the face as Bull squeezes the life out of him. But just as it looks like he's about to pop a rib, Gloves drives his leg back at an awkward angle and hits the big man in the balls with his ankle.

Bull drops Gloves and goes to grab his crown jewels, and I grab my own in sympathy, but Gloves isn't sympathetic, and he crouches down, spins, and jumps, his leg blurring through the air in some ninja shit, and his foot only hits the poor bastard in the gonads for the second time.

The crowd laugh as the red-faced Bull stumbles back, his twice bitten balls firmly held in hand.

259

Gloves dances on his feet, sticks out his hand and gives Bull the *come-hither* hand signal.

This kid's got balls, man. I tell you that.

Bull puts all his pain into anger, and comes screaming at Gloves, face red as a fire poker, neck tendons standing out like a scarlet spider web, and he lashes out with his right, Gloves dodges, his left, Gloves dodges. He's just about to throw a third when Gloves steps in and drives the heel of his wrist into Bull's throat. The big man stumbles back, grabbing his throat, eyes popping from his head, face gone from scarlet to deep purple. The big man hits the floor on his knees, and Gloves spins, bringing his leg around in an arc, and drives his foot into the side of the big man's head.

He hits the floor. Down and out for the count.

The ref counts, but everyone in the audience can see he ain't getting back up. The kid, the fucking kid, cheeky bastard, walks over and steps out of the ring before the ref even gets to four.

"Told you." Gloves picks up his tunic and pulls it back on. I shake my head.

"Where'd you learn to fight like that?" I ask.

Gloves smiles, cracks his knuckles, the metal studs bulge.

"Guess I'm just lucky."

*

We left *The Bloody Nose* to cheers, the both of us bandy legged,

drunken from the small brewery of ale and whiskey we've been bought

by the crowd. I've one and a half million waiting for me back with the

bookie in the Bronx, who won't be happy to have lost but fuck him.

I sling my arm around Gloves' shoulders as we sing our way

through Brooklyn. Getting back to the Bronx, inside we find

Belladonna sitting with Chameleon.

"Nice of you to join us," says Chameleon.

"Are you both drunk?" says Bella, smiling.

"As drunk as a... As a..." I can't think of anything smart to say.

"As a fish farting in your cup," says Gloves.

"What? No, that's shit... As drunk as a..." I fade off. My mind is

blank.

"Well, we just received word from Gamma. She's heard I'm back

and wants to meet."

"Oh, Gag-gaga. Gamma. Yeah, nice tits." I hold up my hands to

my chest and Gloves laughs. I point my finger at him. "Buh... But

don't teh-tell her I said so." I tap my head. "Woman's got a bad temp-

temper..."

"You both need to get to bed. We've to meet her at the northern

tip of Manhattan early in the morning. You need to be sober, Jackson."

I salute her! Which doesn't win me any favours.

I nod. "OK, OK… We'll get to bed."

I turn to leave. Then inspiration hits me!

"As drunk as a squirrel shitting on barrel of drunken squirrels!" I shake my head. "No… It sounded better in my head."

Chapter 19: Knuckles

I am never drinking again.

The kid looks like he could run a fucking mile, all-the-while my insides feel like they could fall out my ass at any moment. I meet Belladonna and Chameleon in the courtyard, and the kid is working the bag. I stare at him with an open mouth.

"You'd swear I was the one in the ring last night," I say, sitting down and grabbing the bottle of whiskey on the table. Hair of the dog.

"You remember what I told you?"

"What, about Gamma? Yeah. She know I'm alive?"

"No. She just knows I'm back. She knows nothing about you. You can let her know if you want." Bella lights a cigarette. "Or not. I know it's dangerous letting her know, being in Crystallini's company and all."

"Hmm."

I consider the odds. While it would hurt me not letting Gamma know I was alive, now wasn't the right time. Better to leave her in the dark, what was it called?

Yeah, plausible denial. That would be best.

"Sounds best," says Chameleon. "If Crystallini even got a sniff that you were alive he would shut up shop and no one would get into the House of Two Faces."

Belladonna places the winnings from the fight onto the table. Guess I must have collected it last night on my way home.

"We're up to three and a half mil'." Belladonna slides the bags across the table.

"Hey, kid, you up for another fight?" I call over to Gloves.

He stops punching the bag. "Yeah."

"Right. Chameleon, look for a higher return fight." I look at Bella. "Any more news about this briefcase guy?"

Bella shakes her head. "Whoever he is, he's keeping himself well hidden. It must be a big player in the city buying the jewels."

"Shit." I take a swig of the whiskey and it burns going down.

"But Gamma might be able to help us on that account," says Bel'.

I nod. "Well then, let's not keep the beautiful Gamma waiting."

*

Gamma stands on the boardwalk alone. Her back is turned to me. I'm wearing my mask, and a cloak, so she won't notice anything is out of place.

I could have stayed in the safe house, but I wanted to see her.

She's as beautiful, no, more beautiful than I remember her. It's been a long year and the sight of those bright eyes as they turn and quickly take in the four of us catches my breath.

Her eyes pass by me without recognition. They watch as we approach, and she nods to Belladonna.

"Good to see you, Bel'." They exchange kisses on the cheek.

"And you Gamma. How's things been?"

"OK. I can't stay for long. I had to slip out while Crystal wasn't looking."

"Is that prick giving you a hard time?"

She shakes her head. "No, I hardly see him, to be honest. I spend most my time on the top floor with Rayah."

"And how is she?"

"She's great. Crystal has her learning all sorts of things."

"Good. It's good she's keeping well." Bella lights up a cigarette. "She's a good little woman."

"Yeah. So how have you been keeping? How's California been treating you?"

"Can't complain. Bought myself a nice plot of land and started growing a vineyard."

"No shit?"

"Yeah." She reaches in her bag and takes out a bottle of wine. "I brought you some."

"Thanks. OK. So let's get to business, Bel', I haven't got long. Here's the file." Gamma takes out a file from inside her coat. Hands it to Bella, who browses through it.

"Looks like you knew about the deal before it was even happening. You have the location, names, times. Wow, Gamma, this is exactly what we needed."

Gamma looks past Bella. "Hey Chameleon."

Chameleon shifts, he's in disguise.

"Don't worry, I didn't make you, Bella just told me you were with her. And hey Gloves, how've you been keeping?"

Gloves nods. "Can't complain."

Gamma looks at me and her eyes narrow. "You I don't know."

"He's just some out of town help. A con man from California."

"He not know how to speak? Or does he like other people doing the talking for him?"

Bella looks back at me. "He's a mute. Can't talk. But he's far from stupid. Saved my life plenty of times."

Gamma points at the file. "It's a conglomerate of buyers from four different boroughs. I don't have to tell you how hard a con like this is gonna be."

"I know. But you know us, we play hard."

Gamma shrugs. "I wish I could help more."

Bella shakes her head. "You've done plenty. Give Rayah my love."

"I will." Gamma turns and walks away.

Back at the safehouse in the Bronx I look at the file.

It turns out Gamma was right. Every borough besides Manhattan was in on this deal. Each boss was buying one million worth of diamonds. Were they trying to gain wealth to get an edge on Crystallini somehow? Buy more muscle? Who knew. All I knew was that their money and the diamonds would be mine. All I had to do was figure out the how.

Gamma had worked out the meeting place, a ship on the east coast of Brooklyn, in two days' time.

If I pulled of this con, then that would bring us up to seven million cash and four in diamonds.

Hey, I know not to count my chickens before they hatch, but a man must think ahead. OK?

*

We worked out a plan. The best way to do this con was if we switched the diamonds after they were checked in the exchange. Chameleon went to a local engineer and offered him some cold hard cash to make

267

us up a special briefcase with two hidden compartments. Why? You'll soon find out.

We then hired four local muscle from the file Gamma gave us.

So, what next?

Why, haven't you ever heard of Bait and Switch?

*

Chameleon used the file Gamma gave us to set up the disguise. There were pictures taken of this man with the briefcase. After half an hour of cosmetics and a new suit, he looked the image of the guy.

We left the safehouse and headed for the first rendezvous. We arrived outside the tavern where the man was located. I entered first and made sure the man wasn't around, and asking the barman had he seen the guy, the barman said he and his four goons had stepped out. The barman was in on the con.

I went back outside and gave the gang the nod.

Chameleon and his four muscle entered the tavern and got the room key off the barman. Once inside the room, they waited.

I was outside, and after half an hour the real briefcase man appeared around the corner. He entered the bar, and me and Gloves followed them inside.

We followed them down the corridor, and after they got to their door me and Gloves started shouting at eachother, the signal to the men inside that they were just at the door.

The four men ignored us and pushed their way inside.

Me and Gloves followed, slipping out the two loaded pistols we had each.

Inside waiting for our briefcase man was five men holding loaded pistols, and at the sight of guns in front and behind them, they had no chance.

The four real guards threw down their weapons.

"You have any idea whose diamonds these are?" growled the briefcase man.

"No, whose?"

"Only the man who runs New York, Crystallini!"

"Really?" I say, loving the news. Gamma hadn't even known that, and that was saying something.

"You guys won't have anywhere to hide after this!"

I knock out the briefcase man as the four guards are tied up and gagged.

"Who said I'm going to be hiding?" I take the briefcase and walk out.

Step one of the con complete.

269

Gloves and the others load the bodies of the now unconscious men out a back door and into a carriage as I slip the barman the ten thousand bucks as earlier arranged to forget he ever saw the briefcase man.

"Who?" says the barman, giving me a wink.

*

I change the diamonds from one briefcase into the other one, the briefcase with two secret compartments. We keep our heads low as we head towards the east side of Brooklyn. We pull up at the docks and Gloves shivers, as he tells me it's the same place he rushed headlong into open fire.

Of course, it is. The tenements are still blown to pieces.

A lone ship sits in the bay. We climb into the boat, me, Gloves, Chameleon and the four muscle who are none the wiser about what's going on.

We climb onto the ship, and there's a gang of men there with rifles. Chameleon wastes no time and approach the four men sitting at the table on the deck. He places our briefcase down beside four black briefcases belonging to the men.

"You're late," says one of the men. "And I thought there were only supposed to be five of you?"

"I was almost mugged yesterday," says Chameleon. "Decided I needed a couple more guns."

The man smiles as he looks around at his men. "You can never have to many guns. OK, let's see them."

Chameleon opens his case, and it's filled with four large black bags, each one containing one million worth of diamonds. They're inspected at length by each of the respective crime-lords'jewellers, and they each give a nod. Chameleon places them back inside the briefcase and hits the switch in one fluid motion. The secret compartment by now will have dropped the real ones into a lower, hidden compartment, while the higher one drops the fakes jewels into where the real ones had been.

"Let's see the cash."

The four briefcases are opened, and we set to counting them out. It's all there.

Chameleon shakes hands with the four men, then we turn and leave.

*

You know what the best part of the con was? It wasn't the cash or the diamonds, it was the shit mess we were after putting Crystallini into. Now he would have to explain why he had ripped off the four other crime lords with fake jewels.

271

Well, fuck you, brother.

*

"May thieves rein!" I toast.

"May thieves rein!" the gang salute.

We drink.

The cash is on the table in front of us. Seven and a half million. Turns out that the briefcase man had also a half mil' worth of bonds secreted away in a compartment in his own suitcase.

Well, thank you very much.

"I missed this," said Gloves, staring down at the cash.

"Well, two and a half is on you tomorrow," I say.

Oh yeah, Chameleon had arranged a fight with a boxer from the Bronx by the name of Jason "Knuckles" Bradley. The kid was one fight away from securing a place in the tournament.

It was one week until the start of the tournament.

One week until I took Crystallini for everything he had.

*

The night of the fight came around, and I had purchased the kid a boxing outfit to wear, after all he was representing the gang and I couldn't let him go in there looking like some bum off the street. I had to get a bookie from out of the borough, as the one from the Bronx wouldn't take my bet after I cleaned him out from the previous bout.

The kid looked good. Black shorts with gold tassels, golden gloves, with 'Gloves' written across his waist. He was ready.

Jason "Knuckles" Bradley was a champion, and he looked the part. His green shorts had a belt around them, as he was the two-time winner of the New York boxing tournament.

This fight would be different. There was no kicking or dirty fighting allowed, strictly professional, and the stage was a far-cry from the rickety piece of shit in *The Bloody Nose*. It was four feet off the ground, with three red ropes surrounding it. The place was packed to the rafters, and everybody who was anybody had gotten a ring-side seat. Even Crystallini was there, surrounded by mobsters of course, he was untouchable, even if I had wanted to get at him.

The kid was two-to-one odds, and if he won this fight, he would have his entry fee to the tournament in the House of Two Faces.

I was stood beside him in the corner, and we made a picture, me with my silver mask and golden cloak, him dressed in his gear, tattoos speaking of a dark past that I had no doubt was filled with violence.

The opponent entered the room to cheers, drums beat in rhythm to his footsteps, and he stopped to shake Crystallini's hand and pay his respects.

Knuckles was tall, lean, muscular, the polar opposite of the Bull, this guy was the icon of an athlete in his prime. I had my doubts that the kid could take him in a fair fight to be honest.

"This guy ain't so tough," said Gloves, cracking his neck from side to side.

I shoved his gum-shields in his mouth and put my hand on his shoulder. "You can take this fucker, Gloves. You know it and I know it. Give him hell."

The referee entered the ring. He walked over and spoke to one of the judges, there were three altogether. Then stepping into the centre of the ring, he waved both fighters over.

"Alright, I wanna clean fight. No biting, kicking, headbutting, or any other foul play. Your opponent falls, you don't hit him. You have ten seconds to get back up and touch gloves, or your out. Understand?"

Both men nodded.

"Touch gloves, gentlemen," says the ref, but neither man offers their glove. The crowd cheers.

A half-naked woman crosses the ring holding a sign displaying the number one.

I reach in and tap Gloves's leg, he looks down at me.

"I have faith in you kid. No one else in this shithole might think you've got what it takes, but I seen you fight, I know you can do it."

274

Gloves nods. "Thank boss. Ain't no sweat."

The bell rings.

Gloves dances forward, Knuckles sidesteps, fists up, circling. Gloves edges closer, throwing a loose jab, then another, and Knuckles swipes them away effortlessly. Knuckles steps forward and Gloves backs off. There's a good head and a half height between them, and Knuckles must weigh twice what the kid does. Knuckles uses his extended reach to corner the kid, swiping at him, left, right, left. The kid dodges them, circles, gets out of the corner, and I realize I'm holding my breath. I inhale deeply.

The kid lunges then, a wide swipe straight out of nowhere, and Knuckles only just brings up his right glove and blocks it. The kid growls as he backs off, he has hunger in his eyes.

Knuckles laughs and shakes his head, then lets out a growl himself as he steps forward and throws a savage haymaker. The kid ducks, the blow glancing off his head, and the power in it makes him stumble. Knuckles closes in, aiming a shot to put the kid down, but he gets his feet back under him just in time and ducks right, avoiding the blow. Gloves dances into the corner once again, and Knuckles laughs. He puts up his fists and shakes his gloves and the crowd cheers.

Gloves shakes his shoulders as Knuckles approaches once again. The man jabs, twice, the third breaking through the kid's defence and knocks his head back. Gloves leans back, up against the ropes, and Knuckles tears into him. One to the ribs, one to the head, another to the ribs. Gloves is blocking them as best he can, but the power behind the shots is telling, and he's red faced as he pushes Knuckles away and makes some room.

"Hit and dodge!" I shout, but it's washed under the noise of the crowd who yell for blood. Knuckles hears them and smiles. He jabs a soft touch, followed by a savage right hand that is fast as lightning, and it hits the mark. Gloves stumbles back, arms akimbo, and he's wide open. Knuckles steps in to finish the job, Gloves regains his feet, but the swipe comes at him too fast, and Gloves goes down in a heap.

"One!" shouts the ref. "Two!"

"Come on kid!" I scream. Gloves is getting back up, shakes his head and nods to the big man. The kid touches his gloves off his head to show he's ready. The ref nods and steps back.

Gloves is steady. His arms unshaking. He steps into the big man and jabs, jabs, jabs, forcing Knuckles back from the centre of the ring, then one to the ribs, two, flurrying a fast combo that Knuckles is trying to block. The next shot rings true and connects straight into Knuckles's kisser. Knuckles spits blood as Gloves backs away, avoiding another savage blow of a haymaker.

The bell sounds and I climb into the ring as Gloves comes back to the corner. I take out his shields and give him some water. "You're doing good kid. He's ahead on points but it's still early, OK? You're doing good!"

Gloves nods. "He's fast for such a big guy."

"Well, you know what they say? The bigger they are…"

Gloves smiles. "The harder they fall."

Woman number two is crossing the ring. I look into the opposite corner and Knuckles's trainer is giving him advice.

"I can't tell you how to win this, Gloves. I can only stand in your corner."

Gloves opens his mouth as I slip back in the shield. "I was born to fight, boss. I know what I'm doing."

The bell rings and round two is underway. I exit the ring as Knuckles comes straight at the kid. He wastes no time and releases a flurry of his own, jabs coming from left to right, high and low, and the kid is blocking and weaving. The kid is backed into the corner, pushed up against the ropes, hugging his head with his gloves as Knuckles tears into him. The kid's ribs are red raw from being pummelled, one blow opens his nose and blood spurts out across the floor.

"Get outta the corner!" I yell. "Get the fuck off the ropes!"

Gloves growls and pushes Knuckles away, circles the ring. Blood drips down onto his chest, staining the upside-down cross scarlet. Knuckles jabs, jabs, breaking through the kid's defence once more, smearing blood across his cheek. A trail of blood follows Gloves, who is still looking fresh besides being used as a human punching bag.

Gloves ducks under a haymaker and circles. Knuckles is controlling the ring now. His size and reach being put to use. Gloves swipes away a right and throws a combo, right jab, right jab, left hook. None connect. Knuckles weaves and bobs, a blur of a giant, too fast.

Knuckles springs one on Gloves from nowhere, rattling his head back and making him stumble against the ropes. The kid's head hangs limp, and only for the ropes he would have gone down.

"Come on Gloves!" I shout. It snaps him awake, and he leaps to the side, as an unmerciful blow swipes past just where his head had been. Knuckles loses balance and falls against the ropes, and Gloves takes advantage.

He steps in as Knuckles is turning and hits him with a beautiful combo. Jab, jab, ribs, nose, making the big guy stumble back into the corner. Knuckles's gloves are up but he's looking rattled. Gloves doesn't let up, bang, bang, bang, a cracking punch to the ribs sends Knuckles down on one knee.

"One!"

"Fucking yes!" I scream.

Gloves dances in the centre of the ring and lifts a golden glove. He gets a few boos but a few cheers too.

Knuckles is breathing heavy, and I say a silent prayer that he cracked a rib. Bastard.

Gloves wipes away the blood.

"Three!" the ref is counting, and Knuckles is back up, touches his gloves and the ref nods, steps back.

"That the best you got?" I hear Knuckles say, but as he steps forward, he's holding his elbow close to his ribs. A good sign.

Gloves dances around him, blocking, weaving, avoiding a savage blow. He's won this round, everyone knows it, and he doesn't fuck up. So when the bell rings, I can't help but shake his gloves and smile.

"That… was… beautiful!" I say.

Gloves smiles. "Told you I could take him. He ain't so tough."

"Now don't go getting carried away. Stick to what you're doing. Don't take no risks."

Gloves nods. "Got this shit locked, boss."

"You focus on his ribs. Work those jabs and force him to expose his ribs, then you break them like fucking that," I snap my fingers.

"Working on it." The bell rings and I abandon the ring once more.

Gloves steps up and does a little dance, and the crowd cheers. Knuckles is cautious, not jabbing with his reach like he's been doing so far. He keeps his elbows locked in, but still holds the centre of the ring. Gloves dances around him, floating like a butterfly, throws a jab here, there, stinging like a bee.

Knuckles is getting pissed off. You can see it in his face.

Gloves soaks it all up, and there's a big smile spread across his face as Knuckles loses it, comes at him, showering blows down on him. Gloves blocks them, weaves, and bang! Right into the ribs!

Knuckles buckles, inhaling deeply. He almost goes down on one knee, *almost*, but no cigar. Gloves is controlling the centre of the ring now, pushing Knuckles from corner to corner, showing no mercy.

Knuckles grounds his teeth, tendons standing in his neck. He clinches Gloves and wraps him in his arms. He looks ready to fall.

Then the worst happens.

Knuckles, knowing he's being beaten, leans back and headbutts Gloves into the face.

The crowd go wild!

The ref jumps in and deducts Knuckles a point. I look up at Gloves and see the headbutt has cut him over the right eye. Shit.

Gloves wipes the blood from his eye, blinks.

Knuckles smiles as the ref backs off. He has no more warnings, but he's done the damage. He jabs the kid, jabs the kid, constantly working on the cut. It opens a bit more.

The bell rings and I jump in and apply pressure to the wound.

Damn dirty fighter.

"Gloves," I say. "He wants to fight dirty. You show him how we play? Got it?"

"They'll cut me by a point, boss."

"It doesn't matter. You're winning by a mile. Show that ugly bastard what you're made of. Got it?"

Gloves nods. The bell rings.

Gloves moves in, the cut has been staunched somewhat but blood still drips down his cheek.

Knuckles works the right side, the kid blocks. Knuckles works his ribs, and then one to the right, at the cut once more, and it opens back up.

"Now!" I shout.

Gloves clinches and drives his knee up into Knuckles's groin. The man deflates. He hits the ground like a sack of lead.

The crowd cheer Gloves on. The ref deducts him a point and gives him his final warning.

It takes two to play dirty, after all.

The count has gotten to seven before Knuckles is back up and touching gloves.

The big guy is seething and comes at Gloves with everything he has. Gloves is a good fighter, but the man is a professional on a warpath and laces into him, opening the cut more, leaving blood trailing behind them in their wake.

Gloves takes a knock to the chin and stumbles. The crowd inhales. Silence. He's on his last legs…

Then out of nowhere he ducks the final haymaker that would have taken his head off.

Moves…

Turns…

The muscles bulge in his back, in his arm, as he slowly brings his fist around.

And **BANG!**

The blow lifts Knuckles from his feet, into the air, and the big guy floats, flies, then hits the ground.

He's out for the count.

"One! Two!"

Gloves lifts his fists. The crowd love him.

"Ten! You're out!"

And the fight was won.

Part 3

There will come a time of fire and night, when enemies rise and empires fall, when the stars themselves begin to die. — **Kevin J. Anderson**

Chapter 20: Dice 'Em Up

Me and the kid bought in to the tournament. I'd use the alias set up by Belladonna back in California, and the kid would enter as a small-time player from Boston. It was three days until the tournament began.

We spent the time relaxing in the safehouse. Me and the kid played game after game of dice and cards to sharpen up on our skills. The kid was good, I'll give him that, and could hold a poker face with the best of them.

The day finally came around and Belladonna wanted to come with us, but Chameleon said he would prefer to stay at the safe house. He was never one much for gambling. It was that morning that a familiar face showed up outside our safehouse.

"Valez?" I smiled as she entered the courtyard.

"Hey, daddy." She kissed me on the cheek. I won't lie, it sent shivers down my spine. That night with her and Gamma had been a steady source of warmth this past year.

"What are you doing here?"

"I sold the tavern. Bought myself into the tournament."

"You got five mil' for that piece of crap tavern?" said Gloves. And he had a point.

"No, I got half. Had to get a loan for the rest, why, not like it's any of your business anyway."

"True that."

"I'm glad you're hear," I say. She took a step closer to me.

"You missed me?"

"Everyday."

She leans in. "I missed you too. Haven't had a bitch like you since."

I clear my throat. "If I remember correctly, you lost the coin flip. So technically you're *my* bitch."

She smiled. "I can be, if you treat me right."

"Always."

She leans in and kisses me.

"Ummh. Yummy."

"Get a room," says Gloves. And he's got a point.

I shake my head. "Sorry, Valez. Nothing personal but I wouldn't feel comfortable until Gamma knows I'm alive."

She nods. "I understand." She pinches my cheek. "Until then."

*

The four of us load into a carriage and we take the bridge to Manhattan. The jagged skyscrapers grow from monoliths on the horizon, to hulking towers reaching, clawing into the sky. As I pass along the narrow

285

streets, they're filled with passers-by, people on the street buying from the stalls on the corners. I can't help but think of the last time I was here, journeying down a path of black roses, on a road to meet my own death.

But I hadn't died. I had been reborn and given a second chance. And I would not waste it. I couldn't afford to.

We arrive outside the House of Two Faces. Its sign hangs crooked. A crooked home for a crooked man.

We're searched outside and enter the foyer, and it's packed with revellers, all heading up stairs to the small games' tables. I show my papers to the gangster with the different coloured eyes. He checks off my name.

Mors Lament.

The kid is right behind me. As are the two ladies and we take a seat at the bar. I order a whiskey, neat, and light a cigar.

"Won't be long now," says Gloves.

Minutes tick by.

"You nervous?" Valez asks me.

I laugh. "Nervous? I'm only not nervous when I'm stealing."

Bella smiles. "With your luck then I guess you're not nervous."

And she was right.

I was a card shark in my younger days. Was a familiar face at all the gambling houses. Now it is my silver face that will lift its brow and bear the weight of fortune. Lady luck was on my side, I could feel it. And if you're not a gambler, then I can't explain it to you. This feeling.

A man approaches us at the bar.

"Gentlemen. Crystallini has invited all V.I.P.'s up to the Floor of Debauchery, where you will be given tokens to use while you wait. Your mistresses may accompany you as far as there, but no further."

"I'm a V.I.P. too," says Valez, showing him the golden card given to us.

I nod my thanks and we follow him to the escalator. A few others shuffle in with us, other players. The elevator grinds as it lifts, and we exit out into a familiar scene of partying, of madness.

There's a man playing a lute up on stage. And I recognize him as the red-haired kid from the bar in Boston.

You remember? When I blasted two of the most powerful men in the city to bits.

We take a seat at a free card table and receive our tokens. I play a few hands, lose some, win some. My luck is only warming up.

"Poker is a man's game," says Valez. I can't tell you how beautiful she looks. If she cut a figure with armoured leather, then a dress of silk only enhanced the raw, rugged attractiveness that radiated from her. "I prefer blackjack. Now there's a game." She cashes out and goes to play at another table.

"You like her, don't you?" Bella says to me.

Gloves watches her go, and he's not the only one, as Valez turns heads. "Why wouldn't he?" says the kid.

"Men," sighs Bella. "Only ever thinking with their cocks."

I laugh and head to the bar to get a refill.

The red-haired lute player is there, and I offer to buy him a drink. He's good after all.

"Thanks," smiles the kid. "Much appreciated."

"What's your name? You play the hell out of that lute."

"Call me Kingkiller."

"Funny name." I clink glasses with him.

"Not as funny as that mask," he smiles.

"A man must keep his secrets," I say.

"Don't I know it."

"You from around here?" He asks me.

"No, you?"

"No. I'm from far, far away." The kid knocks back his drink. "But a man with a lute has the world to explore."

"A man with a mask also."

"Ah, but a man with a mask may find certain doors shut."

288

"Well, that's where I must disagree, as I've never met a door I couldn't pick."

"You a thief?" he asks me.

"As much you are a killer."

"Ah, but I am."

"You are?"

"Yup. A Killer of Kings and Poets."

"Huh?"

"It's my stage name."

"Got a nice ring to it."

"Well, thanks for the drink. Might see you around."

"Yeah."

I head back to the table.

Ten minutes fly by before a man enters the room.

It's Peakers, the silver toothed fucker who took Rayah.

I guess you're probably wondering why I hadn't dropped him to the bottom of the New York Bay. Well, I guess I pitied him. As even looking at him now he looked a shell of a man. Sunken eyes, a limp, combed over hair.

As I said before. I'm not an evil man.

Peakers clears his throat. "Ladies and gentlemen!" The crowd falls silent. "Would all players in the tournament please follow me!"

I lean over and kiss Bella on the cheek.

"Good luck boys," she says to me and the kid.

"Thanks Bel'," says Gloves. I nod to her.

Me, Gloves and Valez join the rest of the players in a large room next door. There's about fifty men and women. Armchairs are arranged in a wide circle, and there's bottles of champagne set on the tables in the centre. Me and the kid pour one each and take a seat. Valez goes to speak to someone she recognizes. I give the kid a cigar and we light up.

It's not two minutes later that Crystallini enters the room. He's flanked by two gangsters on either side of him, all toting dual pistols on their belts.

I can't help but imagine how different things would have been if my shot had been fatal that day. It could've been me standing there. Me ruling this house of paradise. Me worth millions and holding the city in my grip. I had been so close.

Crystallini takes a glass of champagne from one of his goons. "Men, women, thank you for joining me in the first year's celebrations of my victory over the notorious Bronx Bastard."

Oh yeah. That's what the people of Manhattan had dubbed me, well originally it was put out by Crystal and his goons, but the name caught on. But in the other four boroughs I was something of a legend.

To be honest, I kind of liked it.

"Join me in lifting a toast to one year of peace, one year of prosperity."

I don't lift my drink. Neither does the kid. The room drinks the toast.

"Now, please, enjoy each other's company, get to know your opponents, and we shall begin the first round shortly."

Crystallini goes and begins chatting to a man in a fur coat.

"Asshole," whispers Gloves.

I nod and smile.

"Howdy," says a voice. I turn and see the man sitting beside me is staring at me. "That's an interesting mask."

"Is it?" I say.

"Sure. You as ugly as sin under it, or what's your reason for hiding behind a mask of silver?"

"My reasons are my own."

"Jeez, sorry friend, didn't mean to pry." The man offers his free hand, the other is holding a glass of whiskey. He's dressed in a snakeskin suit, with a matching trilby hat. He has a jagged scar running down the side of his face, like he'd been shanked in the past.

"Names Dereck. Dereck McNamara. Friends call me Snakes."

I nod to his sharp suit. "Suits you."

"So, where you guys from? Boston? Detroit?"

291

"From here and there, never one place long."

"Ah, nomads. I can understand that. I'm from California myself. Let me tell you, it cost me a silver shilling getting here."

"Roads aren't safe." I take a drag of my cigar. "Travelled them a few times myself. You run into mutants on your way here?"

"Does a bear shit in the woods?"

"Huh."

"Damn country is crawling with 'em." Dereck takes a sip of his whiskey. "Think the gangs would send out a posse and clear them all off the road, make the transport between cities far more hospitable."

"Gangs only care about lining their pockets." Gloves leans in and joins the conversation. "You want safety, you stay walled up in a city. Everyone knows that. So why risk your life to get here?"

"Why?" Dereck looks around. "'Cos I'm a gambler, friend, plain and simple. Gambling since I was born. I own a small casino in California, but it ain't half as pretty as this joint."

Another man approaches us. He's dressed in a pinstripe suit, a black fedora, and a bad attitude. "That you Snakes? Well fuck me blue, I thought you was dead?"

"Not yet." Snakes smiles and shakes the man's hand. "Gambino, let me introduce you to…"

"Mors," I say, shaking Gambino's hand. "Mors Lament."

Gloves sits forward. "Just call me Gloves."

"You're the kid who won Knuckles?" says Gambino.

"Guilty as charged."

"That was one hell of a fight. I lost two hundred grand." Gambino takes a sip of champagne.

"Well then, I guess you should'a bet one me, huh?" Gloves says.

Gambino nods. "You ever wanna fight full time you gimme a shout. I used to run a fighting club down in Staten Island. I know a few guys who might be interested in you."

Gloves smiles. "That sounds great, but I've got my manager right here with me." Gloves nods to me.

"Is that right? Well, I might just have to kill you to take him. He's got a killer right hook that needs developing."

I look up into Gambino's smile, and it falls.

"I guess we all have a bit of killer in us, hey?" I say. Gambino nods and walks away.

Snakes shakes his head. "You don't like making friends, do you?"

I drink. "I have enough friends, and then some."

"Ah, well, I wouldn't worry about Gambino, his bark is a hell of a lot worse than his bite."

Valez appears.

"Holy hell," says Snakes, "And what might be your name, darlin'?"

Valez ignores him. "You two seem to be enjoying yourselves."

Gloves sits back and takes a long pull of his cigar. "What's not to like?"

"Valez," I say, waving towards Snakes. "Let me introduce you to a gambling man from California."

Snakes had been waving at me, and nodding at me, hinting for an introduction.

Valez looks down at him. "Charmed." She looks away, and I can't help but laugh.

"Valez is as cold as the northern wastelands," I say.

"And as harsh," says Gloves.

"You two can go fuck yourselves." Valez tosses back her drink.

"I always liked a woman who could drink like that," says Snakes.

"I never liked a man who wore a prettier dress than mine." Valez looks down at Snakes, leans over, and rubs his sleeve between two fingers, feeling the fabric. "You compensating for something?"

Snakes blushes. "I… ah. Perry!" Snakes stands up and goes to talk to someone in the crowd.

"You have a way with words," says Gloves.

"Told you my mouth was always getting me into trouble." Valez goes to get a refill. I tap out my cigar as Crystallini is stepping into the centre of the room once more.

"OK, now if you will all follow me upstairs, we can begin our first round of the competition. This round is dice."

Valez stifles a hiss. She hates dice.

We follow him outside, filing into the elevator ten at a time, me, Valez and Gloves force our way into the elevator. It grinds upwards and stops two floors up. We walk through a corridor with four gangsters toting pistols standing guard. We turn left and enter a large richly decorated room. There's a massive chandelier hanging from the ceiling. Ten tables fill the centre of the room. Me, Valez and Gloves take the nearest, as it's facing the entire room.

We sit.

I take off my cloak and hang it on the back of the chair. Underneath I have a sharp black suit, white kerchief, and I tap my fingers on the green felt of the table's surface, eager to begin.

The man from earlier, Dereck, or Snakes, spots us and takes a seat beside Valez, who grimaces as he smiles at her.

Gambino walks by and sees me, and seeing I was rude to him earlier, I think he takes the seat on the far left in spite, as he smiles at me with a half sneer.

The table is full. Gloves is on my left, with Gambino beside him. Valez to my right, with Snakes on her far side. The dealers enter the room, and our man has a pasty smile with a lazy eye. But his hands are sharp as he begins taking the dice from a compartment below the table and moving them around the surface of the table.

"Good evening, ladies and gentlemen," says the dealer. "Today we shall be playing 'Ante Up'. I shall tell you about the rules in a moment, but under Crystallini's directions I am obliged to tell you that anyone caught cheating in these games will be dealt with swiftly and finally. Is this understood?"

I nod, as do the others.

The dealer gives us a golden cup each, and then I check under it. There are five dice.

Ante Up is a game of lying. You shake your cup of dice and slam it down, then check your dice. The first bidder says what he's got, just say one dice has six, then the second bidder must say a higher amount, two threes, or the like. It goes as far as it can, to six, of course, where the man with the highest amount if not challenged wins the stakes. If challenged, the challenger calls him out as a liar, and if he is correct, he gets the stakes. A separate bet can be set up between the challenger and the liar, and the amount of cash that it can go up to has no limit.

In other words, you could lose your fortune from one lie.

It was my kind of game.

"Ladies, gentlemen, please place your bids first, then shake your cups," says the dealer. "Do *not* move your dice once down. Doing so will mean immediate disqualification."

"Five grand," says Gambino, sliding a blue token from his stack.

"Ten," says Gloves, sliding two.

"Fifty," says Snakes, sliding a yellow chip forward.

"One hundred grand," I say, sliding a red chip up.

"Woah," says Valez, "Let's just take it easy now!"

"Any more bids?" asks the dealer.

Gambino stares daggers at me as he slides two red chips forward.

"Two hundred grand."

I slide one and two more forward. "Four hundred."

Gambino nods. No one bets further, but all match the bet. There's two million in the pot.

I shake my cup at the dealer's signal, as do the others, and I slam my dice down. I check under the cup.

I've got two fives. OK. Not bad for the first round. Not great either.

Snakes is the first to bid. "I've got two sixes."

Shit. Out already.

"I've got three threes." Valez stares sideways at Snakes. He stares back just as hard, and I gotta give him credit for holding those sharp blue eyes for more than a second.

"I've got four fives," I say. My heart beats in my chest. I had to say it, or Valez would have taken the pot. If you can't beat the person before you, you lose your bet. You're out.

Gloves looks like he's gonna call bullshit, but God bless the kid, he takes pity on me.

I told you. I'm still warming up.

"I've got five twos."

"Liar!" Gambino calls the kid out.

The kid lifts his cup, and by sure as shit as the devil's balls are black, there are five twos under his cup. The kid bobs his cap to thank Gambino and pulls the winnings to himself.

So, I'm down to four mil' six hundred grand. The kid is the leader, with six million.

The games pass by in a blur. I hold my own, Valez bets small and doesn't raise anyone.

Gambino is the first to go.

"I've got five sixes," I say.

"Bullshit!" Gambino leans forward and lifts my cup. The dealer flips and kicks Gambino out the game, but not before I've taken all his cash, as I wasn't lying.

I've got five beautiful six dotted dice on the green.

Well, fuck you, Gambino.

After that bet I'm back in the lead. I've got nine and a half million under my belt now. The kid's not far behind me, and we don't call out each other, instead we bully Snakes, whose stack of chips is beginning to dwindle.

The man has a sheen of sweat as the kid raises him four hundred grand, a quarter of what Snakes has left. Snakes matches it.

I play the big stack bully and raise Snakes the rest of his holdings, one point two million. Snakes stares into my eyes, trying to read me, trying to figure out what I've got, but I ain't giving nothing away.

A thief never does.

Snakes matches my bet and he's all in.

I lift my cup, I've got four six's, nothing special, but the blood drains from Snakes's face.

"Shit." Snakes lifts his and he's only got three fives.

I reach over and pull in his chips. I've got well over eleven mil' now. Me and the other two play small, biding our time, and soon the other tables are clearing of players.

299

Once the numbers are thinned down to the twenty's Crystallini stands up and claps his hands.

"Congratulations, friends. You're the cream of the crop. You've made it to round two, which won't take place until tomorrow, so please, enjoy yourselves downstairs, and leave your winnings in house if you wish, as they will be guarded safely, you have my word on it!"

I cash mine out. I wasn't leaving nothing to that bastard.

Chapter 21: Poker Face

Exiting the House of Two Faces, three guards were assigned to me to protect the money I had on hand. I was stepping down the sweeping staircase and into the foyer when raised voices caught my attention.

"He'll never get away with this," the man was saying, a lawyer looking man but wearing the red shirt of the Brooklyn mob above his pinstripe slacks. "He went too far. The four bosses are joining together. He's finished."

One of the gangsters in the foyer began to push the man backwards, to the doors. "OK, that's enough. You've said your piece, and Crystallini has already put word on the street that it wasn't him and there's a million dollars on the head of the people who done it. OK?"

"Lies!" shouted the man. People were stopping in the foyer and staring. "Crysatllini's finished. He can't stand against the four boroughs alone! He will fall, just like his brother!"

The gangster had had enough. He grabbed the man by the scruff of the neck and hauled him outside, throwing him onto the ground.

I stepped around the gangster as he made his way back in and approached the man as he stood back up.

"Hello, friend," I say. "I overheard you saying that the four boroughs are going to war with Crystallini?"

"Indeed. The fool tried to con the other crime lords, but he went too far. If you want my advice, sell all your chips now and get the hell outta the city. Things are going to get bloody."

I watched him go.

"It looks like are heist is having unforeseen circumstances," says Gloves, lighting up a cigarette.

I nod. "We might just be able to work this situation to our favour."

*

I get Chameleon on the job to sort out my disguise.

Who am I dressing up as? Why my dear old twin brother. I might have the scars on my face, but no one will be any the wiser that it's not Crystallini.

I get Valez to put out word, a meet with the four crime lords at a location of our choosing. A meet up to work out the mess we put him in. But that was the last thing on my mind.

Chameleon spends the day hunting down the outfit and once I put it on, I look the part. My eyes aren't as cold as his, but still the same pale blue, and I look the image of him.

Valez puts make-up on me to try to hide the scars, and it does an OK job.

We enter the carriage and head to the edge of Brooklyn, where we've set the meet up location.

We arrive before the others, but each crime lord has sent guards to inspect the location. They aren't very trusting, and I wouldn't blame them.

After ten minutes the first crime lord arrives. Valez is back at the safe house in the Bronx, as I knew the crime lord of Brooklyn would have recognized her and might have put two and two together, so it was just Chameleon and Gloves there with me.

The crime lord from Brooklyn enters, a small man with thick glasses, he is a far-cry from the tough and rough Valez that used to rule the borough. But times change. The man nodded his greetings and sat down opposite me. Gloves went and fetched whiskey, pouring myself and the other boss a measure.

"I guess we shouldn't discuss anything before the others get here?" I ask.

The man nods. "It would be unwise."

Minutes pass and another knock sounds on the door.

Two crime lords enter this time, the one from the Bronx is a tall, slender man with a sharp suit and eye. The crime lord from Queens is

303

fat and round, his red cheeks puffing heavily from the climb up the stairs. They sit and Gloves pours them a drink. The last man arrives two minutes later.

The Staten Island cartel boss is a thick muscled man with a ponytail. He sits down in the last chair and takes the offered drink.

"Gentlemen," I say, leaning forward. "I'm glad you have all accepted my invite to discuss recent events."

The Staten Island boss sits forward and points a finger at me. "You fucked us all, Crystallini. You went too far."

The fat man nods. "You'd told me you were hoping to renew bonds with the other boroughs. It was all just a ploy to get us relaxed so you could rip us off."

"And it worked, didn't it?" I say.

The four men blanch.

"I have now the money and the diamonds. I control most the wealth in the city, and if I wanted to, I could hire muscle from Boston and Detroit to set a war on you. We're already matched in power, so if I wanted, I could wipe you all out one at a time."

"You want a war?" says the Bronx crime lord in the sharp suit. "We'll go to war, no matter the odds. We're not the weak borough we were when your brother took over. You'll have a hard time fighting through the streets, ambushes on every corner."

"Not to mention we have you surrounded on three sides. Your only escape will be to turn tail and flee to Detroit, but we'll hunt you down." The small man had a hunger in his eyes, almost steaming up his thick glasses with the anger seething below his tone.

I stood up and walked to the window, intentionally turning my back on them. "That's *if* you win. You do remember how my brother ended up after turning against me?"

The Staten Island crime lord stood up, smashed his glass against the ground. "I knew this would be a waste of time." He stormed from the room.

The Queens boss stands up, his jowls shuddering with anger. "And here I thought you a man of business, Crystallini. You leave me no option but to side with the others. Queens will go to war, have no doubt." The fat man turned and fled from the room.

There were two left. The sharp-eyed man looked at the small man with glasses. "I guess we could turn heel, change sides, crush them and split their territories three ways."

The small man nodded. "My thoughts exactly."

I clap my hands. "Refill our glasses, I think a deal is underway."

The small man frowns. "But we'll want our diamonds, and the cash back as a gesture of good will."

I nod. "Of course."

The sharp suited man smiles, lifts his glass. "To expanding horizons."

We clink glasses.

"So how do we do it?"

I steeple my fingers. "Here's how it will happen…"

*

The next day, once more inside the House of Two Faces. We are up in the Floor of Debauchery, and after Peakers calls us into the room with the armchairs, Crystallini appears, looking a bit worked up, but he tries to smile and show a straight face.

"Ladies, gentlemen, I hope you'll forgive me for being so late this evening, but unforeseen events have called me away."

One of the men across from me laughs. "You call the city tearing itself apart an unforeseen event?"

Crytallini frowns, then looks to one of his men and nods.

Three men approach the speaker and grab him, much to his protests, which earn him a fist to the stomach for his trouble.

"Now, if there will be no more interruptions, we can head upstairs where the next round of the tournament can commence. Please, follow me."

We head to the elevator, we enter first, grind up a few floors and exit into the corridor. We enter the room and take seats. This time Gloves and Valez sit at different seat as earlier organized.

The dealers enter. The cards are dealt and it's Poker.

I'm two cards off a flush of hearts, and I match the opening bet of one hundred grand, then raise another two hundred. The others call. The next card is a heart, so I bet five hundred grand. The others call, the man with the fur coat raises me one million. I call.

The next card is a four of diamonds. Shit.

I bet large, five million, and no one calls, folding like a house of cards. I pull in the chips.

I'm the big stack bully at the table after another three hands. I'm pissing off the man with the silver spectacles, and his face is as flushed as a whore with thrush. I've three aces and bet five million. The silver spectacled man has had enough and calls.

I get a second ten on the river, a full house, aces and tens. We flip and the silver spectacled man has only three tens.

"Fuck it," he curses, as I pull in my chips once again. My luck is in today.

I bet small over the next three hands as the silver spectacled man bets big, trying to regain his chips which are fast depleting. The man in

307

the fur coat calls, and cleans out the silver spectacled man, who stands up and hits the table with the side of his fist.

"Devil's balls," he says. "This game is fixed!"

A guard appears and escorts the loser out, with protest I might add, and the people left share a smile as his shouts fade down the corridor.

"I guess some people can't take the heat," says the woman with the bright green eyes and mole on her cheek.

"Well, they shouldn't poke the fire then," says the man in the fur coat.

"Guess some people just ain't lucky," I say.

I look across at the table where Crystallini is sat. He, like me, seems to be the big stack bully on his table. His chips are stacked high.

There's a few more upsets as the stakes are raised, and I've counted five people that were cleaned out.

I call the waiter for a refill and light a cigar.

I get a good hand, a king and ace of clubs. There're two other clubs on the table. I bet high and annoy the fur coat man, who calls, looking down at his cards once more.

It's his tell.

I raise his bet, five million on his three, and he calls, his face blushing, he only has six million left or thereabouts. I get another sign my luck is in, a ten of clubs, and now I have an ace high flush.

I bet three mil', and the man checks his cards once more, then calls.

The river is a queen of diamonds, but that's OK, I've got the best hand on the table.

I bet three million, and the man calls. We show our cards.

The man has got a queen high straight. I show my cards.

"You fucking kidding me?" he shouts, standing up. "This son of a bitch is cheating."

I lift my wrist and pull up my sleeves, showing them empty. "Guess I'm just lucky."

"I'm not finished with you," says the man, as he is escorted out of the room.

I pull in his chips. The remaining two people have a few million each.

I bet large, making them fold.

The big blinds are raised to one million. They fold.

They're down to two million.

The woman goes all-in. I call. I've got three pair, but I think she's bluffing.

We flip them, and she's got a full house. Shit.

I clench my fist under the table as she takes my chips. She'll regret that.

The man bets all-in in the next hand, and I've got two kings. I call.

I get a ten on the flop. Ace on the turn, and then a king on the river. The man's face drops. He's only got two pair. I take his chips and he sighs as he's escorted out.

There's only me and the woman. She folds her hand on the next deal.

I get an ace and king of diamonds. I bet six million, and she goes all-in.

It's down to this now.

I have a pair of aces, then I get a king on the flop. Two pair. She's got three. Shit.

The turn is no good, and my hands begin to shake.

The dealer flips the last card.

It's an ace.

A full house.

The woman smiles and offers me her hand. "I never stood a chance. Good luck in the tournament." She gets her coat and leaves.

I'm the winner of my table. I've got… over forty million.

Valez has struck out, she's out of the tournament.

"I wish it had been Blackjack," she says with a smile.

Gloves was the winner of his table. The kid is lucky, I'll give him that, and he's got over thirty-five million.

I count ten of us left.

Someone approaches me from behind. "It seems you've the largest pot in the room," says a familiar voice.

I turn to find Crystallini standing there.

I roughen my voice. "Thanks."

Crystallini nods. "Care for a drink. I find your mask very interesting. What exactly are you hiding under there."

I smile. "A scarred past."

"Ah, don't we all have one of those."

We go to the bar, the four of us, the kid, Valez, Crystal and me.

I refill my drink.

"I hear there's trouble brewing in the other boroughs," says the kid.

Crystal narrows his eyes, "Is that right? And just who did you hear this from?"

Gloves shrugs. "It's common knowledge. It's all over the street."

"Yes, it seems someone is getting too big for their own good. I've had some trouble with the local crime lords, but it's nothing to worry yourselves over."

"So, I'm safe leaving my winnings in house?" says the kid.

"Of course. No safer place in all of New York."

"You'll forgive me if I don't share the same sentiments," I say. "It's just that I don't trust anyone."

Crysatllini nods. "Neither do I."

I can't help myself. "This tournament, it symbolizes the victory over your brother?"

"Yes, the Bronx Bastard, biggest thief in all five boroughs."

"Sound's interesting," says Valez. "A man like that, you don't get many of them."

"No," Crystal smiles. "I quite miss hearing of his escapades. But times change. New York is changing. In five years' time it won't be the crime den it is now."

"It'll never change," says Gloves. "The city is ruled by crime, has been for over a thousand years."

Crystallini takes a drink. "But nothing lasts forever. We must change with the times or be left behind."

Valez lifts her drink. "To changing times."

Gloves lifts his. "To luck and fortune."

Crystallini lifts his. "To victory over our enemies."

I think for a second, then lift my drink and we clink glasses. "To old habits dying hard."

Chapter 22: The Last Game

"Word on the street is the Bronx and Brooklyn have gone to war with Queens and Staten Island," says Valez.

We're sat in the courtyard of the safehouse. I have my winnings on the table. It's the first time any of us have seen so much money. The kid, for some reason or other, decided to leave his winnings in the House of Two Faces.

"Bet that'll confuse the shit out of Crystallini," says the kid. "He won't know why the two boroughs have sided alongside him."

"That's just what we want," I say. "Keep him disorganized."

"So, what's the plan for after you win this tournament?" asks Chameleon. "*If* you win. You do know he'll still control Manhattan even if you clean him out?"

"But that's just my plan exactly. Once Crystallini doesn't play ball with the Bronx or Brooklyn, they'll turn on him once again. We've created confusion among the crime-lords, and the first rule of a con is..."

Gloves smiles. "Distraction."

"You have a con in mind?" asks Valez.

"Not a con, no. I want him to be thinking of something else when I spring my trap on him."

"And that is?" says the kid.

"A game of chance..."

*

The final day of the tournament. We enter the House of Two Faces.

It's Blackjack. I best say one thing, it's not the Blackjack that you know. These days the players bet against each other, bidding each other to up the ante, and the player with the higher hand takes the loot. They still play the usual Blackjack downstairs, where it's you against the house, but this wasn't like that.

I bet low and bide my time. I want to narrow down the playing field before I swoop in for the kill.

The tables clear of players one at a time, and an hour into the game we change tables, as we all fit onto one. There' me, the kid, Crystallini and two others.

Crystallini has the biggest stack after mine. He bets big and is lucky, I guess luck must run in the family.

I get twenty-one on the deal and bet big. Ten million, and everyone except Crystal bows out. The fucker matches my bet.

He only has nineteen. He hits and gets a seven, bust.

Crystal smiles. "I guess you won that one."

315

"I guess so."

The kid wins the next hand and clears out one of the other men. There's only four of us left now, and me and the kid must play against one another. We knew it was coming, and I wasn't going to play nice. The kid had the second biggest stack after me, and we bet against each other.

He bets twenty million. I match, I have eighteen.

The kid has nineteen, so I hit. I get a two.

Blackjack, baby.

The kid sighs as he watches me pull in his chips. He's down to twenty mil' now. But we agreed earlier that I'd cut him in and split the pot four ways, between me and the gang, as would Gloves should he win. So, it doesn't really matter which of us wins.

I don't want to take the kids money, but we must make it look real in front of Crystallini.

Crystallini raises the stakes and bets thirty million. I bow out, and the kid matches him.

I watch as the kid flips his cards. He's got twenty.

Crystallini sighs, then smiles, and he flips his cards to reveal blackjack. The kid is out.

Gloves shakes Crystal's hand and gives me a nod as he is escorted from the table.

Crystal is the big stack bully now. There is me, him and one other left.

I clear out the man with the fake eye on the third hand with a nineteen to his seventeen which he busts.

It's just me and Crystallini, the way I knew it would always be.

"Then there were two," he says.

I've got over fifty million in my pot. He's got over sixty in his. The dealer's finish counting out the amounts.

We bet, I bet twenty million, Crystal bets thirty on mine, and I go all-in.

Crystallini matches it.

I flip mine. I've got twenty.

Crystal flips his. He's got eighteen. He hits. Gets a two. He holds at twenty. I can either stand and we go again, or I can hit. I've got a one in fourteen chance.

I hit.

The dealer takes the card and places it down. It's an ace…

Crystallini's face drains of colour. He's just lost fifty million.

I sit back and take a drink of whiskey.

"Congratulations, friend. It seems the better man won." Crystal offers me his hand. I have no intent on shaking it.

317

Instead, I say, "You want to play one more game? My winnings against something of yours that I want."

Crystallini shakes his head. "I'm afraid you've cleared me out of cash. What could I possibly have that you could want?"

I sit forward. "Everything."

"Excuse me?"

"You heard me. My hundred and ten million, against your empire."

Crystallini stares at me with wide eyes. "Tell me why I shouldn't just have you dragged upstairs and beaten, then take all your earnings?"

I spread my hands. "Because your good word relies upon my safety. Where would you be if the winner of your tournament was robbed of his winnings? No one would bother coming here, if they couldn't trust you to deal out the goods when the time called."

Crystal grits his teeth. "Very well. You have my interest. What game did you have in mind?"

I point my hand to my head and pretend I'm pulling a trigger. "My old favourite. Blind Man's Bluff."

*

Crystallini makes a mistake then, one I had hoped that he would, as his vanity wouldn't allow him to pass up such an opportunity of making his name known even more.

318

He spreads the word that he shall accept my challenge. His Empire of Sin against my fortune.

I'm given a suite in one of the upper floors and the gang join me there.

Gloves is ecstatic. "You done it! You bloody well done it!"

I nod. "There's just one more final leg and then I take back what should be mine."

Valez cracks open a bottle of champagne. "Well, here's to the richest dead man I've ever known."

I smile. "You never know, luck has been on my side so far."

"But why would you challenge him to a game like that?" Valez doesn't look happy. "You got away with it once, but that was only because Chameleon was disguised as the referee and had both pistols unloaded."

Chameleon frowns. "She has a point. It's a fifty-fifty toss up."

I know this. "I have nothing to lose. And everything to gain."

*

This is what it comes down to. One final game of chance, and with it I might exact my revenge, take back what was mine. Get back my Rayah, once and for all.

It was a familiar scene as I entered the room. A table stood in the centre, on it ten pistols. Five to each side. One was loaded. A referee

319

had been hired from out of the city, and it had taken two days for him to get here, but it was only fair as we didn't want anyone from within the city, who would be biased to either give Crystallini the edge, loading one of my pistols, or intently loading one of his.

We sat down at the table and themen and women of Manhattan, the creme of the crop, who were paying to watch the game, entered and took their seats around the room.

The four crime lords from the other boroughs were there. A ceasefire had been called until the winner of the game was announced, for after all, if Crystallini lost, which the other crime lords were hoping for, there would be a new leader of Manhattan, and new talks could begin.

The referee came in and shuffled the guns once more, then placed ten of them in a line. We had been given a choice of five or ten pistols, and both of us had decided on the latter. Crystal being the one challenged chose his pistol first, then I chose one, and we went on until all ten pistols were assigned to one side of the table or the other.

The referee cleared his throat.

"Ladies and gentlemen, quiet please! I will read you the rules…"

The ref' told us the rules, but you remember it from last time, right? When I played against Sykes. There would be a coin flip, then the winner got to choose who went first. The player would then shoot

320

themselves, and if the pistol should prove loaded, then the other man would be the winner. If not, then the other man would take the shot, and it would continue until one man either submitted defeat or blew their brains out.

I was hoping for the latter.

"Being as Crystallini was the man challenged, he shall decide which side of the coin to pick."

"Heads."

The coin was flipped.

Tails.

"I'll go first," I say. My hand glides over the pistols. I pick the third one. I place it against the side of my head. "Here goes nothing."

I pull the trigger. It clicks. I replace the pistol.

"So tell me, Mors. It is Mors, yes?"

I nod. "That is one of my names. Yes, Mors Lament."

"An odd name. So, tell me, to come to New York and challenge one of the most notorious gangsters in the city takes balls. How come I never heard of you before now?"

I shrug. "I guess I've just been a… ghost of sorts."

"I can relate. I myself used to prefer being hidden in the shadows." Crystallini picks up the fourth pistol and places it against his head. "But the world changes, and we must change with it." He pulls the trigger, it clicks.

He replaces the pistol onto the table.

"A drink?" I say. Crystal nods and a waiter comes and serves us two drinks.

"It's funny now that I think about it. Isn't Mors Latin?"

I nod. "It is."

"Huh."

I pick up the second pistol, place it against my head, close my eyes. The pistol clicks. I replace it.

I take a drink.

"It's not often you meet someone which such a name. My own alias, Crystallini, you may have heard, is Latin."

"I have heard." I knock back my drink. "Since I gave you it."

"What?"

I reach up as he picks up a pistol.

"I said, I gave you that name." I take off my mask and place it onto the table.

Crystallini's face drains of colour. There are whispers and mutterings around the room, even a gasp.

"It can't be... I saw you die!"

"You only saw what you wanted to see."

Crystal pulls on his trigger, without meaning to, and it clicks making him jump.

"Jackson...?"

"The very same."

"You never knew when to stay dead, did you?" he sneers. "Even as kids you would always best me, going against my wishes." Crystal replaces the pistol. His hand is shaking.

I pick up a pistol, lucky number three. I point it against my head. "I only ever tried to be a good brother to you, Dayton. I loved you, but you betrayed me, on every chance you got." I pull the trigger. It clicks.

I replace it.

Crystallini licks his lips as he looks over the remaining three pistols. His hand passes from one to the other, unsure of himself. He drops his hand.

"I don't want this, Jackson. I didn't want to kill you, you backed me into a corner!"

"You backed yourself into a corner with your greed!" I snarl.

"I only ever wanted to see you happy, but you didn't know when to stop, same as when we were kids, you never knew when a con was too big!"

"Too big? You always were one to look at the half glass empty. You hold everything, control everything, and leave me the pickings to lick off your boots and expect me to thank you for it?"

"I would have shared my empire with you. I would have given you anything you wanted."

"Then why take my Rayah?"

"Your Rayah? Have you no idea what it was like? Watching you raise her? She could be my daughter, have you ever considered that? And you had all the best of it, watching her grow, while I had to stay to the shadows, protecting you both from afar."

"You took everything from me, brother. And now it's my turn to take everything from you. All you have to do is give up, leave New York. I won't hunt you down. I'll spare you your life, as it would be a harder punishment watching you shrivel into nothing, being a nobody in the world, a fate I know you've feared to happen your entire life. You care more about your own reputation than the life of your niece."

Alyssa appeared in the crowd then and approached the table.

"You are both brothers!" she hissed. "Can one of you please see sense? Put down your weapons and stand together." She placed one hand on Crystal's shoulder, one on mine. "I love you both. Can you both just do this for me? If you both love me?"

Crystallini picks up the pistol and sticks it against his head. "My brother died that day on the Hudson." He pulled the trigger, but it clicked harmlessly. Crystal inhales deeply as he puts the pistol back. "It's your turn now, *brother*."

We've two pistols left each. There was a twenty-five percent chance that I was about to blow my brains out.

I pick up the pistol and place it against my head. "I'm going to wait for you, Dayton. In this life or the next, I will find you, and I will make you pay..."

I take in a deep breath and shut my eyes. My heart is beating wildly.

The pistol clicks.

My hand shakes as I replace it.

I cannot deny that I am tired. I am tired of this game I play. Of staring death in the face.

I just want things to return to the way they were. I just want to be that old Jackson who was content to con a life for himself. But I would gladly have walked away if only I could've had my Rayah back. I knew Crystallini would never have given in though. He was my brother, and as stubborn as myself.

"That day on the Hudson," I say. "I wish you really had gone under with those diamonds. My life would have been so much simpler."

Crystal sneers. "And I wish I hadn't watched your back for all those years. You would have been dead only for me a long time ago."

"I never asked for your help. I only ever wanted your presence. But you betrayed the only blood you had left. And for that there can be no excuses."

Crystallini picks up the pistol. It's only one of two he has left. A thirty-three percent chance of death.

"Excuses? I won't lie then. I envied you. I envied the life you had, Jackson. I envied the love you shared between yourself and Alyssa, so yes, I took her. And I might just be Rayah's father. So if this bullet takes my life… Just know that there's as much of me in her as there is you…"

Crystallini inhales deeply. "Fuck it!" He pulls on the trigger. It clicks. He slams the pistol down on the table.

The referee stands forward. "Sudden death, gentlemen. Each man shall take their pistol," he said, loading the empty pistol which had been on Crystal's side. He had come *so* close to losing. "Take twenty paces from the table and wait for me to say turn. If you shall turn before my say-so, you shall be hung for a coward. Is that understood?"

326

I nod, as does Crystal. He is sweating now.

I stand and take my pistol, then turn and take twenty paces. The room is silent. My mind flashes back to the last duel we had, but I had been practicing the past year for this very moment.

"One!" shouts the referee. "Two!"

There are shouts then, and I glance back to see Crystallini turning, bringing his weapon up to bear. I feel my world spin around me... I see my life flash before my eyes, and I can only think of one word.

Rayah...

Something *thuds* into me then. And I'm pushed out of the way as the pistol flashes, the ground comes up to meet me.

I look up to see men rushing towards Crystallini, grabbing him, and punching him. I look down and my heart falls.

"Kid..."

Gloves is lying on the ground clutching his chest, eyes wide.

I crouch over him. "No... Just hold on!"

Gloves shakes his head. "Was just doing my job, boss."

"Don't... You bloody fool, Gloves. Why'd you go and do that?"

Gloves smiles, and there's blood on his teeth. Blood pooling on the floor around us.

"I guess I'm just lucky like that. Not every day you get to save your hero."

Tears fall down my cheeks. There's blood pooling around my knees, but I don't care as I hold him tight.

"Kid... Hold on, I'm going to get you the best doctor in the city. He'll fix you up."

Gloves shakes his head. "Just... Just do me a favour?"

I nod. "Of course, kid. Anything. You just name it."

"Get out of this life. Get your daughter, and just get out." He smiles and then coughs, and blood drips down his chin.

"I will kid. You just watch if I don't."

Gloves nods, smiles, and his eyes glaze over, and he's gone...

Chapter 23: Goodbye New York

We're stood on top of the House of Two Faces. Crystallini is standing along the edge of the building, a rope tied around his neck.

I could have chosen to have him tortured. But I'd had enough bloodshed for one day. The kid's blood was still on my clothes.

"Any last words?" I say.

"I just want you to do me one favour?" says Crystallini.

I nod. "What is it?"

He smiles. "Be a better man than we were, Jackson. Raise Rayah up right. Get her an education, and take her far away from this shithole that we grew up in."

I nod. "Anything else?"

"Yeah. I guess I'm sorry. For everything I put you through. I really do love you, Jackson. I just hope you can find it in yourself to forgive me for everything I've put you through. I only ever wanted the best for us. Only wanted us to have the life that was never given to us." Crystallini. My brother, smiles at me. And I can't deny that my eyes don't water.

I step up closer. "For what it's worth..." I place my hands on his shoulders. "I don't forgive you. Burn in hell, Crystallini."

I push him off the side of the building, and he falls. I stick my

head out and watch, as his neck breaks and he swings from the House

of Two Faces, the home of his undoing.

I have done what I set out to do. I have taken my brother's Empire

of Sin.

*

I walk in and Rayah is sitting on the bed, reading.

"What do you want now, Dayton?" Rayah says. Then she looks

up, and her eyes fill with loathing first, followed by doubt, followed by

confusion.

"Hello, chicken," I say.

"Daddy?" she says.

"Yes, it's me."

"How? I thought…"

Her eyes fill with tears then. She jumps off the bed and rushes

over to me, wraps me in a big hug. I hug her back. It's been a year

since I last held her. And it seems a lifetime since I've last said, "I love

you, chicken."

She leans back and looks me up and down. She can't believe her

eyes, it seems. "I-I love you too." She clings back onto me, and I let her

squeeze the breath from me. "Never leave me again, Daddy."

I kiss the top of her head. "Never."

330

Footsteps then. I turn and see Gamma running into the room. She

runs up to me and stops two paces away. Her eyes are wide.

"Can it really..." She lifts her hand to her mouth. "No, Jackson?"

"Hello, Gamma. It's been a long time."

Gamma wraps her arms around me, and I cling onto Rayah in one

arm, Gamma in the other.

"How?" says Gamma.

"It's a long story."

"Jackson, you better fill me in right this minute!" Gamma laughs.

There are tears in her eyes also.

I fill them both in how Chameleon had brought me back to life.

How I had journeyed to California and worked up enough money to

come back and make a difference. How I had learned about the

tournament and saw an opportunity to get my foot in the door.

"And you didn't think to tell me?" says Gamma.

"I couldn't chance it, Gamma. If Crystallini got wind that I was

back, he would have shut up the House of Two Faces and turned it back

into a fortress."

Gamma nodded. "I understand. I just wish I'd have known. I

guess a part of me had seen something in Mors's eyes. Some form or

recognition."

"What's the plan now?" says Gamma.

"Yeah, Daddy, what's the plan? Are we going to California," Rayah says excitedly. I smile.

"Anything you want, chicken. Daddy just has one more thing to do here and then we'll leave."

"Jackson, no." Gamma seems to read my mind.

"I must. If the crime lords follow us, they won't leave us alone until we're bones for the mutants to pick their teeth with."

"What? What is it?" says Rayah, looking from me to Gamma.

I crouch down and put my hands on Rayah's shoulders. "Daddy just has to take care of some business, and then we'll leave New York, forever."

Rayah bites her lip, but nods. "OK, Daddy."

"OK, chicken. I love you."

"I love you too."

*

Here I was, back in a familiar situation, the four boroughs all there for the taking. All ready to pounce on me if I showed one ounce of weakness.

I called a meeting between myself and the four crime bosses, held a truce so none of them felt threatened. The five of us were sat in an abandoned warehouse on the edge of Manhattan, sipping on whiskey.

"We don't want a war," the boss of Brooklyn says.

"We only ever wanted peace with Crystallini," says the boss of Queens.

"Peace," I nod. "I can't leave this city to run itself. I need you all to swear loyalty to me and promise to kick up ten points a year of your total income."

The Staten Island boss blanched. "This is ludicrous! I thought you were a reasonable man?"

"Reasonable, yes." I drink the last drop of my whiskey. "Foolish, no. If I leave you all to run your own territories, you'll be ganging up on me within the month."

The Bronx gang leader smiles. "Perhaps sooner."

I look him in the eye. "Care to fill me in?"

The Brooklyn mobster sits forward. "You're not as powerful as you once were. If the four boroughs joined forces together, we would crush you."

Comments pass back and forth between us, promising retribution if their demands weren't met, that I was to give away half my territory to be split up by each borough.

I nodded. "So be it. If it means peace among us."

We all shake hands.

They file outside to leave, and that's when the shots ring out.

My gunmen line up the street outside, standing along the pavement, and I watch from the window as they lace bullets into the four crime lords.

Blood pools on the ground, the Brooklyn boss is crawling away. Valez steps up and finishes him.

A truce is meaningless to a criminal.

The word of a thief means nothing.

*

The next few weeks are filled with gang wars, and one by one each borough lays down arms and submits defeat. I hold New York in my hands once again, and I can't deny that the power doesn't feel... good.

I have a path that leads in two directions. One leads away from this life of ours, away from the crime and the killings, away from New York.

The other leads through the fog, to a destination I never wanted, but now I come to hold it in my possession, I find myself asking, why should I let it go?

Isn't this what I wanted? Rayah safe, and no one having the means to harm her. As long as I was at the top of the pyramid, nobody could touch her.

But then what type of life would she lead, cooped away on Manhattan, always shadowed by gangsters, always sleeping with the weight of the past hanging over her head?

No, I decided, I would not place that burden upon her. Everything I have done it was for Rayah, and now that my task was at an end, I found myself warming to the idea of new lands, new beginnings.

I told Valez my wishes, that I wanted her to rule New York in my stead.

She blushed.

"You're sure?"

I nodded. "Of course. I only wanted to make peace in the five boroughs, to have no one hunting me down after I leave."

Rayah was there with us. She barely left my side since we'd been reunited. "Going where, Daddy?"

I sat down beside her. Put my arm around her. "Anywhere you wanna go, chicken."

*

I was a man of considerable fortune. I had over one hundred million dollars. I hired the best team of engineers I could find, even shipped a few up from Boston. They spent two weeks building one of those old air balloons, zeppelins they used to be called, and spent the time with Valez strengthening our grip on the city.

335

We bought two ships and supplied them with cannons, left in the bay off the east coast of Manhattan, a dismal reminder to all the gangs that should they try to rise against Valez when I was gone, she would have the means and the manpower to lay waste to any who stood in her way.

Belladonna, myself, Rayah and Gamma readied ourselves for the trip east. We hired a man who would fly the zeppelin, and once it was built, he practiced moving up off the ground, flying over the city.

Rayah was ecstatic watching from the roof of the House of Two Faces. The zeppelin lifted up, up and away, floating over the cityscape, and my heart and hopes rose with it.

That night we had a going away party. Me, Rayah, Gamma, Valez and Belladonna sat at the table on the top floor of the Empire State Building. The feast was set out before us. What were we having? You name it, we had it. Rayah had a big smile spread across her face.

"I'll miss you, boss," Valez was saying to me.

"I'll miss you too, Valez. But I know you'll do a good job of running this city."

"Not as good as you. Why do you want to leave now you have it all in your hand?"

"It's not what's best for Rayah."

Valez looks across the table at my daughter. Rayah is listening to a story Gamma is telling.

"She's a good kid."

"She is."

"And you're a good father."

I lift a brow. "You think?"

"I know it."

"Thanks, Valez. Who knew that day in Brooklyn when we were trying to murder each other that we'd end up friends."

"Is that all we are, honey?"

I put my hand on hers. "Always more… Hey, if you ever get sick of this cold city, you come and pay us a visit?"

Valez shrugs. "New York is my city. I will die here."

"Well, the offer stands."

Valez looks away from the window, the skyscrapers are faintly red, crimson coloured from the dipping sun partly visible beyond them, and it seems even the sun is escaping this cold and hard city. She looks at me. "Maybe, one day, maybe."

*

That night me, Gamma and Valez make love.

It's sweet, blissful oblivion.

It is our goodbye.

337

*

It is time to leave New York.

I find Rayah on the roof, standing on the edge of the building, staring down at the empty streets far below.

"Chicken?" I say. "What are you doing?"

Rayah looks back at me. Tears in her eyes. In her hands she's holding Edgar. "I don't want him to be locked away no more, Daddy."

I stand beside her and put my hand on her shoulder. "You sure?"

She nods, her face a picture of innocence and wisdom, all rolled up into one heart-breaking scene.

"Then let him fly."

Rayah tosses the raven, Edgar, out into the air, and it takes him a beat to catch the rhythm, but he flaps his wings and threads air, and soon rises.

Rises.

We watch him fly up, up, and away, leaving the shell that was his prison far behind.

Chapter 24:May Thieves Rein

How does a man walk out on everything he knows? One step at a time.

With the blue-sky hovering over us, and the zeppelin anchored nearby, we climbed the steps onto the platform, and I kissed Valez goodbye. The rough and rugged woman was a farce, as she had tears in her eyes as I backed away.

"You were the best bitch a woman could ever want," she smiles. She reaches into her pocket and takes out a coin. "Something to remember me by, until we meet again."

I smile back. "How could I ever forget you?"

"Memories fade, Jackson. Love dies, but hope… hope never dies. So, let's just hold onto hope, huh?"

"That sounds just about right, sweetheart."

Gamma steps up. She kisses Valez on the cheek and bids her goodbye, then climbs the rope-ladder up into the zeppelin. I notice the tears in her eyes.

Belladonna is already on board and waves at us from the window. Alyssa too, she has joined our posse, much to my disapproval, but Rayah needs her mother.

Rayah steps up. "I'll miss you."

Valez leans down and kisses Rayah on the forehead. "I got you something." She reaches into her pocket and takes out a chain, with a silver pendant of a raven. "Your daddy told me you let Edger free. Is that right?"

Rayah nods.

"Well, let me tell you that it takes a strong woman to recognize the true value of freedom. So, you wear this with pride, Rayah, and don't you ever let anyone tell you you're a woman in a man's world. You understand me?"

Rayah smiles. "I think so."

Valez pinches her cheek. "That's my girl."

We both climb the rope-ladder and shut the door behind us.

I stare out the window as the ground tilts and pulls away, and we wave as the figures below us shrink to nothing but smudges.

Rayah looks up into the clouds and her face is brighter than the sun. Brighter than sunshine glimpsed through prison bars. "This is just like the book."

"I know, chicken."

"Daddy?"

"Yeah, chicken?"

"I love you."

"I love you too, chicken."

*

The journey west was a far-cry from the shit-show me and Chameleon, who had decided to stay in New York, I forgot to mention, faced over a year ago.

There was me, Gamma, Rayah, Alyssa, Belladonna, two engineers, the pilot of the zeppelin, and three muscle who would stay on until we arrived in California.

We passed by beautiful scenes, ridgelines covered with pine, lone creeks, where no man stirred, shadowed gorges unexplored that could eat up a man's imagination. On the second day we passed over a valley where a gang of mutants chased us, much to Rayah's wonder.

The zeppelin made good time and within the week we were entering Californian territory.

We travelled toward the west coast and headed north, where the walled remnant of L.A. was, where I had spent most the previous year in hiding with Belladonna.

As the city came slowly closer, I couldn't help but think back on that day I first arrived here over a year ago. How different the world had seemed then. How against the odds my chances of survival were, never mind getting Rayah back.

But I had beaten the odds.

I had infiltrated my brother's House of Two Faces. I had taken

him down, from the inside out, had faced him, eye-to-eye, man-to-man.

It had taken a hard man to push my brother over the edge of that

building, a hard man that I hoped I would be able to bury in the past, a

man that I hoped would slowly erode over the years, a thawing heart

previously frozen from those northerly winters, and the man who stared

back at me in the mirror might one day reflect the person who was

trapped inside.

We touched down and the streets were filled with children, all

amazed at this flying contraption. The gang made our way to

Belladonna's residence, a high-walled and guarded manor, three stories

high, with a pool overlooking the distant hills.

We sat in the courtyard, just like old times, huh? Myself, Gamma,

Belladonna, and Rayah.

Belladonna cracked open a vintage bottle of whiskey she'd been

holding out on me. I supplied the cigars.

"Can I have one, Daddy?" asked Rayah.

"Come back to me in another ten years, chicken."

I lit up. Sipped my drink. It might've been the best thing I'd ever

tasted, senses enhanced by the Californian sunshine, or perhaps the

quality company, or perhaps just the simple sensation of what a man's

soul truly desires.

342

Freedom.

"To the old gang," said Belladonna, lifting her glass. "To No-Name, and Gloves."

Gamma lifted her drink. "To the new gang. And our little protege, who we will have all the boys fanning over her within the month," Gamma winked at Rayah and made her giggle.

I lifted my drink. "To the old ways. To days spent conning a living, living a con. To working the system, and always betting the long odds."

"May thieves rein," said Rayah.

We all laughed.

I nodded. "And may thieves rein."

I knocked back my drink.

What does a man say when faced with death? The burden can only be shared so far, and that extends to keeping death company.

But this time, this time it was, truly, different.

For it wasn't the life of a man simply grieved.

It wasn't the path we all must walk, bound together toward our final destination.

This time, it felt like the simple turning of a page, the ending of a chapter, and the beginning of a new story.

I had played my game, and won.

I had fought my battle, and paid my dues, and earned my scars.

I had saved my girl.

And the world could crumble down around us, for all I cared.

Once my Rayah was safe, beneath the arms of her father, who would

hold its weight, no matter the cost.

I would not falter.

And I would never again be tempted, until my dying breath, to

travel amongst that path.To be a king of a fickle kingdom. A tyrant of a

sickened people.An emperor of an empire.

An Empire of Sin.

THE END

Printed in Great Britain
by Amazon